8/21/14

To Karl,

I return a gift of literature and that that for your books that you provided me in the past. Yours, JB

ONSET

An American's Voyage Beyond Borders

ONSET

An American's Voyage Beyond Borders

A Novel By
JB Gatling

JB Gatling
JB GATLING PUBLICATIONS 2014

JB GATLING PUBLICATIONS

P.O. Box 510
Palm Beach, Florida 33480

Disclaimer

This book is a work of fiction. All references to real people, events, establishments, organizations, or locales are intended only to give this fictional work a sense of reality as well as authenticity, and are used fictitiously. All other names, places, and characters, and all dialogue and incidents portrayed in this book, are the product of the author's imagination. Any apparent resemblance to real characters, circumstances, or events is purely coincidental.

Copyright © 2014 by JB Gatling

All Rights Reserved, including the right of reproduction in whole or in part in any form.

For information about special discounts for bulk purchase, please contact JB Gatling Publications at:

jbgatling@yahoo.com

Or go to the online store at:

http://www.jbgatlingpublications.com/

Cover photography by P.C. Gatlin

Library of Congress Control Number: 2014909797

ISBN 9780990453406 (softcover)
ISBN 9780990453413 (hardcover)
ISBN 9780990453420 (ebook)

Dedication

This novel is dedicated to my wife and her strong support of my efforts, even when I was unaware.

Characters

Howard Family
Granny, Bernard's grandmother
Bernard, Brett's Father
Brett
Nora, Bernard's mother
Dee, Brett's sister
Desmond, Dee's son
Jimmy, Brett's brother
Vivian, Brett's second mother

John, Bernard's father
Sophie, cousin
Charles, Jimmy's son
Joshua, Brett's son

Howler Family
Elisi, Clara's grandmother
George, Oliver's father
Oliver, Clara's father
Clara, Brett's first mother
Pat, Clara's sister

Johnson Family
Staunton
Josiah
Trent
Martha
Samuel
Jessica

CrossCore Family
Eaton Two Ghanaian Students
Steve Two Ivorian Students
Sharon Linda
Blake CrossCore team
Jill Young John

African Family
Ghanaian villagers
Akenboa
Boatwoman

Jensen Family
Dr. Jensen
Aunts
Zena Melody
Ned, Zena's cousin

Hill Family
Beverly
Nina, partner

Arbor Hill Family
Bill Truit
Shirley, Gert, Granny, and James

Smith Family
Carleton
Chauncey, Carleton's son
Alfred
Wilemina
Nathan JoHanson

Aikins Family
George, Lailani's father
Lailani
Keisha, Lailani's niece
Remy, Lailani's friend
Viola, Georges' aunt
Calvin Ward, assailant

Others
Val, friend
Jazz, Brett's mentee
Gwendolyn Russell
Melinda Smith
Bob Baum
Onset Crew
Gjurin Llvala & Croatian Navy
Rev. Sipes
Lieutenant Dorn

Shaka
Boston bus driver
Cy Trowig
Stewart Greenberg
Trunk Thomas
Jason John Paul, Skipper
Willie Helms
Captain Williams
Thunder

Contents

Prologue i

Part One: Early Passages 1
   Chapter One: Father 3
   Chapter Two: Mother 9
   Chapter Three: Returning Home 20
   Chapter Four: Lailani's Pain 33
   Chapter Five: Vast Continent 40

Part Two: Middle Passages 57
   Chapter Six: Lailani's Revenge 59
   Chapter Seven: Chicago 65
   Chapter Eight: Business School 75
   Chapter Nine: Palo Alto 98
   Chapter Ten: Bankers and Activists 116
   Chapter Eleven: Fire 121
   Chapter Twelve: Collaboration 124
   Chapter Thirteen: Trapped 128

Part Three: Origins 133
   Chapter Fourteen: The Ask 135
   Chapter Fifteen: Onset 139
   Chapter Sixteen: Target Practice 143
   Chapter Seventeen: Beginnings 148
   Chapter Eighteen: Lailani 153
   Chapter Nineteen: Croatian Navy 156
   Chapter Twenty: Dreams 160
   Chapter Twenty-One: Gone 163
   Chapter Twenty-Two: Awakening 165
   Chapter Twenty-Three: Sweet Home 167
   Chapter Twenty-Four: Ring-O-Levio 170
   Chapter Twenty-Five: School Days 173

Part Four: Fulfillments 179
   Chapter Twenty-Six: Semper Fidelis 181
   Chapter Twenty-Seven: Betrayal 185
   Chapter Twenty-Eight: Pain 189
   Chapter Twenty-Nine: Hunt for Keisha 193
   Chapter Thirty: All Hands On Deck 198
   Chapter Thirty-One: Crossing the Line 206

Chapter Thirty-Two: New York City 209
Chapter Thirty-Three: Four Square 212
Chapter Thirty-Four: Laughter 217
Chapter Thirty-Five: Destruction 223
Chapter Thirty-Six: Conception 227
Chapter Thirty-Seven: Chaos 233
Chapter Thirty-Eight: Downshift 237
Epilogue 239

Prologue

Their long journey together from Albany to the easternmost tip of Long Island allowed them to bond again. As far as he could recall, he hadn't felt this close to his boy since he was a helpless newborn in constant need of fresh diapers. So Brett Howard willingly endured the occasional leg stiffness at the cramped driver's seat in his crowded van. He was encased all around by the overflow that refused to fit into the bursting rear cabin and back seats. All manner of gear surrounded, them including three jumbo size duffle bags filled with supplies and clothing, four canvas tote bags stuffed with food, games and toys, and the extra large book bag with the boy's required summer reading. They were all front seat companions squashed together for the eight-hour ride.

Although the boy was seven, this marked the first extended road trip they had taken alone together. In between the boy's constant snacking, game playing and periods of intense reading, they talked about pretty much anything that popped out from his active young imagination. He responded as best he could to the rapid-fire questions and comments about life, people, feelings, and things. He could see the boy's emerging identity and personality, and realized that very soon, sooner than he had previously imagined, Joshua would no longer be the little guy in cute short pants, and that he would have to keep up to stay relevant in his boy's life.

Yet that had been harder to do lately. Endless rounds of project management decisions, design and construction meetings, site visits, and the always essential fundraising events had consumed much of his life during the past three years. And here he was again taking another long overland pilgrimage back to the brick and mortar of his passion. He knew it was the embodiment of a long held vision coming together. But this time was special, and he had company riding shotgun next to him. He glanced over the mound of gear to the boy, who was emitting a barely audible snore and taking a catnap.

Has it really been seventeen trips so far, or is it eighteen?

He was keenly aware that his entire family had sacrificed for his dream. He had been so infused with passion for so long, he failed to realize until recently that he had slipped well over the edge into zealous commitment. But his family had endured the frequent long absences and supported him nevertheless. And they accepted his late night telephone calls while he traveled as a substitute for touch and feel. They even grew accustomed to his occasional absences at birthdays and graduations, and at anniversaries. Yet he never felt that they begrudged his efforts or disbelieved in his dream. But maybe, he admitted, he was just kidding himself. Uneasily he wondered whether there was a later price to be paid for his zeal within his own family.

Focus on the road, stay sharp!

After several miles his mind drifted again, this time back to his mother. Before she succumbed to lung cancer, he was able to fly her and his father up to the ten-acre grounds for a visit. They were grateful and they were happy. Dad loved seeing the engineering plans and renderings, and talking for hours with the on-site architect about the details of the amazing transformation that by then was well underway. Richard was kind enough to patiently answer all of Dad's technical questions and commentary about the build-out, without pointing out that the math and engineering assumptions behind the comments were decades old.

That had given him precious time alone with his mother. She never once complained about the long and sometimes jarring tour that she insisted they take around the various construction sites on the property. As he pushed her wheelchair equipped with the ever-present oxygen canister, she ignored the discomfort and asked him dozens of questions.

Your dream is now real, Brett, and the hard work to protect it lies ahead of you.

Vivian had smiled up at him back then and squeezed his hand with all the strength she could muster. Later, they rested together and sipped cold water at the far end of the pier, watching the splendid parade of all manner of watercraft in front of the expansive shoreline. Five months after that, she was dead.

Damn, I miss her.

He knew that she had been a mother to him in all respects that mattered, and he had never once labeled her his stepmom.

How many others can say that they had not one, but two committed mothers in their lifetime? I can. Both are gone, Clara so long ago, and now Vivian.

"Daddy, is Grandpa Bernard coming to visit us this summer?"

JB Gatling

The catnap was over.

"I don't think he'll be able to get away, Joshua. Dad's been under the weather recently and his doctors asked him to slow down a bit and take it easy."

"Daddy, is Grandpa Bernard going to go to heaven like Grandma?"

He knew the answer to that question was yes, and that it would happen within the next few months. He also knew that truth was much too severe for a seven-year-old, even a precocious one like Joshua. His father had helped spark the boy's intellectual curiosity, and they had long ago developed between them a special bond. It would be hard on the boy when the end came.

The reality of his father's terminal illness weighed heavily on him even now, months after they talked about his diagnosis of advanced prostrate cancer. It was a tough telephone call. Before that, he had naively assumed they had twenty or more years ahead of them together. Despite having all the weeks to adjust and to accept the new reality, it still hurt him deeply to realize that his dad would be gone soon, less than a year after Vivian. Then he fully realized for the first time that he, along with his sister and brother, would be alone on the front line of the family, involuntary guardians of the old knowledge and the old values.

"I think Grandpa Bernard will be okay if he follows doctors' orders, Joshua."

Changing the subject quickly before the boy could formulate another question, he asked him about the activities that he was looking forward to participating in during the summer.

"When I get back home next week, I want to race in the Albany lake regatta again like last year, Daddy. I want to win that first place trophy this time!"

Then suddenly, with equal intensity, the boy dug back into one of his favorite games, shutting out the world.

Joshua's bold declaration about sailing made him remember his wife's recent warning as they left the driveway to start the trip.

Brett, keep a close eye on him and promise me you'll keep his sailing up there under control. Promise me!

He'd promised, and he fully intended to keep to that commitment. But her skeptical look as he backed the van out into the street told him she most likely remembered a similar commitment he made to her long ago, when they were kids together. Or maybe his own guilt made him imagine that she remembered. Back then he had pleaded with her to join him for a Saturday afternoon sailing trip on the Albany lake where he spent so much time practicing.

Finally she agreed to come out on the water, despite the fact that water sports were not within her comfort zone at all. Truth was that he wore her down with repeated requests. But she finally joined him on the condition that he promise to engage in no daredevil stunts, and definitely no racing.

He'd fully intended to keep that promise as well. But he couldn't control the weather.

That sail began peacefully. It was a warm and humid July afternoon, with a light five-knot easterly breeze flirting above the water. The blue lake was placid. Many young sailors were out that day; most of them were boys in the same club as him. Several were racing at the northern end of the lake around the temporary course markers. He figured he could race any other day, so he was fine with missing the regatta. He was feeling pretty good about spending time with her and showing that he was a skilled sailor, despite being new to the sport. But when he smiled at her as he was letting out more canvas, he saw the fear on her face as she stared past his shoulder at the sky.

He turned back and saw it too—the thick black squall line racing over the water. It was barreling directly at them, blotting the sky and other boats from view. He dropped down from his seat on the transom and yanked in the main and headsails, securing the lines with rapid lashes around the cleats. Then he grabbed the tiller and moved closer to her, pulling them both low while he checked her life jacket. He put both arms tightly around her and turned her face into his chest just before a high, heavy wave broke overhead, drenching them to the bone. The small centerboard craft was lifted out of the water by the next rolling swell, and then thrown back down several feet, all the while bucking violently but somehow remaining afloat. Then the dark, gusty wind punched them hard and lashed them with stinging rain. They held on to each other. He knew she was praying.

Within minutes the squall passed over, racing away to inland. In its wake, a brightening golden tint spread across the entire lake as the sun emerged.

"Joshua, that's our exit coming up. We'll take Eastern Shore Road out to the point and be in camp within thirty minutes."

The boy smiled wide, showing his missing front tooth.

Part One
Early Passages

Chapter One
Father

Bernard Howard had always been large for his age. At fourteen, he was almost six feet tall. Like his father, he was heavy-boned and solid. It was the kind of frame that made him the natural choice to be catcher for the baseball team. Yet despite the bulk, he was agile as he inched his way forward on elbows and knees down the long, dark hallway. He carried a rifle on his right shoulder. Behind him and breathing hard was his cousin Sophie, who was visiting again this summer from Boston. Three years younger than him, and a bit plump, her fatigue showed as she struggled to carry most of her weight on her elbows and knees. But of necessity she also used her arms, shins, and belly. She tried hard to keep up and stay silent. So far, everything was going the way her big cousin had instructed.

The ammunition bag that she towed also impeded her. In her overactive imagination, she harbored fears that they would never reach the setup point where he would be able to take the shot.

But she struggled on because Bernard was her favorite cousin, and more like a big brother to her. No matter how crazy his schemes, she would rather be here with him than anywhere else, and she wouldn't let him down. Sophie lived for these summers, leaving her divided family behind and visiting Granny every year. Bernard usually came over the first day she arrived. The trips broke up the long monotony of her time at home during the rest of the year. As the child of a second marriage, she was ostracized from the family gatherings back home that were controlled by her dad's ex-wife. After a time she preferred to be alone, and had long ago stopped pretending to be interested in what the half-sisters and half-brothers were doing. Here once again with her cousin, life was thrilling, and she felt involved and alive.

Halfway down the corridor, he signaled her to stop. The temperature in the narrow space had already reached eighty-five degrees, and they both were dripping wet. The brief pause allowed them to catch a little bit of breath. He took a long swig of water from his army canteen and handed it back to her.

"There they are," he whispered, pointing ahead to an open door leading to the kitchen at the end of the hallway. Standing slowly up straight while she pressed against the wall, she could see a round head in the distance, framed in the soft glow of light coming through the pantry window. But to her surprise there were at least four others, and they all huddled around as if to form some manner of protective shield. Sophie slowed her breathing, trying to throw off the mounting stress and focus on what needed to be done. As she resumed her squat position, she steeled her nerves, determined to execute her role. She hauled the bag closer to her, readying the gear.

Without turning around, he reached back with an open hand as they'd practiced, and she firmly placed the tripod rifle mount into his palm. He kept his eyes fixed on the target as he secured the mount to the rifle and raised it into position. Then he reached back for the ammunition. He quietly opened the chamber and loaded the shot, keeping the safety on.

Gradually and silently, he eased his big frame up to a position where his head and shoulders were above the tripod mount. He looked down the long barrel, using the forward sight as his guide. After fixing the target, he signaled to Sophie to come over. He wanted her to look down the barrel at the target. Anticipating this moment, she removed a small six-inch wooden footstool from the sack and stepped up.

It was on target, she said to herself as she nodded back to him. They had done it—almost, at least. Stepping quietly off the stool, she placed it back in the bag along with the remaining ammunition and took her place behind him as he cracked his knuckles and peered once again down the barrel. He hand signaled her to take cover while he nestled the stock of the rifle into his shoulder and released the safety. Then he gently placed his forefinger on the trigger while making minute adjustments. Ever so slowly, he increased the pressure, just as his father had instructed him to do years ago. He stopped breathing and slowly pulled.

He felt the release. Milliseconds later, the round head above the pantry counter top exploded, and the pink insides shattered and covered the back wall. The pellet had lodged deep within one of the other large grapefruits at the back of the bowl, so that no damage to the room would result from any ricochet. The beautiful blue porcelain fruit bowl that contained the grapefruits had emerged unscathed. With a satisfied grin, he looked down at his favorite cousin and gave her the thumbs-up sign.

Together, using teamwork and planning, they had destroyed another fruit display that his grandmother had placed meticulously in her well-kept home. All that remained now was cleaning up the mess in the thirty minutes they had before she got home from grocery shopping. The challenge for him was not only in cleaning up, but also shooting his BB gun in the house without wasting any shots or scratching any walls. And this was not just any house. This was Granny Howard's well-tended and immaculate home. Getting away with it and cleaning up without a trace were part of the thrill for them as they plotted their way through innumerable adventures over the many summer months they spent together.

Granny Howard was a well-known community celebrity in Connecticut. She was the first woman in the county to ride a motorcycle between Hartford and Bridgeport. She also had a spitfire temperament. He loved his Granny, but he could never understand why everything had to be so immaculate in her house. Even his dad seemed to sit on pins and needles when they visited every Sunday after church. Nora, his mother, was even more intimidated by her feisty mother-in-law.

His mother had moved to Connecticut from North Carolina when she was a teenager. Later she met Bernard's dad, John, and they courted and married. Both of them came from families who believed that education was the key ingredient to creating a better life for themselves and their family. Neither of the family branches had yet to produce a college graduate from a major national university, but they were getting closer. They both thought that the Northeast was the best area to achieve that goal. Bernard and his older sister were the objects of that vision.

His mother was also conservative and timid in ways that became harder for him to respect as he grew into in his mid and late teens. Maybe, he often thought, they just grew women differently in North Carolina. His mother used to say that women in the South were much more settled and sedate, whatever that meant. But as he thought about it more, he felt that there was something else deep within his mother beyond her Southern roots that accounted for her caution and fear of living. It was as if the spirit of adventure had skipped over her generation and landed on him with both feet.

Later he began to think that maybe she grew up in a time when making a mistake had such severe consequences that you dared not venture out and explore. He always wondered what the glue was between his mom and his dad, who despite singing in the choir, his deacon status in the church, and solid family man profile, had some of Granny's fire just below the surface. After all, it was his dad who taught him how to hunt and to fire a weapon in the first place.

His grandmother, on the other hand, had been outspoken as far back as he could remember and would offer her opinion on just about any topic you cared to name. But she was always well-read and informed. She kept dozens of books around the house in different bookcases, including one that had been built into her master bedroom wall. Many times he would hear her railing against what she considered the deprivations of women being lorded over in a man's world. Though a widow as long as he could remember, she was not at all like the widows around the neighborhood that seemed to be living on a stretched budget. She even had an early model of the hand-cranked Thomas Edison phonograph from the 1890s, the only one in the neighborhood. It was the center of Sunday gatherings, and the dancing that he loved, after the meal and dishes were finished. And she let him crank it and play as much music as he wanted.

As he grew older, he felt more and more like a prisoner in his own home. His mother never came to support or encourage him embracing the outside world. Whether it was her fear of his love for sports, or her dread that he might be exposed to the wrong elements through his passion for jazz and his skill with the standup bass, her consistent harangue was always that he slow down, stop this or curb that. Those messages were reinforced through his sister, who was two years older and her mother's mirror image—always perfect in school, and always earning this or that certificate or taking another specialized course of study. But in his mind she never really seemed to attack anything big with gusto, and she never got out there and actually did something different, something on her own. He realized much later that his assessments were often too harsh, borne of frustration from what he perceived as the mental straightjacket that surrounded him.

By the time he was eighteen, he'd had enough, and shortly after his high school graduation he enlisted in the Air Force, dead set on becoming a pilot.

"Where you from, boy?" the Mississippi drill instructor demanded to know with a surly Southern drawl. He parked his wide pink face two inches from Bernard's eyes.

"Hartford, Sir," he snapped off crisply despite his body being near exhaustion in the drenching one-hundred-degree Alabama heat.

"I never heard of no Hartford, Alabama, boy," growled the DI, spitting tobacco juice lightly into his face as he talked and chewed at the same time. " So you must be from up there where them Yankees live. That right, boy?"

That was his first day, and the first inspection for his all-black unit at Tuskegee Air Force base. He could feel right away that he and the other black enlisted men were not welcome. It was the kind of feeling he didn't need to guess at. The DI came right out and told them that he was going to wash as many of them out of the Air Force as he had time to boot. Uncle Sam didn't need darkies to win World War II, he would constantly remind them. Bernard soon wondered if enlisting had been a big mistake.

But after his first week, which was all grueling PT, and once enrolled in the basic class curriculum that covered avionics for service men, black or white, he began to warm to the AF. He had inherited a mathematical and scientific aptitude from his dad that allowed him to use his high school classes as a basis for success. That success steeled his will to avoid being boot-kicked out just because a cracker DI wanted it that way. So he ate a lot of crow, but he was among the thirty-five percent of blacks to successfully complete the basic avionics training and move on to specialized career choices.

It was because he had enlisted with the personal goal of being a pilot that the frequent harassment by officers and other white airmen was secondary. He didn't let it bother him too much, because he was motivated to fly and to soar above the clouds. This was a dream he had long held, ever since first seeing the air shows with his dad as a kid. Despite his later understanding of principles like thrust, acceleration, and vectors, to him the very idea of flying remained nothing short of a miracle. To be able to defy gravity and continue soaring high above and beyond the sky overhead was something he just wanted to do.

He had the grades, and he had the desire required to qualify for pilot training. What he lacked was the pedigree to fit into that small class of black Tuskegee airmen who were allowed in and eventually saw combat duty over Europe. Most were a couple of years ahead of him, and were from black families a bit higher up in the social and financial pecking order. A good number of the black pilots were also of a much lighter skin color, he noticed, and seemed to be very comfortable navigating the unwritten rules that governed who would advance and who would not.

When he learned that he wasn't selected for pilot training, it was a major blow, and he thought about quitting and heading back home. The ostensible reason for the rejection was that his large frame made him incompatible with the standard issue pilot seating and cabin areas in the B-52s and fighter jets. The explanation seemed plausible to him at the time, when all he had to do was look around and see that his six-foot-two, two-hundred-twenty pound frame was indeed quite a bit larger than that of anyone else who was selected. That visual reality allowed him to rationalize his exclusion and eventually agree to complete the offered training for an open bombardier position.

Two separate and equally devastating bombing runs over Nagasaki and Hiroshima, Japan, ended any chance that he would see live combat during the War. Instead, he shipped out to Japan as part of the vast American occupation force that ensured the peace. Having never left the shores of the United States, he always remembered the Japanese people fondly as they were the first foreigners he ever met. They were as amazed to set eyes on his giant frame, as he observed their comings and goings as they passed well beneath his big shoulders. While he guarded this post or that post and took his free time to visit different parts of the main island, the ordinary citizens of Japan seemed to welcome him as they efficiently went about the business of recovering from the disastrous war brought to them by their elite and distant rulers.

But the peace back in post-war America brightly beaconed. It promised to be a booming time, and Bernard and his friends wanted to get home and participate as soon as they were able. His very last option was returning to Hartford and to the conservative household ruled over by his mother. Granny had passed on while he was away, so that home away from his own was no longer available. Instead, he decided to settle somewhere else in the Northeast. He followed the lead of his sister, who had recently moved the twenty miles across the border from Connecticut to Western Massachusetts after her marriage.

But he set his sights on the capital city of Boston. His cousin Sophie still lived there, so he would have some family around. He figured that his military education and training, combined with the city's good technical schools, gave him the best chance for success. It was in Boston that he first met his sweetheart, Clara Howler, who had settled from Georgia a few years earlier. She had already started the slow but steady process of supporting her family's northward move away from the limited opportunities in the South. Clara was quiet and studious, though not formally trained. She was a few years older than him, but the age difference didn't matter to either of them. Her spirit was remarkably serene yet strong, and he was drawn to her from the beginning. She fully supported him in his efforts to master his technical education and achieve certification.

Clara's brothers, on the other hand—rough-hewn, working class men—would often poke fun at his constant practice of carrying books and school papers from here to there as he balanced classes along with his part-time jobs. But her sisters extended a warm welcome to him, and were happy to see their younger sibling interested in a man with some promise.

Within a year of their first meeting, they were married. Within five years, they were very busy raising a family of three: Dee, Brett, and Jimmy.

Chapter Two
Mother

Josiah Johnson walked out of the small county land registration office, clutching his recorded deeds in his thick hands. He was now only one purchase away from his endgame—control of five thousand acres of pristine land in the northwest corner of Valdosta, Georgia, a newly incorporated town in Lowndes County. Many other speculators had paid heavily inflated prices for land situated in the middle, south, or east of town. In those areas, drainage and clearing promised to be a lot easier, thereby inflating the price for speculators and subsequent commercial and residential development. But Josiah was not concerned about building houses or establishing businesses. He was focused on exploiting the superior information that he possessed from his uncle, who ran the Bureau of Railroads up in Washington, D.C.

Last Christmas at the family gathering in Marblehead, Massachusetts, Uncle Staunton told him precisely where the Bureau would permit and authorize yet-to-be-announced track beds for the railway that would run between Atlanta and Valdosta. The line would later extend to the Florida border and beyond, opening up commerce and trade for the entire southern Georgia and northern Florida areas. And the railroad would need a depot, stockyards, terminal space, and access to water to fuel that growth. Knowing exactly where the track lines would run was a gateway to enormous profit.

Before executing the final bundle of purchases, Josiah confirmed with his uncle that no changes had been made to the plan and route. Once those plans were published, he would have the difficult but very appealing choice of selling his holdings to other speculators at up to ten times his purchase price, or holding all or part of the land for later development and construction.

As he stood wide-legged on the wooden porch, he looked out over the soon to be explosive area of commercial growth. After tucking the deeds into his satchel, he pulled out his pipe and packed it with moist Virginia tobacco. He inhaled the warm, aromatic smoke, and his mind turned to the only remaining obstacle between him and his well thought out plan. That was Oliver Howler and his half-breed Indian family. He had to clear them off the land and seize the valuable water rights they controlled.

Josiah was a devout man by the standards of the day, and like generations of Johnson men before him, he was a leader in the local church. Since the Mayflower, Johnson men could always be counted on as strong deacons or municipal officers. Yet they always carefully avoided the position of pastor or mayor. Johnson men believed that those executive positions ran counter to their acquisitive nature. They knew that being in those very visible local leadership positions would tie their hands and force them to be more open and equitable with business opportunities.

This most recent venture in Georgia was ninety percent financed by Johnson family wealth, with a ten percent local participation included as a hedge against any opposition that needed to be overcome. It was the deepest Southern penetration so far by a family that began their expansion through the nation with a land grant from King George in the 1600s. Since the time of the earliest English speaking settlements, and after the founding of the country, the Johnsons had purchased, sold and developed land throughout the northeast, mid-Atlantic and upper Southern states.

Savoring the tobacco, he could almost feel and taste the initial exhilaration of his distant ancestors when they received that first land grant of ten thousand acres in northern New England from the king. He imagined they felt very much like he did at this moment, full of promise and endless possibilities. Divine Providence, he believed, had truly smiled upon him and his family for many generations. And he had all of that accumulated wisdom, experience, and wealth in the persons of his fathers and uncles to call upon.

The methods and procedures for acquiring and securing land and property wealth were closely guarded from outsiders, but generously shared within his family. As he struggled to decide on the best method for removal of the thorny impediment that the Howlers had become, he recalled his first uncle's words to him many years ago as they walked along the seaward jetty heading to a twenty-foot tender. It would take them across the bay to the deep anchorages, where his uncle's fleet of clipper ships waited far out in the harbor.

Before you let a man set himself firmly, without being dislodged, between you and your fortune, Josiah, ask yourself if that man and his family are more deserving than your own blood line, and then make your choice.

Over the centuries, the Johnsons had seen no families more deserving than themselves.

Looking quickly at his gold pocket watch, he was jolted back to the present moment and he stepped off the porch to his horse and buckboard. He didn't want to be late for dinner tonight, where he and his deacon board would discuss solutions to his problem. As local investors, they had every interest in helping him find a permanent remedy.

Walter Sherwood, William Trent, and David Teacher all arrived that evening together, but by separate horse or buckboard. Even with the pacification of all pockets of Indian resistance long ago accomplished, the folks of southern Georgia continued to practice the same travel precautions from decades ago—travel in groups after sundown, and travel well armed.

They were all prosperous men whose families had greatly benefited from the auction of Cherokee and Choctaw lands a generation before. In the last few years, they each had significantly extended their own holdings to include formerly unattractive parcels outside of the Treaty provisions. These were *appropriated* from Indian families who remained on the fringes.

Among them was the strong bond of hard work, faith, and a shared belief in the political system. It allowed for consensus around most issues of importance, to them and to the community. It was a very comfortable partnership. On this evening they assembled for a good meal at the very capable hands of Mrs. Johnson, and to help Josiah solve his problem with Howler.

As usual, Martha Johnson served a wonderful supper, this one consisting of fresh killed venison, pork loin, sweet carrots, green beans, mashed potatoes, and deep-dish apple pie. Expressing the surest sign of appreciation, belches were heard all around the large dining room table. Even Josiah's ten-year old son, Samuel, tried to make his own belch, which came out as more of a squeaky burp. Five-year old Jessica, not to be outdone by her big brother, managed to grunt her approval and dribble water down the front of her dress.

"Gentlemen," he said after he belched again and eased himself back from the table edge to provide additional room for his girth, "shall we retire to the front veranda to conduct our business?"

They nodded in agreement and thanked Martha for her generosity and hospitality. She promised to pack a big plate for each of them to take home to their families. On the way out, Josiah grabbed a tray with a large lead crystal decanter full of his best brandy, along with four snifters.

As they sat back in comfort on the screened-in porch, the grandeur of early summer Georgia spread out before them. They were surrounded by the fragrance of pine and magnolia, and a cacophony of sound from crickets to pond frogs. All was stirred by the muted noise of scores of animals settling in for the evening in the many barns and stables that dotted the large property. He poured generous glasses of brandy and shared with his friends.

Walter and David had already lit their hand-rolled cigarettes, and William was just completing a good pack of his pipe. He handed the leather pouch over to Josiah. Each man drew heavily on the tobacco and followed it with long draws of drink. They paused and appreciated the wonder of the evening, taking it in slowly, as was the pace of the time. They asked one another about family and children, and talked about what the future held for their own legacy in the rich land where they each had planted deep stakes.

In time, Josiah set his pipe down in the large shell ashtray and moved it to the center of the heavy oak table. After taking another long swallow, he reached for the decanter and refilled the glasses. As he sat back he looked at his friends.

"It's such a lovely evening, I truly hate to interrupt it and turn to this Howler business. But that damn fool refused my best and last price to buy his property. And I took the time to personally go over there to his cabin to make him that offer. Looks like we're going to need to be creative to drive him off the land."

David, a burly dark-bearded man of ruddy complexion, spoke up first after draining his glass.

"I'll tell you what I heard," he said after a deep, thunderous belch. "Them Howlers are devil worshippers, burning midnight fires, sacrificing animals and chanting incantations around them totem poles scattered over the property. And don't tell me that noise is real Indian chanting, cause I know for a fact that the last real Indians headed down to Florida twenty years back to hook up with them Seminoles."

William, a thin, studious man and a bit of an amateur historian, sipped his brandy and chimed in.

"Not too sure, David, about that devil worship thing. I do recall from my title search on the property that there was a land grant to Howler's father, George, who fought for the Confederacy against the Yankees. Apparently, as suggested by other local records at City Hall, he joined three hundred or so Indians from scattered tribes to stand and fight Sherman's savagery. Thirty or forty slaves were with him. His land grant was similar to the others given to the Indians that fought. Unlike those, however, Howler's title didn't identify any tribal connection. But it's safe to assume it would be Cherokee or Choctaw, since the women living at the cabin are from those tribes. Howler's claim appears to be a valid and lawful transfer through the will of his father in the amount of ten acres."

"Ten acres smack dab in the middle of our claim," David growled.

Josiah reached over and drained the last of the brandy into the glasses. He took a sip, waiting for other comments.

Always reluctant to speak first until he knew which way the wind was blowing, Walter cleared his throat and snuffed out his cigarette. He stood up as if to add authority to the words he would deliver, swaying unsteadily.

"Allowing our claim to be devalued by Howler is out of the question. I'll be damned if that man is entitled to that land. He doesn't fool me with his crazy Indian act. I think it's all a charade. Damn it, if Howler won't sell, then we'll have to move him and his half-breed brood off the land."

"Well, it wouldn't be the first time for that, would it?" Josiah asked with a grin. "Andrew Jackson gave the boot to 130,000 of them in the 1830s. The deal was that they got Oklahoma, and we got Georgia. By refusing to accept my fair offer to buy, isn't Howler welching on that deal?"

Rather than setting out to correct that cloudy view of history, William decided it was too formidable a task, and instead continued to sip his brandy.

Josiah was impatient, and he turned the meeting to action.

"Gentlemen, if what we really have on that land is a squatter, I would like to talk about how we permanently remove him."

"Elisi, Elisi," Clara pleaded as she strained forward and raised her hand for attention. Clara was four and the youngest among her sisters, brothers, and cousins who sat in a neat ring around their grandmother. Elisi, as she was called in the Cherokee sign of reverence for age and position, was now an old Cherokee woman with long white hair, a tan complexion, and high, rounded cheekbones. Despite her age, that she had once been a stunning beauty remained for all to see. Her dark oval eyes were serene, and she seemed to be able to follow the frenetic comings and goings of her grandchildren without moving her head. But they all had learned the hard way that she was immediately aware of any trouble they might attempt to get into, even when they were playing outside.

"Please tell us the story of the three wolves, Elisi, please."

She intended to tell them a story, as she always did, to ease them into the dream world. But first there was order to achieve, and she quietly commanded that they change into clean clothes for tomorrow after washing their face, feet, and hands. The eight children scattered quickly, competing to finish the tasks and be the first to return to their favorite place around the story circle. After this, she required that the young girls comb and brush each other's hair and plait it in long braids. Clara brought her a brush and matching comb, and began her nightly chore of preparing Elisi's waist-length hair for the evening. It was a chore Clara loved, because it allowed her to be close and touch her grandmother, and look at her face from all sides. Her face and skin and black oval eyes were a part of Clara, who had been in their loving and patient presence since before she could remember.

With all chores completed, Elisi looked proudly around the story circle at the children of her daughters and sons. They were a broad range of colors, from nutmeg brown, to cinnamon, to pale tan. Their hair was black or brown, straight or curly. Seeing them, she recalled fondly her husband George, who died many moons ago. He was from the tribe across the great waters, and was of the brown-skinned people who had settled with her tribe generations ago when hundreds had escaped the great slavery. His blood was alive before her eyes, and she smiled. Her oldest son, Oliver, had taken Sarah, the squaw of her tribe, as his wife. That union blessed her with Clara, her favorite, who shared her spirit. Turning to each of the eager young faces in the circle that waited on her every word, she finally began the ancient tale of the three wolves.

"Listen carefully now, children. It was a time many moons ago, the time of the great trail of tears for our people, the time when the people walked and died and were always in the cold or the frozen snow. And many would fall and speak no more. Our entire nation had to walk, had to move forward to a new home and a new beginning. And along that trail, after many moons, they entered the place of the great vast plains where all was different and strange to them. Even the hills and mighty pine trees were no more to be seen. The sky above, with its guiding lights over the ages, had also changed, and the people were lost when they looked up to it. Then the many soldiers with long guns who had made the journey with them turned back, and the people were alone.

But from not far off in the bush, the people were being watched by three big, hungry wolves with large green eyes and long sharp teeth. They had thick black coats of fur, and big claws. These were not the wolves the people had known before. These were the magical spirit wolves of the high plains, and they had learned to talk among themselves like men, and to think like men. As they looked down upon the people, wolf one smiled and bared his sharp white teeth.

He spoke to the others:

We have a choice today for dinner, and it has been many days since we have eaten.

Wolf two, agreed but added something important:

The people before us are tired and weak, but they still carry the long bow and the spear and the knife. Perhaps we should go back on the trail where they came from and find food that is already dead, and that carries no sharp weapons.

But that food may not be fresh, said the third wolf. And if not, when we return, the people here may be gone.

Then we should attack the people now!

Wolf one then opened his mouth wide, raised his head high, and stretched his long strong neck."

Elisi looked around at all the children and could see their tiny eyes filled with fear for the people.

"Can anyone tell me," she whispered softly, "what wolf two said to this?"

All eight of the children raised their hands and strained their arms for attention.

She picked a young girl child to provide the answer.

"Wolf two said he was hungry, Elisi."

The other children laughed, but Elisi spoke gently to Pat.

"You are right, my child. Wolf two said he was hungry."

"Then wolf one spoke up again and wondered whether there was a way that they might have much food from the people, and not worry about the long bow and the spear and the many knives.

Wolf three, the wisest of them all, responded that if they could turn the people to be friends with them, they would enjoy many meals, and not just one meal. Then the people would always bring them food.

Wolf two asked how that could be, because the people were afraid of them and acted out of fear.

Once again, wise wolf three had the answer to the question. He said they should go to the sandy plains after they rolled around in the tar pits. The sand would then stick, he said, and turn our dark hair to light brown. That is the color of many of the dogs that walk even now with the people, the dogs the people love.

Then wolf one thought he finally understood the wise wolf at last. He smiled and showed his long, pointy teeth. He asked wolf three whether they should wait until the people held them close, and after that time he was very sure that they must be eaten.

No, no, not at all, said the wise wolf. When we look like the dogs the people love, we will return and lead them into the green lush valley on the horizon of the plains. They will travel safely, and they will be grateful to us. Out of their affection they will always provide food for us and hold us high in their esteem.

Wolf two asked what would happen when the sandy color faded away, and they became the black wolves that they really were.

The wise wolf had the answer.

By that time you must make sure you are friends with everyone, and then your true color will not matter."

She looked calmly around the circle and saw that all of the children were sleeping except for little Clara, who was smiling back at her.

Elisi rose, and they led the others to the rear of the cabin, laying them down on the straw mats.

Alone in the thick undergrowth of the backcountry, Trunk Thomas was in his element. His worn moccasins quietly moved over the pine needle carpet on the forest floor as he picked his way. He had walked an extra ten miles through the darkness to arrive by this less-traveled approach and was thankful for the low cloud cover that rendered him virtually invisible against the trees. Just ahead, he spotted a towering stern-faced totem pole staring down at him, marking the southernmost edge of the Howler property line.

Trapping and hunting had long been in Trunk's bloodline. Four generations of his family had ground out a harsh but profitable living in the thick, overgrown Georgia forests. In the old days they hunted bear, wolf, and beaver. Then gradually, the high price to track and capture Indians and slaves made that living unprofitable. In time his family made their skills available for hire for any reason, to any man with a good purse. But tonight was not about hunting, he reminded himself again. It was about terror. Josiah had laid down the rules clearly to him, and had him repeat those rules.

Break, but don't kill.

He knew that his most pressing order of business was to tame Oliver Howler. After that, he figured as he smiled with a ragged gap-toothed grin, he would have his way with the unguarded women and the girl children. Even that old white-haired squaw was going to be included in the party. As for them mongrel small ones, it would only take a thump of his thick, rough hand to put them out.

But Howler had to be hit hard and solid. He intended to take no chances, and would strike him down with every muscle he could muster. If he killed him while doing so, that was just too bad.

The large log cabin was now barely visible through the darkness, just over the rise beyond the clearing. No light came from the structure, and he grinned again as he reckoned they were sleeping off the liquor used in some devil worship ceremony. His hand went to his waist, and he pulled out his heavy war club. From past experiences he knew it was silent and lethal. Any contact at all with Howler's stubborn skull would put him under. Solid contact would put him under forever.

He crossed the clearing to the cabin and paused, crouching at the door. Snoring could be heard from within. Had to be Howler, only man in the house this time of year. He quietly eased the door open and paused again. The snoring continued. He moved down the left inside wall to where Josiah said Howler slept with his squaw. He could see a faint glow coming from the straw mattress some ten feet ahead. Two dark shadows were lying there, and Trunk knew then that his stalking had been successful. He summoned all his rage and approached, raising his right arm high and cocking his thick wrist to release the war club with maximum power. As he crouched and smashed the club straight down, his mind wondered uneasily why Howler would use blankets on such a warm night.

The Bowie knife that ripped through his back and scapula below his right shoulder was the answer to that unspoken question. The sharpened tip lodged deeply in Trunk's lungs, deflating them. The heavy blade had been in Howler's family since his grandfather's time. It was 10-inch hardened Swiss steel with a weathered brown hilt weighted in the outer part to increase rotation. A young Oliver had learned to throw it through his grandpa's patient instruction when he was ten years old. He practiced with it daily after reaching manhood.

Trunk collapsed and pitched heavily forward onto the mattress. Howler waited patiently. Then he approached from the shadows across the room, moving with no sound.

He yanked the blade out of the limp body with both hands after placing his knee in the middle of the back. He wiped it clean on the leather britches of the intruder. He checked for breathing and pulse, finding neither. Then he quickly pulled the blankets from over the two mounds of clothing on the straw mattress and placed both under the side of the corpse, spreading the excess out on the dirt floor. After rolling the body over twice in a tight wrap, he lit a match and peered into the face of the would-be assassin. He recognized the grizzly visage of the bounty hunter called Trunk and wondered why he had come to kill him and his family that evening. He knew at once that it was a bad omen.

Then he spat into the face of the ancient hunter of his people.

He thought further and reasoned that there also was a good omen to consider. That was the bounty hunter's noisy approach to the cabin that he'd heard all the way from the great Totem pole. Maybe, he hoped, the bad and good omens would cancel each other out. But as he hoisted the heavy corpse up on his shoulder he knew that the bad omen was much stronger.

That's why he wasn't as surprised as most folks in Valdosta when he was convicted of first-degree murder. The judge, however, had seen fit to be lenient with his sentencing, allowing him and his brood to leave the county free and clear, so long as the title to his land was forfeited. Four members of the judge's church ended up qualifying to purchase the land, since they already owned abutting property that could benefit.

He accepted the deal because he could not risk leaving his family to fend without him. Thus began the family's long separation from the land, and years of decline. Much later, his youngest child, Clara, was instrumental in bringing most of them north after she secured a position in the retail trade in downtown Boston. Howler, however, died of a heart attack and was buried in his native Georgia one week before he was scheduled to depart.

CONFIDENTIAL

Secretary of the Bureau of Indian Affairs

UNITED STATES OF AMERICA

January 14, 1895

Dear Secretary Brunell:

This will respond to your recent letter inquiring about the loss of Indian lands in Georgia during the past several years. You included in your examples, among others, the 10-acre lands formally owned by Oliver Howler in Valdosta, GA. You have also asked for recommendations from our Regional Office to discontinue what you characterize as the *disturbing pattern of land loss among the remaining Native American tribes in the Region.*

From my personal summary of local interviews and a review of extant records, the following seems clear beyond peradventure.

    1. Oliver Howler, for unknown reasons, tricked and lured Trunk Thomas onto his property and viciously stabbed him in the back. The

badly mauled and partially decomposed body of Mr. Thomas was discovered wrapped in two wool blankets downstream from the Howler property, five or six days after the murder.

2. No motive was ever established for the murder, but we know from local reports that Howler may have harbored an ancient blood feud against the Thomas family for alleged bounty hunting in the distant past.

3. Our independent research confirms that the Thomas family had for generations engaged in criminal apprehension activities, all sanctioned by local authorities and pursuant to valid and outstanding warrants of arrest.

4. At trial, Oliver Howler failed to mount a credible defense to the murder charge, and usually spent his time in court chanting Native American songs of unknown origin. He was rightly convicted of murder and duly sentenced. His sentence was later commuted.

5. Finally, neither Oliver Howler nor his father included mention of Cherokee or Choctaw wives on any deeds of conveyance or testamentary instruments, thereby, according to our local advisor, eliminating any potential title issues arising from the sale of the land to the present owners.

As to your remaining inquiry concerning improvement in the Bureau of Indian Affairs' Native American ownership inventory in the southeast, I would strongly urge that a dialogue be established between the United States and the local and respected leadership in the affected communities. After careful consideration, we believe that the clergy in these areas, along with their deacon boards, are the best place to initiate a dialogue. Local political leaders would in our view be a disagreeable choice. If you concur, I will proceed to open up channels and establish appropriate committees under my leadership at the earliest opportunity.

Very truly yours,

James W. Hump

Regional Administrator

Southeast Region

Bureau of Indian Affairs

Chapter Three
Returning Home

Brett walked over to the corner table in the college dorm room and grabbed the half-gallon of cheap vodka that he and his college buddies had seriously dented during the last two hours of their celebration. It was Thursday evening. Normally that was one day early to start partying for the weekend. But with the pressure of submitting term papers lifted, and with all finals completed, they were not partying alone. In every dorm and residence house, there were celebrations among the students. All would soon leave for home or other places at semester's end.

Their small Ivy League New England university had lived up to its reputation as a place with serious academic standards that challenged the best and the brightest. For the past two weeks, between pizza, Greek salads and endless junk food snacks, these friends had pushed the limits, logging twelve-hour study days. None of them dared to try skating by on raw intelligence alone, even though they were all top academic students at their high schools the year before. Brett was the only public school graduate among them, and thus was a bit of an anomaly. The other three came from various prestigious boarding schools around the nation, which they began in the sixth or seventh grade.

He had felt added pressure from his peers during the semester, despite his honors and advanced placement classes at Queens High School. That was clearly because the private school students, who were the large majority of his classmates, brought extra academic preparation to the table and usually bent the grade curves higher. Having to work twenty-five hours a week while others were studying during that time also helped put him in a disadvantaged position. But so far, he was still holding his own.

Simon was from Richmond, Virginia, and was a graduate of an elite prep school there. He was their host. He glanced at Brett as he approached with the remains of the vodka while he reclined in his favorite stuffed green chair from his study room at home. His parents had airmailed it to him after he complained about butt calluses from the military style dorm furniture that was standard issue for freshmen

"Brett!" he shouted gregariously. "We've been pounding that half G hard for at least two hours, and every one of my damn drinks has been warm as piss. I thought you were in charge of laying in the ice cubes for this shindig, my friend."

"Damn warm, indeed," he agreed, a slur lacing his speech as the vodka continued its slow assault on his senses. "Simon, I think you're fried from all that warm vodka. Even if I handed you some cubes right now, they would melt through your fingers before hitting the bottom of your glass."

Gerry and Stan, both stretched out along the floor on opposite walls of the room, broke into convulsive fits of laughter, spurred by the effects of the potent marijuana chasers that Simon had provided from his private stash. He regularly received FedEx packages that contained some of the best reefer Brett had ever tried. How he paid for it, or where it was sourced from, was Simon's little secret. But he was always generous.

When they all had regained a small amount of composure, Simon chimed in again.

"I'll tell you what, chums, I'm getting close to the bottom of the barrel with my Thai weed. And sure as hell I don't want any of that stale shit that I know one of you has balled up in a plastic bag in your pocket. Let's drain this bottle, toast to the end of hell—otherwise known as exams—and then take a few hits of the Thai before we call it a night. After enduring y'all for two hours, I'm going to fetch some TLC from Brooke before she flies home tomorrow, and then on to St. Barth's."

"We love you too, Simon," Brett replied as he splashed the remaining vodka more or less equally into their upturned glasses.

Gerry raised his glass first from his supine position and belted out an appropriate toast.

"To halfway to sophomore year, gents, with good drink and smoke. We'll be doing this again in three months."

'Hear, hear!" they all shouted.

The cool New England air on the way back to his dorm room was a refreshing blast that sobered Brett up enough to prevent him from stumbling across the quad. As he pushed open the old wooden doors that guarded the glass entry to his dorm, a poster stared back at him. In bold block letters, it asked a simple question.

How would you like to go and work in Africa this summer?

"I would like that very much," he said out loud. He snatched the entire poster from the door and marched up to his dorm room on the third floor. He followed the instructions on the poster and began the arduous process of completing the application and drafting the required essay. He worked until sunrise peeked through his east-facing window, and then passed out on the floor.

Five weeks later, he received his acceptance letter. Two months after that, he finished packing his duffle bag and was dropped off at the airport, on his way to the departure orientation.

The regional flight from White Plains to New Brunswick was the first time he had ever been on an airplane. Despite knowing very little about G forces, acceleration vectors, or climb-out vertices, it turned out that takeoff, which scrambled all of those sciences, would forever remain his favorite part of flying. And whenever he flew from that day forward, the poem he first memorized in junior high school came back to him.

Written by American pilot John Gillespie Magee, who died in a spitfire crash at the age of nineteen, Brett could still recite the poem from memory.

Oh, I have slipped the surely bonds of earth and danced the skies on laughter-silvered wings. Sunward I've climbed and joined the tumbling mirth of sun-split clouds and done a hundred things you have not dreamed of..."

When he arrived late that afternoon at the New Brunswick College campus, the contrast to his university back home was apparent. The campus was large and sprawling, with parks and open space. A separate bus line provided transportation throughout. It was vastly different than the tightly woven beehive campuses in New England. It would serve as the command center for an intensive three-day orientation. From the study of local culture, including family, tribe and clan, to tutorials on public health and economic conditions, he would learn the basics for successful integration into African culture. After that, the national group of students would depart from Kennedy Airport for destinations all over the African continent.

It was the nationally known CrossCore program, founded by Professor Mitchell Jamison. In total that year, they would insert ten groups of students to locations in different countries with a variety of local needs. Each country had agreed to the CrossCore code that resembled a miniature Peace Corps declaration. The countries also worked out a logistics plan, as well as a vigorous work schedule for each team. Every team would be joined by four to six university students from Africa, who would work with them for the duration. Team leaders would accompany the students in country, and they were all experienced travelers with proven leadership abilities. At the end of the work site assignments, the teams would participate in a two-week overland excursion to view regional and local sites of interest. No work, only rest and recuperation, was planned for that segment.

At the plenary session, the executive director welcomed everyone and said that they represented almost every state in the Union. He gave a special welcome to the international guests and national scholars who had joined them for the orientation lectures. He went on to outline the program and workshops for the next three days, including a quick briefing about the Air France flight that would take them to Dakar, Senegal. From there, regional jets or overland transport would take the various teams to their final destinations.

As Brett took notes and listened to the other speakers, he continued to have a hard time believing he was actually selected for the program. He would later joke that it was the power of cheap vodka and other unnamed substances that were responsible for his good fortune. But even after being selected, getting to his seat at the table had been a real challenge. Each selectee had been required to raise two thousand dollars in sponsorship support from local businesses, family, or friends. The remainder of the cost, roughly twenty-five hundred dollars, would be funded by the CrossCore endowment.

To meet his obligation, he had started working right away to organize what he believed was an effective campaign to raise the necessary funds. Knowing that he couldn't rely on family and friend donations, because there just wasn't a lot of extra money floating around in his circles, he concentrated his efforts on calls and visits to local organizations and neighborhood business in Queens. He had been naively confident that the Boys and Girls Club, the neighborhood YMCA, the NAACP, and others would be very willing to support his return to Africa to work alongside local villagers.

But after numerous rejections, he began to fear that he'd never be able to raise the money. In the end, mostly from family, he raised five hundred dollars. But along with his tender of that amount, he submitted a detailed prospect list and contact sheet that showed all the letters he'd sent out, and all the doors he'd knocked on to raise the money. He asked CrossCore to grant him additional scholarship aid to help him make the trip. Despite his substantial shortfall, the program decided to make up the difference. He wondered as he sat there if he was the only one unable to raise the full two thousand dollars.

The executive director's closing remarks snapped him back.

"You are a small but especially talented group of 140 students. We know from experience that your efforts will make an enormous difference to the cause of mutual understanding and trust that must lay at the foundation of peaceful international relations."

As he listened, he saw that the director had a very tanned and benign face, with a touch of sadness around his eyes. There were flecks of gray throughout his healthy mane of combed black hair. According to the bio that he received in his orientation package, the director was a forty-five year old Harvard trained Ph.D. in international studies. His entire career so far had been devoted to international efforts to bridge the gap between Americans and diverse people around the planet. Two years earlier, he had led a similar outreach program to China. It dawned on Brett as he looked over the director's impressive skill set that he could have been making far more money working as a consultant or a businessman. Instead, he was working with him and other students to make a difference.

"In three days' time, we fly out to explore the great continent of Africa, an enormous place of endless diversity. You will be ready for that diversity, as your workshops over the next three days will provide the knowledge you'll need to successfully work with the communities that have asked you to join them."

"But tonight we have our opening reception, a moment for you to get to know your fellow travelers and team members. I look forward to greeting each of you personally this evening. Now, we'll take a twenty-minute break and return for our first speaker, who will discuss important yet mostly invisible social and cultural distinctions between the Christian and Muslim communities."

"Thank you so much for your attention."

During the break, Brett introduced himself to one of the students that had attracted his attention during the morning registration.

"Hello, I'm Brett," he said as he smiled and bent slightly at the waist in a mock formal greeting.

"Well hello there, Brett. I'm Linda." She smiled back and managed a pretty good deep-kneed curtsy. "I'm so relieved that our name tags omitted surnames. It gives us something to solve for later as we get to know each other."

She smiled her perfect smile, and they shared a good laugh together. In just that moment, a bond was formed between them, based on their mutual sense of ribbing humor.

It turned out they were both in the Ghana group and would be traveling together for the entire summer.

"Of course, that had to be the case," he said when they combed through the final posted list of team assignments that afternoon.

"If not, we would have worked out some kind of switcheroo with one of the other teams to make it happen," she added.

Before returning to hear the afternoon speakers, they got to know each other a little better and agreed to meet that evening at the opening reception. Linda called it a mini date night out.

As he strolled around the campus grounds later that afternoon, when the workshops ended, he felt an incredible sense of freedom. It was almost a head-clearing feeling that sharpened his senses. Other than his first week at college, he couldn't think of a moment like this before, where he truly felt he was making a significant move on his own. It was a clear step away from the ordinary and regular. He felt, without really knowing why or how, that it might affect his life for years to come.

During the stroll, his mind returned to a more immediate concern. He was painfully aware of his razor-thin finances. They had barely gotten him there at all. Although he'd managed to put together an additional eighty-seven dollars for the trip, that had to last him almost three months. He calculated that he could double the amount by using the black market currency exchange that was common practice in Ghana. Because room and board was taken care of with his team's provisions, he wasn't overly worried about running out of money on the trip. But shopping sprees or splurging of any kind were not in his future.

Linda met him a few minutes before nine in the large lobby outside the reception hall. As he approached, he could see that she was finishing up a call on one of the pay phones in front. She wore tight pink skinny jeans and a white cotton top with a synched waist. He wasn't certain, but from his vantage point he suspected she wasn't wearing a bra. But the outfit was tasteful as well as sexy, and he admired the way it complemented her tall stature. The elevation from the high heels she wore brought her to within two inches of his six-foot-two frame—the perfect kissing distance, he believed.

She turned when the call was done and walked over as he waited by the entry door.

"Well, Brett, aren't you going to say *hello* and give me an obligatory peck on the cheek, or are you going to keep checking me out?"

"Oh, was I staring?" he said with genuine embarrassment. His peck to her cheek was clearly in keeping with the obligatory tradition as he tried to regain his balance with her. "Yes, busted. I admit I was checking you out, but only in the most clinically correct sense. You look great this evening. I'm glad we decided to do the reception together."

"Thank you, sir." She smiled. "And I must say that back home on my campus, very few if any of the available males manage to make a simple set of jeans and a dress shirt look quite as good as you do!"

"Well, thank you, Miss Linda! But please, tell me why women have the knack of staring without being seen doing so. It's not fair."

Not letting his clinically correct comment go unnoticed, Linda looked at him quizzically, furrowing her brow. "That's a secret all women are sworn to keep, I'm afraid. But I am going to follow up later with you about that clinical comment. I thought you said you were a history major, but maybe you meant to say you were pre-med."

"You know, even history majors are skilled in observational techniques." Smiling, he held his arm out to her, and they entered the large inner hall together.

They went right to the dance floor, where a large crowd had already gathered under the multicolored lights. The sound system commanded by the DJ was first rate, and between his tape recorded collection and dual platters, there was hardly any letup in the flow of popular dance numbers. Brett tried to be subtle this time as he admired her style on the dance floor. She seemed to flow between the rhythm and the treble beats, moving with an effortless grace. At times she would partner up with him and mix in a few spins and turns. She clearly enjoyed dancing. He admired her nutmeg brown complexion and high cheekbones that suggested a mixture of Native and African American blood. She also wore her black hair smoothed back and in a chignon. He remembered it was the same style that his mother and his aunts often wore their hair when he was small. She smiled back at him, and he could tell that she was checking him out as well.

After almost two hours on the dance floor, they took a much-needed break. They grabbed some water bottles and went out into the garden area in the rear of the building that surrounded a large three-level fountain. It was a clear and beautiful New Jersey summer evening and he began to acquire an entirely new appreciation for the Garden State, which he had always viewed with derision as a New Yorker due to the I-95 chemical plant parade.

Linda broke the silence first after they both nearly drained the first water bottle.

"I can't wait to complete the orientation and fly out to see Africa, Brett. I'm usually pretty laid back about things, but this one is really getting me amped up. What about you? How are you feeling?"

"Me? It's all just a dream, Linda. I think it won't become tangible for me until I step off the plane in Ghana and actually touch the soil under the African sun. Don't get me wrong, I don't plan on kissing the ground or anything."

"Thank God for that," she said quickly, "I heard they have the same dirty tarmacs over there that we'll see at Kennedy."

Then she turned serious.

"Is it just me, or did you notice some of the students today who, how to best say it, seemed hardly interested at all in the orientation topics and solely interested in cornering some of the women and making aggressive moves?"

"You must mean that less than honorable contingent from Trenton. It was my pleasure to spend a little time with them at lunch, when I made the mistake of sitting at their table. I hope they're not planning to wear those loud, colorful clothes when they get to Africa. The insects will have a field day."

"It takes an insect to know one," she said. "So they'll be right at home over there."

"I think they have one primary purpose, and that's keeping our egos in check. After all, we were at risk of buying the Kool-Aid about our being an elite group of students, nationally selected, cream of the crop, and all that. Those guys will forever keep us humble, since they're in the same group we are."

"You're right about that," she laughed. "No way we can fall for that elitist line with those knuckleheads in our midst. One of them practically pinned me in a corner this morning after the inoculation workshop. And we were only chatting for three minutes before he made his move!"

"Whoa, that's pretty aggressive. He should have been in my workshop that covered cultural differences we'll l run across once there. If he pulls that crap in some of the local tribal areas that we covered, he may end up going home in little pieces, complements of the village men who don't tolerate that behavior with their daughters and sisters."

"That workshop is being repeated tomorrow morning at eight. I'm tempted to slip a reminder note under his door personally, inviting him to attend. But something tells me no one in that crew has ever made an early morning class before."

"Speaking of early classes, it's a little after 11:30 now."

She checked her watch and nodded. "Where did the time go? Want to have a couple of last dances before calling it quits?"

"Sure. But don't expect me to always be willing to quit this early," he said with a sly grin.

Linda looked at him, and then gave him a quick kiss on the cheek. "Believe me, Mr. Brett, the last thing I would mistake you for is a quitter."

They held hands and walked back inside to the dance floor.

Brett's sleep was broken early in the morning by shouting voices coming from down the corridor outside his second-floor dorm room. What first startled him, however, was a thudding, crashing sound. He rolled off his bed, pulled on his boxer shorts and slipped into a tee shirt. There was no need to flip on the light switch, because his room was illuminated with pulsing red, blue and white light from outside. Looking through the curtain, he saw five or six police cruisers and one EMT vehicle haphazardly parked on the grass in front of the dorm.

Opening his door slowly, he leaned out and peeked past the facing to the far end of the hall, where the ruckus originated. A large crowd of students blocked his line of sight, so he walked down to the perimeter. His height allowed him to see over the heads of the twenty or so students who had formed a spectator's gallery around a flurry of police activity. They had cordoned off the end of the hall. Officers were stationed outside of room 202. Three students were soon brought out in handcuffs. They were barely dressed, and officers held their cuffed hands behind them. One of them had a bloody, swollen face and smeared blood down the front of his white tee shirt. Another was crying and trying to wipe away the tears with his shoulder. The third one appeared in reasonable shape, until Brett noticed that the officer pushing him forward had his right hand on the student's head. He was pressing a large gauze pad against it.

Right away, he recognized them. The Trenton guys.

"Stand back! Back it up! No cameras, or you'll be joining this party downtown," one of the bigger officers bellowed.

"Move it back!"

They all pressed against the wall and made space. One student was stupid enough to focus a small camera at the room door in anticipation of what might be coming out next. He was roughly grabbed by a burly officer, shoved, and cuffed up against the dorm wall. Then he was taken out behind the others.

Within seconds, two EMTs wheeled a large metal stretcher out of the room and began following two other officers down the hallway. One of them steadied a rolling IV station attached to the right arm of the young woman lying prone and unconscious under the blue sheets and brown blankets that tucked her tightly into the stretcher. Brett stared in disbelief at the once-beautiful girl that he'd first seen from a distance during one of his orientation classes the day before. She had apparently been violently beaten about her face. Her left eye was swollen closed, and he could see trauma marks on her cheeks and forehead. The hair that had been impeccably coifed yesterday was ragged and appeared partially uprooted from her head. A weave ripped out, he suddenly realized.

Oh my God, she must have been gang raped.

He watched the gurney recede slowly down the hall to the elevator.

What about Linda?

He ran back to his room and pulled on some jeans and sneakers. He raced down the north stairwell to ground level and ran the four hundred meters across the lawn to her dorm in what, if timed by the race clock, may have challenged some of his best outdoor track times. As he bolted up the front steps to the entrance, he could see the graduate student proctor sitting peacefully beyond the glass doors behind a desk, completely oblivious to the gruesome scene that he had just witnessed.

He drew deep breaths to catch his wind before entering the double front doors. He realized that his appearance alone at 4:00 in the morning could provoke a panic response from the proctor. Stranger things had happened to black males on largely white campuses across the nation. So before he entered the lobby, he composed himself and ran through what he would say in his mind.

Then he pressed the intercom buzzer and waited.

"Yes, may I help you, " the surprised graduate student asked.

"Yes you may. I'm here to check on the safety of a friend of mine, Linda, who is a resident in room 414. You may not be aware, but there was an incident at the male dorm over on Stedwell. The perpetrators were arrested. And the victim has been removed and taken to the hospital. Even though everything looks peaceful here, I would like to call my friend to make sure she's okay."

The proctor looked wide-eyed at him. Then, finally comprehending what he'd just heard, he hit the intercom and replied.

"Give me a minute and I'll patch you through to your friend."

Before doing so, the proctor called some type of central dispatch, and Brett could read the facial expression of shock and disbelief as his story was confirmed.

'Hold on, please. I'm patching you through to room 414."

Linda must be a sound sleeper he realized impatiently as the phone rang six times before she picked up.

"Hello," she said groggily.

"Linda, it's me. Brett. Sorry to wake you so early."

"It's four in the morning. Is everything okay? Why are you calling so early?" She was quickly coming on board now, he could tell.

"There was an incident, a rape of one of the women in the program in my dorm, on my floor. She was taken to the hospital ten minutes ago. She's been hurt bad. It was the Trenton guys."

"Oh no! I knew they were out of control. I should have reported their actions to the director. I could have helped prevent this."

"Hold on. Maybe you could have, but it's really hard to say. You can't take the blame. Nobody knew how out of control they were. If someone knew that, you've got to believe they would have never been accepted into the program in the first place."

"I know. I guess...I suppose you're right. I weighed those same issues when I had the run-in yesterday. They didn't seem like felons, just over-sexed throwbacks."

"Brett." Linda paused. "Why did you come over here to tell me this tonight? Why didn't you wait until morning?"

He hesitated, then he decided to put it out there. "Because I was really worried about you, Linda. I had to know right away, tonight, that you were safe and unharmed. I hope you don't mind."

"Thank you. No, I don't mind. Thank you, Brett."

It was doubtful that morning whether they and seven other CrossCore students would be joining the group at Kennedy the following day for the flight to Africa. Rather than participating in the ongoing morning and afternoon orientation sessions, they were all invited down to the New Brunswick police department, based on their contacts with the victim or with the rapists. They were told they were likely to be classified as material witnesses in the prosecution's case. If that happened, they would stay home that summer.

In a small, windowless conference room, Detective Arthur Maloney took off his crumpled suit jacket and placed it over the back of the metal framed chair at the head of the steel conference room table. His sleeves were already rolled up, as he had learned that this saved him countless rolling and unrolling of his sleeves during his twelve-hour shifts. No serious meeting ever happened in the precinct with jackets on and shirtsleeves unrolled.

The students were seated around the table watching him.

Detective Maloney was totally focused on casting the widest net possible for witnesses to convict the accused suspects. He had a personal bone to pick with rapists, as a different set of them had violated his fifteen-year-old niece years earlier. His record of convictions was the best in the department.

He adjusted his suspenders and turned to face the students as he loudly cleared his throat.

"I want to personally thank all of youse ladies and gentlemen for coming down to the precinct on short notice. I have heard that youse have got classes and what not that youse are missing today. When the PD learned about your leaving the country soon, it became necessary for us to start this conversation immediately. You have important information in your heads about the perps in this case. With that information, we're gonna convict those S-O-Bs, after a fair trial of course. But that will require your presence here in the good old U.S. of A. Africa will need to wait. I know I can count on each of youse to make the sacrifice and put off that trip for another year."

The speech was a body blow. Linda and Brett looked despairingly at each other. It wasn't like they didn't want to help. But for the life of them, they couldn't understand why their assistance was essential. The thugs drugged the girl, took her to their dorm room, and raped her. Those were the facts, and they just couldn't see why any color commentary they might have on the issue made a bit of difference in what should happen: conviction and jail time.

After another long hour with Detective Maloney, they sat outside the police station. Linda started working the pay phone, beginning with her father. After a fifteen-minute conversation where she filled him in, she hung up and said he would be in New Brunswick that afternoon. He was driving from Trenton and would get there by about two o'clock. She seemed to be encouraged, and said that her father was a long-time politician in the New Jersey state capitol. He might be able to fix this, she said. That was pretty much what he had done throughout his political career, she explained, and he knew a ton of people in New Jersey.

Because Linda was encouraged, he felt less anxious about their predicament. They all went to lunch at a local sandwich shop. The food was passable, but the cost was very agreeable from his perspective—it was free of charge, compliments of the New Brunswick PD.

Unfortunately, they had to return to the station after lunch for what Maloney had said would be further group and individual interrogation.

They had just reassembled in the stuffy, windowless room when Detective Maloney removed his crumpled jacket and started in on a speech about the department's need to have accurate contact information for each student. A knock on the door interrupted him and he opened it irritably, ready to ream whoever had deigned to intrude. A tall, well-dressed detective whispered something to Maloney that caused him to grab his jacket and leave the room.

"Youse all sit tight," he said before he closed the door.

Linda looked at Brett.

"My father should be here by now, if he kept to his schedule. Keep your fingers crossed." She held his hand.

Detective Maloney never returned to the conference room. Instead, the students were ushered out 20 minutes later by three uniformed officers, who escorted them to the front of the station house. A white transport van was waiting at curbside, and the door was opened from within as they approached. They were instructed to board. When they were seated, the older officer entered and stood at parade rest in the front of the van, his arms behind his back.

"Listen up, folks. We have determined that your further cooperation will not be necessary in this case. New Brunswick PD is confident that it has sufficient facts and evidence to obtain a conviction. You are free to resume your travels without restrictions."

Cheers erupted from all of the students. Brett and Linda hugged each other for a long time.

Chapter Four
Lailani's Pain

Lailani Aikins chose to walk the two miles to and from her high school every day rather than brave the trauma of the Albany public bus system. Except for the very coldest days of winter, she preferred the solitude of her thoughts to the noise and rancor of city busses packed with students. Many of those kids were there only because it gave them a chance to exploit and bully real students.

She also knew that those same bullies had been known to follow girls from the bus that refused to give them the right smile or deference to their crude solicitations. She remembered that last year a tenth grader was assaulted as she walked home from the bus stop. The local newspapers extensively covered the tragedy, reporting that she was a shy, sweet girl who apparently offended the toughs by failing to smile at their antics and lewd jokes. After what they perceived to be an affront to pride, they laid in wait for her a couple of days later. According to witnesses, some of them got off the bus one stop before her and others remained and left at the same time she did. Soon they surrounded her as she walked to her street. She recalled reading that her clothes were cut off her body with a straight razor, and that the girl was forced to run almost naked to her house, clutching her sliced-up dress and undergarments. She also suffered severe lacerations from the razor.

Chills went down Lailani's spine at the memory of it all, but she overcame them and calmed down. She would not be a victim if she could help it. In her coat pocket, she tightly clutched the large butcher knife she carried with her every day.

Despite the weekday tensions of coming and going from school, she liked her neighborhood, where she had lived all her life. Older now, and in her senior year of high school, she was able to contribute to those less fortunate and also give back to her community in other large and small ways. On Saturdays she volunteered at the local nursing home, where she helped feed many of the infirm patients. For others she would read them a favorite book, or summarize sections of the newspaper that they were interested in hearing about. But mostly her time at the nursing home was about providing basic human contact to the many who rarely received a visitor and never left that enclosed space.

In addition to the nursing home, she was a member at her local church, having been baptized in the basement pool when she was eight years old. The women's group accepted her as a junior member, and she assisted them with prayer intercessions on behalf of the faithful as well as with local outreach missions to the neighborhood. Her faith came largely from her mother, who before her passing had instilled in her young daughter a strong belief in the power of the unseen.

But there were also big changes ahead for her, and she could hardly contain her excitement. She had been accepted into the registered nurse program at Slater Memorial. That four-year course of study would begin in August, and she tried hard to control her growing anticipation.

As she turned down her street she relaxed a bit, knowing that she was safely in sight of her house. Then suddenly a strong sadness came over her. She still deeply missed the close times with her older sister every day after school, even though she had moved out years before. Together they had overcome the sadness of their mother's passing. It was one of those unexpected waves of sadness, equal in intensity to her more occasional memories of her mother. But seeing her best friend Remy waiting on the front steps with her head in a book lifted her spirits, and she left the past alone.

Remy had fallen one grade behind, due to a bout with pneumonia last year that kept her home for three months. But she was smart and still motivated to get good grades, even though she missed being in the same classes together.

"Hi, Remy. I didn't see you in school at all today."

"That's because I wasn't there, Lai. My baby brother had a bad cough this morning, so Ma had me stay home with him. She can't afford to take off a day from work."

"Did you get all your homework assignments? I would've gone around for you if I'd known."

"Yep, no worries, I have everything. I asked Gloria to bring them to me this afternoon, because she was leaving school a little early for a dentist appointment. I have all two hours' worth!"

"Well then, girl, I guess we'd better head upstairs and have a snack, and then get to some serious work. I'm not sure if Dad's still sleeping, so remember we have to creep up those noisy stairs."

Her father had been a single parent raising his daughters since his wife had passed. He worked the night shift at the Union Railroad yard, one of the largest employers in Arbor Hill. His best friend also worked there, and she always called him Uncle Calvin, even though she knew they weren't related by blood. She remembered hearing that he was also a good friend of her mother back in the day. Calvin Ward worked the day shift at the rail yard. That worked out well for her dad, because Uncle Calvin lived across the street from them, and he'd always check on things around the neighborhood at night to make sure she was safe. She'd worked out a secret signal with him to indicate that everything was okay inside the house. She would always leave her small table lamp on by the window, and it would remain on until morning.

Later as they were finishing up their homework, her father came down the hall and peeked into her room. She was sitting on the floor, leaning against the wall with her legs crossed at the ankles as she finished the last of her calculus homework. Remy was at the study desk completing a writing assignment.

"How you doing, Lai?" he said in his deep morning voice, one that seemed to rumble in his chest until he had his mug of strong coffee.

"Hi Dad, we're good."

He smiled at Remy and nodded hello.

"How was work last night?"

"The usual, girl. You know no one's interested in breaking into the railway yard and stealing a locomotive. It was slow, just the way I like it."

Lailani glanced back over at her Dad and smiled. He seemed to have a little more belly fat than she could recall, and she wondered whether he was supplementing the healthy dinners that she made for him with junk food.

"Dad, do you want me to put some more fruit and maybe a bit more meat and carbs into your lunch box before you head in each night? I could also add a healthy treat for you that you wouldn't see until you unwrapped it on your break."

"That would be great, Lai. Sometimes I could use a snack around five, just before the sun starts to peek out. It would help keep me sharp"

"Okay then, you're going to find some extra special things in your dinner pail from now on."

She was happy that he agreed to her idea. She would make something tasty and healthy that would keep him away from the calorie- and sugar-laden options around the neighborhood.

"How was your day, Remy?" he asked, realizing that he had not properly greeted her.

"My day was pretty good, Mr. Aikins. I had to stay home to tend to my brother, but I got all of my homework from school and I'm just about finished."

She knew, of course, that Mr. Aikins placed a high premium on completed homework, and that her report would make him feel good about her and Lai.

"That's wonderful to hear. So many of our children out there would take advantage of a day like you had, and not even do any homework. I'm proud of you, Remy."

"Thank you, Mr. Aikins."

"Lai, is Remy going to join us for dinner after you all finish?"

"No sir, she has to get back home soon to make sure her brothers and sisters are fed."

"All right. But Remy, you make sure Lai gives you a big slice of that deep dish apple pie that we got from the church yard sale yesterday. We picked up two pies, so make sure you take enough for your brothers and sisters."

"Thanks, Mr. Aikins."

Lailani knew that dessert treats were a rare thing at Remy's household, where her family lived from paycheck to paycheck, supplemented by food stamps, to meet the basic nutritional needs.

After her dad left for work later that evening, she kept to her usual routine. As night approached, she turned on her upstairs safety lamp. Then she took out several novels that she was reading simultaneously and decided which one she would continue in that evening. She decided to read more of *The Catcher in the Rye* by Salinger. After washing up, brushing her teeth, and changing into her nightie, she scooted across her bed and leaned against the wall, pushing her favorite pillow seat cushion behind her back.

Two hours of reading passed quickly, and she was a little bit hungry. In the kitchen she cut a small wedge of pie. She boiled hot water and filled her favorite glass mug, adding an herbal chamomile tea bag. She took everything upstairs on a small tray. Once there and settled, she continued reading about the exploits of Holden Caufield, Salinger's intrepid protagonist. Yet his exploits, exciting as they were, failed to keep her from dozing off into a deep sleep within the next half hour.

Sometime later, a loud pounding on the downstairs front door jarred her awake. As she got out of bed, she realized that her room was completely dark.

The bulb must have burned out.

More noise came from the door, and it sounded like it was being unlocked. She eased across the room and out to the hall, crouching behind the big rail post at the top of the stairs. She heard the rattling of keys and the sound of the latch turning open. Then the slightly sticky door was roughly pushed in.

Dad must have come home early for some reason.

The yellowish glow from the nearby street lamp cast a long, narrow light shaft across the entryway, and Lai saw the figure of a big man enter the doorway. She stood up from behind the banister, thinking it was her father.

The shadowy image looked up the stairs and bellowed her name. "Lai, Lai, you all right, child?"

"Uncle Calvin, is that you?"

"It's me, girl." He slammed the door closed. "Your light was out, and I came over here to see what was wrong."

He quickly climbed the creaky stairs toward her.

"I'm okay. I'm fine. My light bulb must have burned out when I dozed off, that's all."

Soon he was standing unsteadily two steps below her. He was breathing hard, and she could smell the pungent strong liquor washing over her. He stared down at her short nightie that was well above her knees and showing her smooth legs. Then his eyes rose to her chest, braless beneath the thin cotton material.

Instinctively she folded her arms in front of her and stepped backward toward her room.

"Thanks for coming to check on me, Uncle Calvin. I'm okay, as you can see. I never knew that you had a key to the house. Did Daddy give you that?"

His balance wavered. To steady himself, he pulled his bulk up the final two stairs.

She shined her flashlight at his face and could see that his eyes were red, and his face was flushed from the liquor. She began to back up quickly.

"I always had a key, girl. Got this years ago from your mama. We was real good friends back then, before she got into all that church business."

Fear took hold and she felt her knees shaking. But she had enough strength to slip through her room door and latch the lock before Calvin could react to her movement.

She stood with her back pressed against the door, catching her breath and listening for any sound. The hallway was quiet, and then she heard what she thought was the creak of stairs.

He's leaving.

Daddy's got to get those keys back. That was weird. Why would Mama give Uncle Calvin keys to their house? And what kind of friends were they?

She put on her coat to cover up her nightie and listened at the door for a few more minutes. Everything was quiet. She was about to go out and take a peek when Calvin crashed the door open with his heavy body and she was thrown back across the room, landing on her backside. As he approached her, his eyes lowered to her legs. She realized that her nightie was ruffled up above her waist, exposing her hips and belly and white cotton panties.

She grabbed at her nightie, trying to pull the light cloth down while scrambling backwards on her elbows. She tried to stand up straight, but Calvin locked his meaty hands onto her ankles and dragged her to him, spreading her bare legs wide apart. He pulled her up around him and fell down between her thighs, smiling. She was crushed under his bulk.

"Come here, girl. You as pretty as your mama was, and looks like she done left me a gift to take the place she used to have."

He splayed his big body over her and grabbed at her hair with his left hand, ripping it down from its neat bun and spilling hairpins over the floor. Then his right hand slipped under her and he squeezed her cheeks hard, causing her to wince in pain. Before she could scream, he clamped his foul-smelling mouth over hers and moved his tongue roughly back and forth.

She could hardly breathe, and her eyes glared wide in the dark room. She was pinned. Frantically, she knew she had to play along to loosen his grip. So she moved her head slightly to the side and started to kiss him on the cheek and ear. The pleasure relaxed him, and he responded by easing up off her as he smiled. Then he let her right side free as he reached in to yank down his zipper.

In that instant she pushed her hand into her coat pocket and gripped the handle of the butcher knife. She stabbed the sharp blade into his flabby side again and again, until she was covered with blood and he was still.

Chapter Five
Vast Continent

For the second time in a week, Brett was on an airplane. But this one was a massive trans-ocean Air France jet. The flight crew was based in Dakar, Senegal. Two forward cabin stewardesses greeted him warmly as he boarded. He felt a tinge of pride as he passed the cockpit door where two African pilots were fully engaged in completing the final departure checklist, not noticing him at all. Having very little flying experience, he had no idea how rare that sight was in the world of aviation.

He relaxed a little after he was seated and managed to tamp down some of the anxiety that had been gnawing at him for the past few days, when the full realization hit him that he would be crossing several thousand miles of open sea at an altitude of thirty-five thousand feet.

Before touchdown in Dakar, the flight plan had them landing in the Azores to refuel. It was a small nation consisting of nine volcanic islands, situated far from land and surrounded by ocean; it lay almost a thousand miles west of Lisbon, Portugal. For a first-time international traveler like he was, surviving the approach into the Azores was nerve-wracking. It involved descending from thousands of feet and landing on what was akin to a postage stamp in the sea. As he watched the jet descend through the small cabin window, it seemed to be smoothly dropping into the water. He grabbed Linda's hand and closed his eyes. He just hoped those pilots were as good as he first thought they were. He hardly felt the wheels touch the runway when they landed.

There was also a somewhat exotic aspect to the long flight. French was spoken first, followed by English. Linda was completely attuned to the French language, having taken four years of it in high school as well as during her freshman year in college. But he was dependent on waiting for the English version to understand what he was being told to do. He smiled inwardly, recalling his Dad's insistence that he not take French, but that he study Latin instead. Nobody alive spoke the Latin language, he had protested. But his father's argument back then, which proved to be fairly accurate, was that Latin would improve his reading comprehension and writing. Ultimately, he was told, it would enable him to score higher on standardized tests. He gave his old man some credit, as his scores did end up helping him enter a highly rated college.

But pushing his luck further, his father insisted that he take German as well during his junior and senior years. The rationale was that German would boost his academic success in chemistry. That turned out to be a mentally painful crock of crap, as he never saw any connection between his study of the difficult German language and mastery of the periodic table or the balancing of chemical equations. So he gave his father a 50 percent score on the language front.

"Did you get that last instruction, Brett?"

Linda looked at him and smiled mischievously as she laced her fingers into his. "It said that all tall, handsome black men had to report immediately to the rear cabin and change into silk pajamas provided by Air France. No underwear allowed."

He smiled at her and shook his head. She was a hoot, and he had really grown to appreciate her in the short time they had known each other. He wondered what the future might hold for them.

After the refueling was complete, the captain eased the lumbering jet slowly down the tarmac to the number one position for takeoff. Of course we're number one, he said to himself, there's no one else taking off.

The plane turned slowly onto the runway, then paused in position. After several minutes, he wondered whether some mechanical issue might have surfaced that prevented them from moving forward. But then the captain pushed the throttle full forward, and the big quad engine jets roared to life. As the G forces pressed him hard against the seat, the runway clamor and vibration was soon replaced with smooth acceleration that drove them cloudward to Africa, beckoning from over the horizon.

―――――

Brett's few first days in Ghana were everything he hoped for. The team of ten had grown by four as they welcomed two male students from Cote d'Ivoire and two women from the University of Ghana.

Along with Eaton, their leader, who was a doctoral student at U.S.C., they provisioned for the motor trek north from Accra. The overland journey to the worksite in the Volta region would take them roughly eleven hours, including a relaxed stopover in the regional capital of Ho to refuel and enjoy some local hospitality.

The team's final destination was a small village with the unassuming name of Anfoeta Chebe. They would soon learn that the toniest living quarters in that far-away outpost was an old two-story former regional administration building. It was being prepped for their arrival. Since the end of British Colonial rule fifteen years before, the stately old building had remained unoccupied and boarded up. In preparation for their guests, the villagers removed the boards, swept and washed away decades old dust as best they could, and repaired and painted the interior rooms and exterior façade of the building. While the building had no plumbing, electricity, or exterior window covers or panes, each of the rooms had been equipped with double beds and full mosquito nettings. The villagers were proud of their accomplishment and confident that their soon-to-arrive American guests would feel very pampered indeed.

They left Accra at seven o'clock in the evening, since it was important that they arrive at the village soon after sunrise the next day, rather than late afternoon or early evening when the villagers would already be sleeping. Every day the villagers arose at three or four o'clock in the morning, depending on the particular responsibility they bore. The earliest risers would trek long distances and return with fresh drinking water, walking sometimes more than four hours in total. Along with gathering firewood, that chore was always carried out by village women.

They filled the compact and sturdy coach bus, leaving only two empty seats. Many separate animated conversations were happening among team members at the same time, and everyone was excited and energized to at last be on the way to the worksite. In the brief time together they had gelled, despite the vastly different personal histories they each carried with them.

Brett sensed a mutual respect among the young group of students that would have been unanticipated by an outside observer merely reviewing resumes about each of them. It was the unusual synergy evolving over time within the team that caused him to think more deeply about the reasons that accounted for it. In many ways, it helped him to form the early contours of his basic view of the world, one that he would sharpen and refine over the decades.

The earliest kernel of his thinking actually began with a question: Given that his CrossCore teammates ranged from rich to poor, from black to white, from American to African, how in the world would they ever be expected to accomplish anything of real significance together? After all, he thought, they were not getting paid, had not signed up to some central philosophy or creed, and the impetus that drove them was volunteerism, not forced labor. He gradually began to appreciate that it was the mission itself, and the activity required to accomplish it, that held the team together and allowed them to achieve something tangible despite adversities.

Halfway through the journey north, and to the great joy of all, they adopted an eleven-year-old African boy named John while they were dinning out in Ho. He was an orphan working as a bus boy at the restaurant. Those wages, he said, helped his younger brothers and sisters at the orphanage survive. John energetically proposed to lease himself out as a tour guide and porter for the team. He was fluent in four European languages, and five or six local languages and dialects. Those skills alone were worth far more than the wages they would pay him. He also willingly pitched in to provide manual labor support. That alleviated some of the toil that fell on the team members as they schlepped supplies and luggage throughout the three-month adventure. After Eaton concurred, John returned with a small satchel with extra clothes and sat proudly in his seat at the front of the coach. He was the one who seemed to have adopted the entire team, and no one felt bad about that.

Soon after departing the town, the ebony evening blackness over Ghana was complete. A vast front of thick clouds obscured the mesmerizing display of southern hemisphere stars, a display so brilliant that Brett and Linda had sat together two days earlier outside of their temporary quarters in Accra and leaned back against a terrace wall, gazing up at the sky for hours. Neither of them wanted to run inside and retrieve the sky map that would have enabled them to precisely label each constellation and star. Time for that later, they agreed as they absorbed the grand stellar rotation above the vast continent.

When they were two hours north of Ho, the darkness and monotony of the road had lulled everyone to sleep except the driver. Linda crashed with her head on Brett's shoulder while he was completely knocked out and reclined deep within the comfortable coach seat. His mouth was slightly open, and he made a soft snoring sound as he slept. But some unexplained and barely audible presence gradually woke him out of that deep slumber. He raised his head, but kept his shoulder level so not to awaken her. Between the hum and bump of the tires over the narrow, uneven road, and the rev of the engine as the driver worked the gears for the best traction, he listened. He was sure that something was making a different noise in the background. Slowly he reached down to his knapsack and took out his flashlight. Aiming it above his head, he turned it on.

"Oh my God," he cried as his light disturbed a dense parade of bugs across the ceiling. "It's crawling with bugs!"

Exposed to the light, what seemed to be thousands of insects began a zigzagged dash to cover, partially disappearing by the time the other team members were awake enough to look overhead. The driver followed Eaton's frantic orders and turned on the interior lights. Then he pushed hard on the brakes and brought the coach to a skidding halt in the middle of the pitch-black night. By that time, no more a dozen or so quarter-inch long black bugs remained on the ceiling. And those were fast disappearing. Several women who saw the bug parade screamed and stood up, running in panic to the front of the coach.

"I think they're under the seats!" shouted an otherwise quiet young woman from Wisconsin.

Everyone spilled out of the front coach door, including the driver. They all backed away and used their various flashlights to illuminate the otherwise complete and utter darkness surrounding them. Then John went over to Eaton, and they whispered back and forth. Eaton finally nodded, and John spoke to the group in clear, British-accented English.

"My dear, wonderful friends, it is advisable that we all should not long remain here in the middle of this road, and in the darkness you see. There are much bigger things out here than the little roaches that make their home in the coach. In fact, we are the visitors to their world, as this is a common problem in parts of Ghana. These particular roaches have quite good taste indeed, as they have chosen a beautiful German coach for their home. They will do us no harm, my brothers and my sisters, as they do not bite and carry no disease. If we keep the bus clean and free of food, you will hardly notice them. At night if we are traveling, we should always keep the lights on, and only a very few, if any, will be seen. But believe me, we really must not stand out here in the bush at night. For you see, there are much bigger dangers that we attract to ourselves."

With that sobering report, Eaton instructed the team to board the bus quickly. With interior lights on, they continued the journey to the small village. The roaches were no bother, just as John advised.

When the team arrived at the village shortly after dawn, they were greeted with a magnificent welcome pageant. School children from all of the lower grades were adorned in local costumes, and there were singing, dancing, drumming, and welcome speeches. The villagers had all turned out, some seventy of them in total, it appeared. This was their first time viewing Americans from America, and none of them would miss that opportunity. The smaller children who were not part of the pageantry crowded around the team members, and several children touched the skin of the white students. Then they would run away giggling when they learned that what they thought was white paint did not rub off.

The two Ghanaian women who had joined the team were of a different tribe than the members of the village. They were also from the capital city of Accra, and that caused the villagers to view them with great awe. The Ivorian students, on the other hand, spoke French as their primary language. They were also supremely sophisticated students and very trendy dressers. The villagers found them fascinating. But despite the French-inspired flash and dash, they achieved an instant bond with the village children because they were accomplished footballers. They would conduct soccer matches with the local kids every late afternoon using the ball of choice, a healthy dried coconut pod.

What really struck Brett about the welcome ceremony was the almost perfect melodic pitch of the voices. And there were no wind instruments accompanying them to provide a starting note for harmony. Only traditional local drummers played along to provide rhythm. Yet the voices rose in a stunningly perfect harmony that enveloped and surrounded them all in the small clearing. He would always recall the Ghanaian words of one particular greeting song, feeling its welcoming spirit while having no idea what the words actually meant.

In the days that followed, he and the other African American students on the team heard the rumor circulating that they were considered by the villagers to be black Englishmen. It turned out that neither the village parents nor their children had ever been taught about the transatlantic slave trade. So they had no concept of Africans in America, who were distantly related to Africans on the continent of Africa. During the early weeks of their stay, Brett and some of the other team members talked with small groups of children about those topics, and the youngsters eagerly listened. He would soon learn how big a mistake that was.

Meanwhile, the daily grind of appearing at the work site at five-thirty in the morning was the norm for all. Team members also burned the candle at both ends, at least in the villagers' eyes. When the village went to bed at dusk, the team members were still up laughing, playing cards, and having fun with board games. Or they were drinking beer or palm wine. So another rumor circulated widely—that the Americans did not require sleep to live.

Despite their late night activities, the team ate breakfast together at five and then walked the quarter mile down the pitch-black road past the Forbidden Forest to the work site. The most peculiar aspect of that quarter-mile walk in absolute darkness was that every invisible villager who passed them said hello to them, using their individual names. How they could see anything always remained a mystery. On one walk to the site, Linda and Brett were startled by a cheerful hello from an invisible source only a foot or so behind them. The source of the greeting was apparently on a bicycle with a friend on the handlebars, and could be heard but not seen peddling away from them.

"When we get back stateside, I've got to get my eyes checked," Brett said.

Linda nodded in agreement.

At the work site, they spent their hours assisting villagers from their home village and two neighboring villages construct the school. It was a simple two-story cinderblock design that would house ten new classrooms and several expansive enrichment areas. Mortar and bricks were made near the site at a local quarry. The CrossCore team worked as unskilled laborers, with skilled work teams from each of the three villages. The presence of the international team acted as a common adhesive, allowing the different villages to work together despite a history of friction that had often driven them apart.

After the fourth week at the site, the tall, lean headmaster, Mr. Akenboa, who would be in charge of the new school building when it opened, invited the team to the old school house for an afternoon chat. He stood at the front of the classroom while the seven of them who were curious enough to make the walk over sat in the small student desks in front of him. His arrogance was apparent to everyone, and it simmered just below the surface as he regally conducted the meeting.

Brett remembered him as the same man who had mediated an intra-village squabble a couple of weeks earlier. The squabble back then was over the distribution and equal sharing of cacao beans. They were handed out daily at the site like candy from large buckets to each of the work teams. In addition to keeping energy levels high, the beans had several other positive health effects and had long ago been incorporated into West African diets. When the argument among the three village work teams reached a peak and emotions flared, there was a work stoppage. Akenboa was called in to mediate and get things back on track, since he was apparently held in great respect by all three villages.

But at least in his eyes, Akenboa's harshness was on display during that mediation. One quite short and stocky villager had stood up to explain why his village had always been shorted when the beans were passed out. Brett knew him as a decent fellow who had given many team members patient instruction in how to lay brick and mortar in a straight line. But he had not even completed his first sentence before he was strongly admonished to sit down immediately by Akenbao. The publically stated reason for the command to sit was that the man could hardly know anything at all, due to his short stature. No villager supported the man or challenged Akenboa.

Brett and his teammates were shocked to learn back then that an ancient tribal prejudice favoring height and punishing shortness was alive and well before their eyes. That hadn't been covered in the otherwise thorough New Brunswick orientation. The mediation continued, but soon turned into a one-sided arbitration that was settled by dictate rather than consensus. He tried hard to see the deeper cultural reasons for the manner in which the dispute was handled, but they were lost on him.

And so he wondered with some apprehension what Akenboa was up to this time.

"We are here to speak about the stories you have revealed to the children, such things as the slavery of men and women, and ships crossing the sea from our country to America that were carrying such slaves. These stories are very bad indeed for my students, and you must tell them soon that you were only making big jokes with them."

Steve Woodland, a white sophomore from the University of Chicago, had a real problem with Akenboa's demand.

"Slavery was no joke at all, sir," Woodland said in a loud and clear voice. "More than twenty million slaves, including men, women and children, were extracted from West African shores and transported to the Caribbean Islands, and further on to North America or South America. Others were hauled off to the Middle East, North Africa, and other parts of the world. The exact numbers will never be known. The slave trade persisted for more than four hundred years, twenty generations. These, sir, are conservative estimates that have been published in peer-reviewed journals. I can send you the citations to these articles if you want to review them."

It was clear from the sour expression on Akenboa's face that he was unaccustomed to pushback of any kind. But he was crafty, if nothing else, and quickly switched his tactics.

"You must see, my good friends, that a history of slavery is completely irrelevant to my students. They are members of a sovereign nation, and some of them will grow up to help run Ghana. That is what we educate here in the Black Star Nation—future leaders and strong citizens. What can slavery information do for their future? These students have many more important things to master."

Then he strode back to his desk and sat down on top, continuing his vertical dominance of the space.

"My good friends, have you heard about the Forbidden Forest from the village people?" Several team members nodded. Akenboa became slightly animated as he continued. "This is the one you pass every morning on your way to the work site. It is the one where those who have entered have never been seen or heard from again."

They had each heard the stories and seen the fervent belief on the faces of the villagers who told them to beware and not step even one foot from the road into the forest, lest they be consumed by it and never seen again. Many team members, including Brett, were tempted at times to step quickly into it and then maybe jump back out, but in the end they decided not to tempt fate.

Akenboa then rose to his full height and spoke loudly. "I have a potion that once ingested by you, will allow you to enter the Forbidden Forest and reemerge unscathed. Who among you will volunteer?"

Brett looked around and didn't see any hands shooting up. He, for one, thought that the meeting was beginning to take a really strange turn.

Akenboa was very surprised there were no takers. He had heard that all Americans were brash risk-takers. So he decided to up the ante.

"And there is much more. I have a mighty potion that will allow you to be struck by a razor-sharp machete without damage to your skin. Believe me, no blood will escape your body. And finally, there is a strong potion that will enable you to launch an arrow into the air, which will travel miles before returning back to your hand. You will then see what the arrow has seen."

Brett raised his hand, and for a moment Akenboa believed he had enticed one of the Americans to take advantage of his offer. But he fooled him.

"Excuse me, sir, but what kind of potions are these, and where do they come from?"

"Ah, you see, my American friend, these potions are from the ancient medicines built upon the old knowledge of the ancestors. I am able to command these things because I am the regional witch doctor."

Brett always remembered that it was Linda who suddenly manufactured some excuse whereby they all had to immediately return to the campsite for an important meeting. She, of course, always denied that charge.

Later that evening, after the usual storytelling and games and palm wine drinking with the team, they both returned to their spacious open-air bedroom. They had an expansive view of the outdoors through three large windows frames. Since mosquito netting was the only defense against innumerable bites, they undressed and quickly dove beneath the billowing white gauze netting. Ensuring its full effectiveness required that it be tucked in completely at every side and corner. The effect left them thoroughly cocooned, but prepared for any possible aerial assault by the incessant pests, some of which could be carrying malaria.

When they were both partially covered under the white cotton top sheet, he turned on his side to face her.

"Lin, I think this nightly adventure into our gauze house has given me a completely different perspective about intimacy between couples and the need for them to stay together."

"You know," she said, turning fully to him and resting her head on her hand, "I was thinking the same thing the other night. After tucking in with you, the last thing on my mind is to contemplate any kind of separation during the night."

He smiled. "I think it's a testament to night-long bladder control on both of our parts. Or maybe it's only a healthy fear of being eaten alive by our pesky, buzzing friends."

"You're absolutely right," she said, gently stroking his forehead.

As she moved her arm, the white sheet slowly slid down from her shoulder, revealing her taut breast. He gently messaged the back of her hand and soon placed in on his chest while kissing each of her fingers.

They had grown so much closer to each other in this vastly different world, where even the most familiar things turned alien if given enough time. But they were now a constant to one another, something familiar and something solid. And their intimate times together were patient and tender. He learned this way from her as she guided him away from stereotypes about male performance and female needs and desires. They felt no pressure to perform on some regular schedule when they were alone, which made moments like this more intense and passionate.

He moved next to her and cradled her face in the palms of his hands, drawing her closer to fully kiss her lips. She responded, pressing her warm body against him. They felt the familiar heat rise between them, further charging the humid temperature that was a constant evening norm. They encircled each other with a long, athletic hug, where even their ankles and toes seemed to entwine.

He gently relaxed his embrace and kissed her shoulders and chest and legs and waist, savoring all of her for what seemed like forever. In time she drew him in completely.

They would continue pressing deeper into each other, until their love was finally exhausted. Then they passed out and slept together beneath the enveloping white canopy and the bejeweled African sky.

At breakfast the following morning, Eaton suddenly appeared at the long table where they always shared the early morning meal. He frantically gestured at everyone to come in close.

"I just came from the supply tent, where I finished the inventory check. Someone got there before me, probably very early in the morning. All of our prescription medicine is gone, including penicillin, morphine, codeine, and the rest. It's been cleaned out. That medicine had to last us all summer. It was probably worth five thousand dollars."

Brett spoke up quickly.

"I know what you might be thinking, Eaton—that one of the villagers took the stuff, and that we should pack up and leave. But I gotta tell you that in the weeks I've been here, I believe I could leave my wallet on a tree stump and return a week later to find that it had not been touched, not by the people here. Now it might be soaked from the rainfall, or filled with ants or bugs, but the money and cards would still be there."

Others in the group seconded his assessment about the remarkable honesty that surrounded them.

Knowing his precarious financial circumstances, however, Linda couldn't resist ribbing him.

"Brett, we all know there wouldn't be any money in your wallet in the first place. And as for credit cards, what would a villager do with your library card and student ID?"

Her humor brought a little bit of relief to the tense atmosphere, and there was laughter all around. He looked at her, and raised both fists in a mock threat.

Eaton responded, "I agree with your sentiment about how honest the villagers are, Brett. But if not them, then who?"

That's when Steve spoke up from the far side of the circle.

"Someone's missing from breakfast," he said. "Where's young John?"

When they got to John's room, they found that all of his personal effects and his satchel bag were gone.

School construction was 85 percent complete, despite the occasional work stoppages. It was time for the CrossCore team to depart. They were confident that the villagers, who were now working smoothly together, would put the finishing touches on the structure and open the doors to students sometime in the fall. They envisioned the influx of dozens of fresh, smiling brown faces eager to listen and learn.

For Brett, the memories from that summer would always remain, augurs of what was possible when a community pulled together and overcame differences. The experience was etched in the stone of the building site, memorialized in the clatter, dust, and din of the work. It was preserved in the metallic scrape of trowels on cinder block bricks and the fervent cries among the field of bricklayers demanding *mortar, mortar, mortar.*

They packed up, and it was time to say farewell. Team women said their goodbyes with long hugs and tears, surrounded by the many women from the villages. They had all come to know each other well over the past weeks. They were sisters now. It was evidence of the eternal bond among women that could transcend vast distinctions in social or financial class. Among the men, the bond was as deep, but of a different kind. The mutuality of strength and persistence through several near calamities during the work had drawn these men from vastly different cultures together. Brett and his fellow teammates stayed within the cultural norms they had absorbed long ago in New Brunswick. So there were no hugs, embraces, or tears among the men. Instead, firm hand holding, stout shoulder bumps, and bold gazes into the eyes of their friends signified a lasting respect.

Everyone knew it was now finished, and they would never meet again.

They team set out after dawn, along with the roaches, for the two-week land cruising adventure that would take them eventually to Senegal for the long flight home. But a few of them, including Brett, persuaded Eaton to allow them to set foot on Nigerian soil, if only briefly. Eaton was also a student of history and was aware of the significance of the request, although he was still not easily persuaded. Finally he relented when the coach driver assured him there was a village that straddled the border, and that would allow safe crossing over water to Nigeria. His decision was not reached lightly, since deadly civil war had wracked parts of Nigeria for the past two years.

The interested group of eight team members, some black and some white, were taken to the boat dock in the morning, while the others continued to luxuriate at an overnight bed and breakfast. They were met at the river by a boatwoman in a large, wide canoe with a small outboard engine. She gave them a gap-toothed smile and greeted them warmly.

"Come, we go now together. Move slowly into seat. Thank you good." She smiled again.

They all gingerly boarded the beamy water taxi and shoved off. The destination was the Ghanaian village of Ganvee. Then, if she later agreed to their plan, they would head to the Nigerian border.

Ganvee was a thriving village with stick and thatch houses, and larger public buildings. All were elevated above the water. Brett saw ongoing construction projects along their route, as well as large, fully functioning produce and fish markets. All transportation within the village was by water vessel both large and small. The population seemed to be busy and motivated, and he saw no signs of idleness.

Blake, one of the most affluent and widely traveled students on the team, joked that the village looked like a budding Venice without the eroding concrete and falling plaster that was in abundance during his last visit. Linda thought that it actually might have predated Venice, based on the migratory patterns from East and Central Africa that dated back several thousand years.

When the scheduled tour ended, Brett made his pitch to the boatwoman.

"Ma'am, we would like to cross over to the Nigerian side, just to see it for a few minutes. Could we ask you to take us over there and bring us back? We're willing to pay you well for your time."

The old woman frowned, and the almost permanent smile she had worn during the tour disappeared.

She looked at them and grimaced.

"Nigeria bad place, they fight Christians and Muslims together. No peace. Ghana is good place for tour, no?"

Linda spoke up, hoping that a little woman-to-woman persuasion might help their cause.

"We won't be asking you to wait long at all, you see. Just a ten or fifteen-minute stop to wait for us. We have come so far, and the blood of Nigerian tribes flows within some of us."

Steve sealed the deal by pulling out a fifty Cede note—twenty-five dollars U.S. at black market rates. That represented almost twenty days' wages for the old woman and would help meet many family needs.

"We go and come back quick!" she said, her smile returning.

She pointed the boat slowly to the west and glided across the shallow marsh areas. Ghana receded behind them, and only water and bush lay ahead. They could feel roots or other hard objects occasionally scrape against the hull of the boat. But whatever path the old woman was following was more than deep enough, for the most part. Then the thick bush and trees seemed to close in on them, and Brett and the others clutched the side of the boat and ducked low.

At any moment it appeared they would run aground as the marsh bed began to get clearer and closer beneath them. The old woman steered the boat on an arc to the right, and they drifted through thick vegetation, forcing them all to lean in and crouch even lower.

Suddenly, they emerged into a clearing, and spread out before them was a twenty-foot outcropping of mud brown sand. The old women cut the engine and quietly glided the boat up on the beach.

"Nigerian land," the old woman said quietly, looking around.

They jumped down and started moving inland. Brett turned to the old woman, pointed to his watch.

"We'll return in fifteen minutes"

Linda couldn't resist busting his chops as they walked away.

"You realize that the old woman wasn't wearing a watch, don't you?"

He smiled at her and nodded.

"But I bet she'll have a good sense of time, even if her skin watch runs slowly, to earn that fifty Cede note."

"Over here!"

Blake was kneeling next to a well-worn path that pointed inland. "I'll bet it's an old smugglers' route in from the shore."

"I think you're right." Brett had figured toward the end of the boat ride that the old woman's navigation was just too precise, and that she must have taken the route many times before.

Linda spoke up before they all went down the path.

"Let's follow it for five minutes on the clock, look around at that point, and then take five minutes for the return. I'll keep time."

They all nodded and headed down the path. Brett took the lead.

As they approached the five-minute mark, he frantically signaled them to stop. Everyone followed suit as he crouched low on the path and motioned no talking. He pointed 45 degrees ahead to their right. One hundred yards ahead, they saw a bluff in the direction that the path would lead them. The small hill was set back about thirty yards from the path. Movement could be seen at the top of the rise. It could have been just treetops swaying in the breeze. Or maybe it was something else.

From his crouched position Brett grabbed a baseball-sized rock and balanced himself while remaining low. He heaved it some sixty yards at a tangent to the hill. It landed with a loud thud.

Immediately, heavy weapon fire erupted in the direction of the rock. Flashes of light and smoke were coming from several areas on the hill. Brett recognized the heavy, muffled thudding of a 50-caliber machine gun. He remembered that unmistakable sound from past naval exercises offshore in high school with his ROTC unit. After the machine gun bursts and small arms fire quieted, the metallic scraping noise of mortar-launched devices held sway. Upon landing, the rounds uprooted the forest floor. The group stayed crouched as the onslaught continued and backed slowly down the path toward the boat. Once covered by the tall bush, they turned and ran to safety. When they arrived, the old woman awaited.

"You back early," she said pointing to her imaginary skin watch and showing her gap-toothed grin. After they all scrambled on board, she glided silently away from shore and returned to Ghana.

No one in the group that day admitted the truth—they had wet their own underwear when the gunfire erupted.

The remainder of the two-week road trip was almost uneventful. As Brett gazed out the coach window, he was constantly in awe of the incredible lushness of the countryside. At one point they crossed a broad savannah plain that narrowed gradually, and then sliced through a thick blue-green forest that framed the savannah on each side. A narrow clear-colored river meandered through the scenic view. It was so idyllic that he wondered aloud to no one in particular, what would happen if you just walked from the road to the savannah's edge, and then beyond into the forest? Were there crocs or snakes or other hidden hazards?

Indeed there were, all of the above and many more, said his Ghanaian friend from Accra, *which was why you'll never see folks out for idle walks away from the village.*

Blake confidently opined that the dangers were probably overblown and based mostly on superstition. He went further and said the next time he traveled to these parts, he would do an overland hike and pitch a tent for a few days. Blake was the son of a wealthy New York banker. He sort of did his own thing, avoiding any strife or tension that would inevitably flare up from time to time among team members.

And he was always cool, always laid back. During the weeks at the work site, he also effortlessly flaunted the rules. It was his private way of defying gravity, one that he had practiced from his earliest days when he learned how to defy both of his Scandinavian au pairs.

Brett couldn't help but smile and shake his head as he remembered a particular instance back at the village earlier in the summer that should have cured Blake once and for all of his desire to wander in the bush. But based on this recent comment, it hadn't. Back then, Blake and his inseparable companion Sharon, a strawberry blond from Michigan, decided that they'd had enough of the bucket shower routine, which was standard procedure for the team in the village. Basically you were outside, and one of the villagers lifted buckets of cold or lukewarm water above your head and dumped it down while you stood naked on the other side of a high wall.

Tired of that routine, Blake and Sharon decided to take a swim in one of the rivers close to the village. Why they wanted to do that was unclear, particularly since the villagers themselves always walked many miles to fetch clean water, carefully avoiding the local rivers. None of that seemed to matter, and they were determined to swim and catch up with the team later.

And so they did. There were no attacks by crocs or piranhas, or whatever else the rest of them conjured up in their vivid nineteen year-old imaginations. When asked how the swim turned out, Blake was low-key, but that just made everyone feel that it must have been a grand time. Brett and the other team members were starting to feel a bit paranoid and foolish as they all gathered later that evening on the porch of the compound. They were all talking about going for a swim the next day.

Gradually during dinner, Blake let out a few more details about the river, and Sharon casually shared how great the swim was. It was clear to all that they did more than just swim while they were there.

Later that evening, with the mosquito nets down, the porch-side veranda at the colonial house was once again the gathering spot.

Then a strange thing happened. Blake and Sharon were both seated at one of the round tables, holding court and dribbling out more information about the great time they had at the river. As Brett remembered it, there was a card game or some sort of board game going on, so he went over to see who was on top. Blake was doing well and was racking up the winnings. Of course the men were shirtless, and the women wore very light dresses or local clothing. All tried to catch some of the light breeze in the ninety-degree evening heat.

That's when Brett thought he saw movement on Blake's bare white back. As he looked closer, it was the most unbelievable and freaky sight he had ever seen—a dozen white worms were hatching and burrowing out of Blake's skin. Of course, after he pointed this out, Blake lost all pretense of cool and ran to Eaton for emergency medical treatment. But he recovered and finished the trip with the team. Sharon escaped a similar fate because of early medical treatment.

I wonder what he'll catch when he hikes across the country...or what will catch him?

They continued to enjoy the relaxing pace of the meander northwest to Dakar, shopping at small village outposts and sharpening their skills at bargaining for value with the local people. They also paused at several points of interests, including one significant historical monument that remained forever engraved in Brett's mind. It was the infamous whitewashed Elmina castle, a major deportation point to the *new world* for millions of captured souls. One of his favorite team members from Nebraska named Jill kept trying to herd him and others into a group photo in front of that gigantic slave house. To this day, he was sure that poor Jill probably didn't understand why they politely refused to follow her direction.

Part Two
Middle Passages

Chapter Six
Lailani's Revenge

George Aikins was an uncomplicated man who continued to cling to a small set of core beliefs. Through the years they had served him fairly well. They were faithfulness to his wife and daughter, loyalty to his few friends, and his paramount duty as the protector of his family. These he garnered from his parents and his aunts and uncles. His family, like many others, had slowly migrated out of Alabama during the post-war years to cities like Albany and other urban areas in the north.

His aunt, Viola, his dad's older sister, was the first to leave. She was the free spirit in the family. As she grew into her teens and looked around at her small, rural Alabama town, she rejected the idea of spending her whole life in that box of limited opportunity. Everywhere about her, she saw folks merely existing day to day. Even at that young age she knew that her spirit was just too big to be confined like that. So at the age of sixteen, she just up and left town after another bitter argument with her mother. Stories say that she hitchhiked and ended up in Albany only because that was where the trucker who provided the ride was heading. Before she stepped down out of that big rig, he was said to have looked across the cab at her and asked if she knew the Lord. As she slammed the heavy steel door behind her, she shouted back yes.

Once in Albany, she soon learned that getting a job would be very tough, because she was a high school dropout with no credentials, no references, and no family in the area. Walking the neighborhoods streets, she filled out an endless number of job applications that led to nothing. But over time, as she became familiar with the neighborhood and the small businesses, she realized there was one occupation for which she was highly qualified, and that was doing hair. She had done hair for her nieces, cousins, second cousins, and just about every other female head in the family since she was 8 years old. It was a skill, and it took patience, and at least in that realm she had developed both. After getting her first job as an assistant stylist in Arbor Hill, she established herself as a pretty good hairdresser. Then she went to school and got her license at night.

Most of all she was reliable, and over time every shop sought after her and her customer list, because his aunt *could do some hair*. But she was also loyal, and she stayed with the same shop for many years, helping to make them very successful. Over time she saved her money and put together a small nest egg that to her Southern family would have been considered an enormous fortune. Over a ten-year period, she singlehandedly pulled all of her nine brothers and sisters and their children, including George the youngest, from Alabama. George and his brothers were able to slowly enter the building and construction trades in and around Albany, starting as common laborers and slowly working their way up.

Making good and steady money, George's older brothers soon were attracted to the gambling and party life that was pervasive in Northern cities. That affliction controlled many of the young black men relocating from the south. Bars, broads, and gambling houses were all well practiced in the art of liberating cash from those unsophisticated entrants. Over time, George buried all four of his brothers, who had each succumbed to the shiny but deadly allure of the sporting life.

He couldn't understand why he was thinking more and more about his long-dead brothers.

But he did know that ever since the attack on his daughter, he'd had a very tough time coping and returning to his normal routine. Usually a gregarious man by nature, he started to keep his opinions and feeling bottled up on the inside. Lailani had tried hard to shake him from his increasing withdrawal, but her efforts only seemed to push him farther away. Sometimes he just wanted to be invisible in her presence.

He increasingly brooded over the fact that he had worked hard to provide a home and a stable life for Lai after his wife's passing. Lord knows that wasn't easy. Back then, he had to overcome deep feelings of remorse, sadness, and guilt. The most difficult thing of all for him to swallow was that he was powerless to intercede and to help his wife in any way. The cancer had total control, and he couldn't do a damn thing about it. He couldn't protect her at all.

In the months before they diagnosed the large spot on her lungs, she suffered with a bad, rasping cough. The cough persisted and she grew weaker. In denial, they both refused to consider the obvious possibility that she might be seriously ill from her pack-a-day cigarette habit. But she had trusted him then, and trusted his judgment.

So they delayed seeing a doctor, and she kept praying. But he knew that wishful thinking and saving money had a lot to do with his own reluctance to seek prompt medical attention for her.

Then one night she had a monstrous coughing fit at the supper table. Young Lai looked at her mother, and he could see the distress on her seven-year old face as her mother kept coughing and hacking to release what was tormenting her from deep within her chest. She covered her mouth with a napkin, and then grabbed another from the table belonging to Lai. When she removed them, they were covered with blood and mucous.

He remembered that as the end approached, Lai had been loyal and attentive to her mother's needs. Even the treating doctors commented that she was the most involved and caring young girl they had ever seen. One of the physicians mentioned that she might be a doctor herself at some time in the future, and they encouraged him to give her that chance. He thanked them. But his plan for Lai was far more practical—complete high school, learn a good trade. That's what her big sister was doing, and that was how his family had always made a way.

When his wife returned home from the hospital for the final time, she did so under the care of a hospice program. It took him a while to make the adjustment and absorb what that really meant. Conceptually he understood that it was terminal care, based on what the doctors had described to him. But then she started resting comfortably at home, and her spirits picked up. For a time he really believed that she might recover. But the truth became apparent as her pain medication was radically increased. She quickly drifted away.

Young Lai had understood the reality of a future without her mother long before he caught up with her. She was prepared when the hospice care provider began to arrive for only an hour a day, and she calmly asked to stay home from school to be with her mother. He agreed, but he fumed at all of the changes. While he worked, Lai took over most of the hospice duties, bathing, changing bedpans, and swabbing her mother's brow with a cold face cloth. She would read from her children's books and make jokes even while her mother slept.

Somehow he had managed to bury his own despair from those times, and create a safe home and a future for Lai.

But it wasn't safe at all, and that's a fact. I let the wolf guard the hen house.

It was 3:00 A.M. in the railway yard that George had faithfully guarded since his retirement from the construction gangs that built and repaired the company's stockyards and track beds. That was work for a younger man, and after the physical strain caught up with him, he was rewarded for loyal service with the coveted night watchman position.

The yard was always eerily quiet at that early hour. He took irregular routes around the property as he made his rounds to ensure that no one could anticipate his arrival at a particular location. As the only guard at the site, he was autonomous, with no boss and no underlings.

The yard would show very little activity until 5:00 A.M., when the engineers arrived to begin the detailed procedures involved in tuning their electric and diesel locomotives. After that, they would pick railcars and cue up for the 6:00 A.M. departures.

He had two hours before then to finish his business.

He walked to his truck that was parked around the corner from a security camera. He took off his jacket and lumberjack shirt, along with his boots and jeans, storing everything in a duffle behind the front seat. Removing a plastic bag from the passenger side, he quickly donned green medical scrubs and a pair of black comfort clogs, all purchased at the medical supply store across town. He started up the truck, made a U turn, and pulled slowly away from the yard.

In twenty minutes he reached his destination and stopped at the same vantage point he had used for the previous three nights. His earlier reconnaissance assured him that activity at the hospital was entirely predictable at that time in the morning. But soon, the triple bay emergency area should begin to heat up with activity. Stabbings, shootings, gang fights, and domestic assaults all seemed to take place after 4:00 A.M., as if maintaining a ghoulish schedule. He hoped that pattern would repeat itself again tonight.

After grabbing a brown bag from the glove compartment, he secured it at the small of his back, covering it with his scrubs. He stepped down from his truck and walked across the street to a position around the corner from the ambulance bays. He waited no more than fifty feet down the block, remaining out of sight in the recessed doorway of an abandoned medical equipment business. Even though he didn't smoke, he pulled out a newly purchased pack and lit a cigarette. Having watched countless smokers in his day, he duplicated the motions without inhaling the noxious fumes. At worst he would be taken as a shift worker taking a much-needed break.

Within moments he could hear opportunity approaching, and he smiled. The distant wailing of three or four ambulances was fast approaching. Mixed into the chorus were a cacophony of short burps and bleeps, indicating Albany police escorts. He snuffed out his unfinished smoke.

The arriving group was much larger than he anticipated. Five ambulances and four squad cars crowded the emergency bays. Unlike previous nights, the police parked randomly, failing to form an exterior barrier around the EMT vans that were jammed tight in front.

Big gang fight.

A large team of trauma doctors, nurses and administrators spilled from the access doors, joining the EMTs and police as the ambulances were emptied of victims. The entire area looked totally chaotic.

Immediately he left his perch, rounded the corner and walked purposely over to the frenetic scene. He continued straight ahead and through the middle bay double doors leading to the triage and reception room. Many patients, who apparently arrived earlier that night or during the previous day, were still warehoused in beds, piled along the walls, or stored at the entryway of corridors leading from the main area. He looked ahead, making no eye contact, but he could not help thinking as he passed the waiting crowd that this was the last place he would ever want to come in an emergency.

Years ago he had spent several weeks at this same facility, visiting his wife in the highly rated oncology unit. That gave him the knowledge to quickly access the back stairwell. Once there, he climbed to the fourth floor and listened at the door. Then he slowly opened it and peeked down the hall.

No one.

At the far end of the hallway, past the dozens of open patient doors, he saw the faint glow from the nurses' station. He stepped out and moved quietly to the nearby janitor's closet. Once inside, he placed a small device behind a mop bucket after flipping on the green switch.

Retracing his steps to the stairwell, he quietly closed the door behind him and walked down to the third-floor landing, where he waited at the entry door. His watch showed thirty seconds remaining. He opened the door and started walking calmly to the far stairwell at the end of the hall. Then he heard the muffed sound of the explosive. He remembered the broken English on the faded, greasy brown label of the device.

This make more smoke than fire but maybe make small fire two!

Once in the stairwell, he climbed back up to the fourth floor just as the fire alarm started and the canned emergency warning messages cycled in. Accurately, the automatic system indicated an alarm at the northeast corner of the fourth floor, and it warned everyone to stand by. As he eased open the door, he saw several nurses and a police officer running down the hallway toward the janitorial closet that was belching smoke and flames. The trailing officer was shouting into his shoulder microphone.

He walked quickly into the room that the officer had been guarding and came face to face with a sleeping Calvin Ward. He punched him hard in the chest. Ward's eyes blinked open. When he recognized George, they bulged wide and he opened his mouth to speak, or maybe to scream. That's when George clamped the pillow down hard over his face, leaning heavily with his beefy shoulders and torso to jam Ward's mouth and nose through the bed frame. Even in his weakened and bandaged condition, Ward twisted, kicked, and struggled for life's breath. Gradually the struggling stopped.

He carefully replaced the pillow and removed any signs of struggle. Then he retreated down the stairwell to the first floor and walked back out through the emergency bay doors.

Chapter Seven
Chicago

The return to college after Africa turned out to be a real struggle. For the first time in his life, Brett had a great answer to the old question: *so, what did you do on your summer vacation?* But very few people at school seemed interested, particularly his financial aid officer, who cut him off two minutes into his description of the trip and bluntly asked how much money had he saved for the fall semester. Of course the answer was exactly zero, and that began a series of negative consequences for him that quickly brought to the fore the ugly reality of his precarious financial position.

The most significant impact was an extended delay in receiving his funded financial aid package. That led to a delay in purchasing books. The result was that he could not begin studying until days after his peers. Because he wasn't registered, it restricted his ability to qualify for work-study employment on campus. That caused him to take a position at a warehouse off campus. But the added commuting time to get there and back worked against him as the academic requirements intensified during the semester.

One bright spot was his frequent calls to Linda, who actually called him the majority of the time to save eating up his limited free cash. They spoke at least twice a week, even as the crush of papers and exams began to strain that schedule. The summer hadn't exactly cemented them as permanent lovers. But it had bonded them into a friendship that would endure for some time.

Linda became concerned when he called her in November and mentioned that he would be leaving for Chicago over the Thanksgiving break. He apologized for changing the original plan that had him traveling to visit her at her home in New Jersey for the holidays. But it was his reason for the change, rather than the change itself, that took her by surprise. He recounted his selection by his school's African American Union to be their representative at the national

Black Muslim convention in Chicago. He was very curious about the Muslim programs and thought he might learn a lot, while also representing his college at the event. And besides, he went on, they were paying the airfare as well as room and board.

"Brett, let me ask you this. How many other students were selected for this honor?"

'Well, I was the only one, really. I had the flexibility in my schedule."

"Did it ever occur to you that no one else was selected or volunteered because most people spend the Thanksgiving holiday with their family and loved ones? Except, of course, the Black Muslims, and now you apparently."

She was steamed because she wanted her mom and dad to meet him. And now she would have to manufacture some reason for his absence, as she was unwilling to tell her parents that he had chosen to have his turkey and stuffing with a radical organization rather than at their home.

"I'm sorry, Linda. I should've mentioned it to you before I signed on the dotted line."

"Brett, having traveled halfway around the world with you, I know your penchant for pushing the envelope. But have you considered that this organization can be dangerous? Aren't they the ones that killed their own leader a few years back?"

He gave her a serious answer, the one that really motivated him to accept the offer and view it as an opportunity.

"Truth is, Lin, I felt that I needed to go because I'm still in the discovery phase when it comes to race, my own identity, and exactly what I want to believe. But I'm clear so far about one thing. I want to invest some of my own energy and resources into making a difference for my community, a difference for those born without a silver spoon in their mouth, or any spoons at all. Without a couple of good breaks early in life, I could have been right there among them. That's part of it."

"But also, one of the big things the Africa trip did for me was help me start to sort through some of the rhetoric we hear all the time about the so-called global black struggle. I always doubted that the rhetoric squared completely with the facts. I came back this summer understanding how far off the mark much of it is. You saw it too, Lin. Africa will be shaped by its own history and people, and the same thing will happen here in the States, in a different way. That trip helped me shed a lot of romantic notions."

"All right, I grant you that. It was enlightening and clarifying, particularly after our witch doctor friend refused to even consider the relevance of the shared history between Africa and North America. But what do the Muslims have to do with anything other than blaming the *white devils* for every ill that afflicts the black community?"

"Actually, when I looked further into it, they seem to put much more stress on individual accountability than they get credit for. They run some very disciplined and successful programs that produce results. Some of the over-the-top rhetoric that we hear obscures that. I want to see how they do those things on relatively modest budgets. At the end of the day, I'm beginning to believe that programs and tangible results outweigh rhetoric, or at least they do for me."

"Okay, Brett," she said, masking her disappointment, "let me leave you with two thoughts. One, enjoy your trip and call me when you land, and two, stay on the reservation and watch your butt in Chicago. It's a sketchy town in certain parts, and I wasn't there all that long ago."

"Well, dearest, I would rather you watch my butt. However, since my choice has made that impossible, I promise to keep an eye on it myself."

She smiled. "Have a safe flight. Maybe we'll see each other over Christmas."

"That would be great. I'll call you from the Windy City when I land."

"Be safe."

"I will."

On the approach into O'Hare Airport, Brett realized that he was nearing the fifteen thousand mile mark on his frequent flier card. With the return trip miles added on, he should have more than enough points for a free round trip down to Linda's house in Jersey. Without it, there was really no way he could afford to see her. He'd let her know he was definitely coming when they spoke next.

Then his mind turned back to how best to approach the Chicago conference. He knew that for the most part, he'd be among a large group of true believers. But he also understood that it was far from a monolithic movement, and that there would be different points of view on display. Linda was right, though—one of their own leaders had been killed, and there were at least three strong factions still vying for national control.

Lacking any real guidance from his college, he figured the best approach was to assume the role of roving reporter. In that way he could remain detached and uncommitted to any point of view, while also being somewhat of a loner.

It turned out that his call on the partisanship of attendees was on the mark. Every person he met during the opening day and workshops checked him out during conversations to judge his political bona fides. He rebuffed, as politely as possible, at least seven separate attempts to enlist him in one cause, march, protest, or recruitment effort happening in different parts of the country.

But the breakout sessions covering the range of programs currently up and running were well worth the trip. It was clear that there was one common organizing principle that made the programs successful—basic, uncluttered messages, repeated often, that were reinforced through action and direction. That approach had changed lives and kept lives on track. Folks were kept busy in each of the programs, and they were encouraged to achieve a goal. The principles seemed to him to be consistent with some of the learning from his African experience, albeit in a much different context.

He decided to skip the group dinner that evening, because the propaganda and recruitment efforts directed his way were already wearing on him. One thing so far had been reinforced on this trip: he was no radical, and he was firmly rooted in the American experience, the good, bad and ugly parts.

He slipped on his boat shoes and decided to go for a walk to get some fresh air, and to enjoy the big, bustling city. Before he was even aware, he had strolled for more than four miles. But the neighborhoods looked safe enough. Other than a few small groups hanging out on stoops on certain streets, he hardly passed any pedestrians after a while. That gradually began to strike him as unusual, particularly given the beauty of the late afternoon fall day.

But the thing he failed to notice about the various groups of young men on the stoops that he passed was the different color handkerchiefs or bandannas that most of them casually wore. He later learned that those colors signified allegiance to one of two violent gangs, the Crips or the Bloods. These gangs also populated other large urban cities, including Los Angeles, Detroit, Houston, New York, and Philadelphia. Each gang, no matter where they were based, was extremely protective of their territory. Without realizing it, he had been casually ambling through Crips or Bloods territory for the past forty-five minutes.

And he almost pulled it off, until a group of four young black men left their stoop and fell in behind him, keeping a distance of about twenty yards. He finally noticed the additional company, but was not sure yet if he was being followed. He crossed the street and took a random right turn down a broad tree-lined avenue, and then he crossed to the opposite side. The four young men did the same and closed up the distance to about ten yards. He had a sense of foreboding about what might happen next. It was a sense that he first felt many years ago as young five-year-old boy in the wrong place at the wrong time.

Weighing his options, he realized they were all bad. Standing his ground in confrontation would probably end with his own serious injury. Running was unlikely to be successful, since they were probably as fast or faster than he was. Besides, they knew the neighborhood much better, and he could only approximate the best route back to the hotel. He finally figured that the smartest approach was to turn back toward them after he got to a street with some activity on it. But now that he was focused on it, cars and pedestrians were extremely hard to spot.

He turned onto Crenshaw Street and was relieved to see some pedestrians, as well as a few vehicles. He took a deep breath and turned back to the four young men. When he was within a few feet, he stopped. They also stopped, spreading out to block the sidewalk.

Figuring that he had nothing to lose by breaking the ice, he spoke up.

"Hello guys, my name is Brett Howard and I'm visiting your great city this weekend. I'm here for the Muslim convention, reporting on the events for my school back east."

The largest of the four, about two inches taller than he was and a good twenty-five pounds heavier, looked steadily at him as he dangled a toothpick from his mouth. He spoke without removing it.

"Yo man, what you doin' cruising our hood? You gonna file some reports on what you seen?"

The others, clearly followers, laughed at their leader's funny opening gambit.

But toothpick man didn't smile, and he didn't move from his position directly blocking Brett's path.

He could feel the danger wafting toward him.

"No, no. No reports, no pictures." He managed to smile. "Just getting away from all that talking downtown, just started walking to get some fresh air. I was doing just that when I passed you all back there."

Toothpick man glared at him with what appeared to be bemusement, but he couldn't be sure.

"Yo, you got no clue, do you, my man. You been kickin' all afternoon through Crips and Bloods hoods. Since we Crips, I'm thinkin' why the Bloods let you pass if you weren't spyin for them?"

He realized then the enormous mistake he'd made by not consulting someone at the hotel about what might be a safe route to take for his walk. He had carelessly strayed way off the beaten path, like some stupid rube in a comedy movie. He knew instinctively that the ending here would be anything but funny.

Making one last plea, he looked at each of them as he gave his speech, hoping in vain to get some kind of committee vote in his favor.

"I have to apologize to you guys. I had no idea at all that I was walking on your turf. I should have gotten better directions. But believe me, I'm not working for the Bloods, and I am not spying for anyone."

Seeing no facial response from the four toughs, he continued, more out of nervousness and rising panic than a belief that his words would do any good.

"This is going to sound real lame, but would you guys give me a pass? It was an honest mistake and one that I won't make again."

Toothpick man appeared to consider his request for a moment as he glanced over at his boys, who were waiting for his reply. Then he zeroed in on Brett's eyes to deliver the verdict.

"You right, bro, that was one lame-ass plea you just copped. But I tell you what, if you can pay the toll, you might get that free pass you talkin' about. Flip me your wallet real slow, nigga."

He tossed it slowly over to toothpick man, who opened it and removed the cash. After counting it, he was not pleased.

"Shit man, less than two bills in here. Toll gonna cost you a lot more than that."

Then he removed Brett's bankcard and snapped it over his index finger with his thumb.

"Let's take a stroll over to the bank on Gleason, real slow and friendly like. You gonna take five hundid out your bank to finish payin' me, you hear?"

He knew he had more than that in his account. He also knew that his financial aid money had to last him until the start of the second semester next year. So he took a big chance and replied that he wouldn't be able to pull any cash out, because his account was overdrawn due to this trip.

Toothpick man seemed more annoyed than angry. He probably believed the story about lack of cash. But in front of his soldiers, he couldn't afford to show any kindness. So he casually approached while holding out the wallet in his left hand. As Brett reached for it, toothpick man closed the distance between them and kneed him hard in the groin. As he doubled over, unable to breathe, he was roughly shoved to the ground. Then he felt the full-booted kick delivered to his lower back. The pain flared up to his shoulders and burned in his neck and chest. Defensively he curled up into a fetal position to protect himself.

"Get up an' take your lame ass outta here. Don't wanna see you again, or someone will be carryin' you outta here face up an' foot first." He threw the wallet back in his face.

Brett was able to get up, grab the wallet and stagger away. After getting some cash later at Gleason, he found a jitney taxi and went back to the hotel.

Linda tried hard to be sympathetic on the phone, but she wasn't happy at all after she heard the circumstances leading up to the robbery. She just didn't think he fully appreciated how lucky he was to be alive. Although he acknowledged some carelessness on his part by striking out on a random walk in a tough urban environment, she got the feeling that he didn't really appreciate the full measure of his folly.

"Brett, you've got to promise me that you'll take this near disaster in Chicago to heart. We've known each other for less than six months, and in that time you've flirted with major trouble twice. I worry about you. Are you trying to tempt fate?"

In the back of her mind while they talked, she began to wonder whether he was just a bit too much of a risk taker.

"I know you're concerned, Lin, and believe me, I've been doing some serious after-action review on my own part. If there is a pattern going on here, I want to identify it and control it. Nigeria, Chicago, those were scary situations, and if I'm subconsciously falling into patterns of high risk behavior, I'm going to change."

She was pleased to hear him say that. They left the subject and talked about local issues on their respective campuses. He also confirmed his plans to visit her at home in Jersey over Christmas. But he put a bit of a damper on things when he talked about the upcoming San Diego regatta that took place during the mid-semester January break. Lacking the funds to fly, his current plan was to hitchhike across the country and back.

She resolved to herself to be patient and take one more stab later on at getting him to cancel the California trip.

When the call was over, he continued to think about her concerns. She was important to him, and he knew she wasn't trying to hurt him or unduly limit him.

Am I too much of a risk taker?

The answer to the question, he realized, was probably apparent as he considered his barely adequate checking account and his nebulous financial plan to complete his undergraduate studies. Further evidence—he had taken a physical beating in Chicago largely because he had no way to replace the money in his account. That beating could have been far worse.

The truth was he was living from week to week each semester, with no real contingency plan in case something went wrong. And it didn't have to be that way at all, he admitted, had he not had decided in his junior year of high school to rewrite the plan for his education that his parents had worked out. The financial pressure wouldn't exist, because he would have been enjoying a full boat scholarship to the Naval Academy. It was a great plan, he recalled as he eased his long frame into his only comfortable chair and put his feet up on the hassock. But it wasn't his plan.

He remembered his dad sitting him down in the electronics workshop in the basement when he was fifteen to make the pitch to him. They were surrounded with transistors, test equipment, and a variety of devices in need of repair from his dad's skilled hands.

Full boat scholarship, Brett, then four years active, four years reserve.

Plus his dad added a kicker, knowing Brett's love for sailing.

You get to sail all over the world as a naval officer. You might even captain an aircraft carrier or battle group.

He was hooked, and he enrolled in his high school's three-year ROTC program, where he wore the Navy uniform once a week, participated in drills and classroom learning, and periodically traveled off-site on two-day field trips to various naval facilities.

At first the program was everything he wanted, and the idea of eventually attending the Academy seemed really cool. Going out on destroyers, mine sweepers, and supply ships on various weekend training missions added a special spark to the program, and more than compensated for the dull classroom lessons taught by retired naval personnel. Crashing through rolling twenty-foot waves in a fast-moving loaded destroyer had been the most exciting thing he had done through that point in his life.

But things began to sour, starting with his junior year visit to Annapolis for a preview of the campus and what college life would be like. To him it wasn't college at all, at least not the academic and personal freedom that he envisioned college to be. What really turned him off was watching how the freshman plebes were treated by the upper classman. The final straw was when he had lunch at the Academy dining hall, and saw that freshman had to eat their food using an exaggerated and squared-off manner, like robots. No, he thought back then, he couldn't go from the box of his nearly all-white high school to another box that was run by the military, despite the scholarship.

When he got the nerve to approach his father about that decision, he thought his old man would be angry and pressure him to go forward regardless. But to his surprise, his father told him he respected his decision and hoped that he would find another way to support himself in college.

He didn't fully grasp then that his dad was dead serious. But when the time came in his senior year for his dad to fill out financial aid forms and commitments for college, he learned that there was no extra money lying around to cover his college tuition or room and board. Paying the mortgage and expenses on the suburban home and putting food on the table took up most of his father's income, and the rest he was putting away for retirement.

The reality of his future life at college on a shoestring hit him hardest at his high school graduation, when the scholarship awards were read. He had expected to receive a decent amount from his school. After all, he had lettered in three sports and had been National Honor Society, along with solid participation in several other activities. He still recalled the shock and disappointment that he felt when the five hundred dollar, one-time award was read after his name.

He twisted in his lounge chair to ease the tension on his still-sore back.

Okay, he admitted, he had made some pretty careless snap decisions in life, and it was time to grow up. Linda was right.

So he resolved to be more deliberate, a little more boring, and a lot more focused during his final years in college. His last real fling was the San Diego regatta, but he decided to take a bus rather than hitchhike. Linda showed a little extra appreciation for that decision when he told her over Christmas.

He returned from the San Diego races with a second-place trophy. While he didn't skipper the boat, he served as forward deck crew in charge of the spinnaker and genoa sails, both key elements that added necessary speed and enabled them to medal. Not bad for a sailor from Albany, he thought as he placed the small trophy on the bookshelf in his dorm room.

But a decisive break came when he qualified for an MLK scholarship based on his decision to focus specifically on African American history. His essay turned out to be the deciding factor in his selection. He drew from his unusual background, having being raised in both a segregated, urban elementary school as well as in a virtually all-white junior high and high school—six years in each. He was able to weave those experiences and lessons together with the learning from his Africa and Chicago voyages. He convinced the selection committee that he had both depth of understanding and the required commitment to advance the cause of underserved communities, consistent with the MLK vision.

With room and board and tuition and books paid for by the scholarship fund, he was able to buckle down his last two years and drive up his GPA to a competitive level. Drinking far less and eliminating smoking of any kind also contributed to his success.

History had always been a natural choice for a major to him. The virtual lack of any focus during his education so far on African American history made that choice of study under the scholarship particularly appealing. But he had no desire to remain in school four more years after graduation, seeking the necessary Ph.D. He knew that would lead to a comfortable professorship. At heart he realized he was a doer rather than a talker, so he prepared for the GRE and set his sights on business school. With a business degree in hand and a successful career, he figured he could provide a lot more tangible resources to help inner-city kids than he would accomplish by teaching at a university.

Where to apply and spend two years in graduate school was an easy choice for him. Some would later suggest that the choice demonstrated once again his impetuous streak, particularly since he didn't consult with parents or friends about his thinking.

He applied to UC Berkeley as his first choice. They had a top-ranked business school, and he knew from his contacts during the San Diego regatta that the school was close to San Francisco Bay and world-class sailing.

This last decision, which he announced to Linda without even talking with her beforehand, seemed to permanently tear the fabric of their relationship. In her mind and despite his apparent buckling down, she had come to accept that he would always remain somewhat of an adventurer, always willing to take a walk on the wild side. But for her, the wild side was too much risk. It was something you did when you were in your teens. She told him that she had spent way too much anguish worrying about his safety over the years. And now, without even a discussion, he had set his mind on studying on the West Coast, when he knew that she would only pursue her graduate studies in the east.

By the end of senior year they had become occasional friends, speaking less and less often on the phone. He realized belatedly one day that he hadn't seen her in person for over a year.

Chapter Eight
Business School

Brett still found it hard to fathom how quickly college had come and gone. But in the end, he felt that he had accomplished something tangible.

His mother and father were proud. His dad, never a person to display a lot of emotion, hugged him at the graduation ceremony. His mom was much more emotional in her praise. As he looked at her, he realized how remarkable Vivian was in her own right. After all, he thought, how many thirty-seven-year-old women would marry a widower like his father, who at the time had children aged ten, twelve, and fourteen? She had done her best and made a clean, safe home for them. His graduation seemed to vindicate for her that she had done a good thing by them. He would miss her and try to get home once or twice a year to see both of them. Then his father took him aside before the celebrations and photograph sessions ended. He quietly said that he would be able to contribute some money each semester of business school, to help him pay the bills.

At home, Brett finished zipping up his father's faded green duffle bag that he had used for the past four years in college. It was the same bag his dad took with him to Japan years ago. He remembered asking him back in high school whether he liked leaving home for good and joining the Air Force. His dad looked at him and said that he joined the AF for two reasons: the freedom to fly, and the determination to get away from his mother and sister. He was also honest about his initial disappointment at not being selected for pilot training. But he was clear that he never regretted leaving home.

As for Brett, he didn't think he would ever regret leaving, either.

He was heading out early in June to spend the summer in Berkeley as a sailing instructor at the marina. That would allow him to boost his bank account and give him a chance to train about seventy-five inner-city kids in the art of sailing and seamanship. He was also able to secure an agreement with the marina owner to use a spare back room at the base for free sleeping quarters. The job and the consideration derived from the sailing experience he had in San Diego two years ago. One of his fellow crewmates lived in San Francisco, and his father was a long-time member of the Berkeley Marina. That contact helped him land the job and the bed.

When the owner interviewed him by phone in April, he asked him what he hoped to accomplish before heading to business school in the fall. Brett replied that beyond providing instruction to the regular members and their kids, he would like to increase sailing opportunities for some of the kids from the inner cities of Berkeley and surrounding towns, who had no exposure to the sport. The idea turned out to be very appealing to the owner, who was an old California progressive in the true Teddy Roosevelt vein. Years ago he had hoped to launch something like, that but it just hadn't happened on its own. He gave Brett a modest budget and asked him to work with a couple of local community organizations to line something up. Within six weeks, working with the Boys and Girls Clubs and the Urban League, he pulled together the outline of a program, including the all-important transportation component between the inner city areas and the marina. The owner was thrilled, and he told him to get out there and recruit some young urban landlubbers for the program.

It turned out to be an opportunity for him to apply some of the principles he had come to believe in. He realized that to some people, seamanship and sailing seemed like exotic sports for the rich and famous. Of course, it was true that the well-heeled were the ones that garnered all the attention. But he knew that there was another side seldom told. Maritime history, whether in Britain, the early colonies or further back in time to the South Pacific, Egypt, or elsewhere was based upon a few simple principles: teamwork, discipline, and pride in learning your station and responsibilities. Those principles, he believed, had enabled ordinary men and women to accomplish extraordinary things.

But another thing he was also sure about was his own lack of experience in running any kind of program, let alone one aimed at city kids. So he reached out for advice from a number of sources. He also remembered that one of his other friends from the San Diego Regatta organized a program for inner-city kids from that area last summer. He leaned heavily on him to understand what he would be facing in Berkeley. One key piece of advice he received was that the classroom sessions were as important as the hands-on learning in the boats. Got to give them some *head food*, his buddy said, so they can make the connection with their everyday experiences.

On the flight across the country, he thought more about his own good fortune and the connection to sailing. He realized that in part it was the discipline from the early years of sailing in Albany that prevented him from going off the deep end during those five years when he and his siblings were under their grandmother's care. Because she was uninterested, or perhaps simply unable in her older age to closely monitor them, he had way too much free time to run unsupervised around the inner-city neighborhoods of Albany.

Idle time and lack of motivation, he said to himself for the first time.

He had experienced too much of both of them when he was young. They were the dangerous pitfalls of his early years in the inner city.

Thinking back to those days, he remembered that making friends as an outsider at the age of seven had not been easy at first in Albany. Eventually he came to know a few of the boys in the neighborhood from common classes in school. But his house never became an area where his friends would gather and play marbles, or run their toy trucks up and down the yard on make-believe construction sites. He realized that he had been ashamed to bring any friend over to his grandmother's house, because he knew they wouldn't be welcome.

It wasn't just her irritability that made him feel that way. It was very connected to his own realization that neither he nor his brother and sister considered Albany, and the house they were living in, to be home. In the back of their minds, Albany was always a place from which they would be rescued. It took a full five years for that to happen.

During that time he developed some risky habits, a natural outgrowth of idle time and lack of motivation. His best friend back then was a kid named Calvin, who would frequently invite him over for dinner. A chance to avoid eating his grandmother's terrible cooking meant an automatic yes to those invitations. But he never asked for permission to leave the house. He would wait until his grandmother went to bed, which was always around seven o'clock, and he would just leave the small house on the dead-end street where they lived.

Calvin's place was not a house at all. It was more of a strange-looking large building with seven floors. It had orange and yellow tape surrounding certain areas, and the front was completely blocked because the concrete stairs were crumbling. Years later he realized that it had to be a squatter building, condemned by the city, where mostly children and very few adults lived.

It was located across the street from a big city lot that housed an assortment of vehicles, including school busses, trucks, and light pole tenders. Calvin's apartment was on the second floor, accessible only from an unlighted stairwell in the back. The hallway always had a strong, musty smell to it.

Dinner at Calvin's place invariably turned out to be a big bag of potato chips that they would share, and a couple of hot dogs for each of them that Calvin himself would boil in a dark pot on the stove. Sometimes there would be buns, but most times they put the hot dogs between white bread with either catsup or mustard, depending on what Calvin brought out.

In all of his visits, he never saw or heard a mother or father in the house. He could hear what he assumed were Calvin's brothers and sisters running and screaming in the front area of the apartment, but they never came into the kitchen.

He liked Calvin a lot, because he seemed to operate in his own world and pretty much do whatever he wanted to do. He did meet Calvin's older sister once in the schoolyard, but he never saw her at the apartment. Calvin was a good runner and a broad jumper, both highly respected skills in Albany. It meant that you were sought after by a lot of school teams for the biannual races among all of the elementary schools. Relay races, individual sprints, and jumping competitions were a male rite of passage, and he and Calvin were most often on the same team and did very well together. Many times they would be seen running together throughout the Albany neighborhoods, two boys who believed in their imaginations that they were the fastest kids in the city.

After the chips and hot dogs that evening, which they ate without bread or buns for some unexplained reason, Calvin pulled a big stack of comic books out of the kitchen cabinet and put them on the floor between them. They dug into their favorite characters. Sometimes they would read for two hours before he headed back home. But tonight, Calvin looked up after an hour and asked if he wanted to go outside and do something really cool.

Of course he did.

They put away the comic books and headed out.

Once there, Calvin pointed down the alley that passed behind the rear entrance to his apartment. It was the same alley that further up crossed several busy streets. Last year they set up their homemade slingshots up there and fired rocks from the alley at passing cars. But one time, a truck stopped and backed up after being pelted with a lot of their good shots. The driver put his arm out of the window and turned to see who fired the stones. It was the biggest, hugest arm Brett had ever seen. As the driver jumped down from the truck and ran after them, they abandoned their slingshots and took off running as fast as they could. They ran until they could hardly breathe, and at every corner they nervously looked around for that driver with the giant arm.

But they were off in the opposite direction this time and turned up a narrow dirt path toward the main street in front of Calvin's apartment. They crouched down and were partially hidden by the ragged three-foot high hedge growth on both sides of the footpath. Darkness had fallen, and they moved about unseen. Calvin signaled for them to cross the street and head to the truck yard. Then he went along the fence to find a hole that had been cut in the bottom. They scrambled through to the other side.

After Calvin looked around for any guards, he took off running low and fast for a hill in the rear of the yard. Brett followed. At the base of the hill, they dropped down on hands and knees and scrambled to the top. Several trucks were parked up there. All were pointed to the other side of the hill, and some were parked pointing slightly down the hill. Calvin approached one of them parked on the incline that seemed to have a big, circular balloon shape on the back of it. He whispered that he never saw that type of truck there before. Then he eased around to the driver's side and tried the door handle. It was open. Calvin looked back with a big grin on his face.

"Watch this!" he whispered.

He climbed quickly up into the cabin and put both feet on a pedal on the floor, pushing it down low. He grabbed a metal bar with both hands that was between the seats and pulled back hard on it. Then he pushed it down fast. He jumped back down, and they backed away, keeping low in the darkness.

Seconds later, the balloon-shaped truck began to slowly roll down the hill.

Calvin turned to him excitedly.

"Remember we learned all about gravity in science class? This truck's going to roll all the way down the hill to the back fence, on nothing but gravity!"

Brett nodded and smiled, sharing Calvin's excitement. Then he swiveled and looked down the hill through the darkness to where the truck was heading. In the glow of a backyard light on the other side of the fence from the city yard, he could see small children running back and forth. Some seemed to be very young, maybe babies in diapers.

The balloon truck kept lumbering downhill, picking up speed.

It was moving much more quickly than Calvin had seen in his other times. "It's going to smash the fence, Brett, it's moving too quick!" He could see that Calvin was concerned, but whether it was for the truck or the kids or both, he never learned.

The truck impaled itself on the fence, but didn't smash through. The children in the back yard stopped playing and stood still, staring. The crash alerted women in the house, who ran outside and began frantically grabbing and pulling the children back with them away from the wreckage.

The balloon part of the truck cracked open like an egg and sprayed what they thought was water over the fence and into the yard, just after the last child had been dragged away. But it wasn't water. In a couple of moments, the glow from under the truck began to follow the spray that was arcing into the air. Within seconds the vehicle and part of the yard were engulfed in orange fire. But for the fence, the flames would have destroyed the nearby house.

They hurriedly retreated down the hill and retraced their steps. No one noticed them. Brett was still shaking when they emerged from the path and ran down the alley to Calvin's place. He looked at his friend and said he had to get back home. Calvin seemed shaken as well as he turned and headed for the stairs.

Brett woke from his memories when the captain announced that they would be landing in San Francisco in twenty minutes.

Idle time and lack of motivation

He would run several classes and on-the-water training sessions that summer to address both problems.

At the marina during the farewell party, all of his students seemed to mix pretty well together, both the privileged and the underprivileged. His inner-city graduating class had grown to one hundred students from the word-of-mouth endorsements that they shared with friends. They all wanted to know if he was coming back to teach next summer. He was honest and told them he wasn't sure, and that he would have to see how school went that year. As a parting gift, he gave each of them a small sailboat key chain with his room number and dorm telephone number at the business school. He invited them to call him if they needed to talk. They gave him a yellow foul weather hat and a slicker, with the words *No. 1 Skipper* monogrammed in blue on each item.

Despite the rigor of the summer, he felt rested and mentally prepared for the challenge of business school. He'd managed to take six days off during the three-month stretch that allowed him to compete in two races held in San Francisco Bay. It was big boy sailing for sure. Full foul weather gear and boots were essential. The Bay's wind patterns and explosive gusts down the mountains were the stiffest challenges he had faced to that point as a sailor, far exceeding New England coastal cruising in intensity. The Bay tides and currents upped the ante tremendously, with both working against or at cross-purposes to the bow more often than not, making each upwind leg of a race more like a thundering cold shower.

He recorded a third-place and fifth-place finish out of some seventy competitors in each regatta. And he skippered both boats during the races, complements of owners with deep pockets, little experience, and no available crew. Yet they were eager to enter their toys in the race and reap some bragging rights, maybe even stealing the first-place cup.

He remembered how lucky he had been to get those skipper positions. He'd followed a hunch after seeing several nearly new boats in the marina that rarely put to sea. So he looked up the contact information for a couple of them in the membership log. When he finally managed to reach the owners on the phone, he proposed a turnkey operation. He would recruit and train the crews, tune the boats for the regatta, and at the podium ceremony give total credit to the owners' vision, foresight, and preparation. Each owner got a kick out of his sense of humor and hired him based on the telephone call and his references. The real surprise was when he showed up in person. They never expected a black skipper from Albany.

More important to him than the glory of high finishes in San Francisco, however, were the personal connections he made with his students over the course of the summer program. A sophomore named Jazz was his favorite, likely because he reminded him of himself in many ways. Even at sixteen, Jazz had an emerging political awareness and the ability to make observations and connections between seemingly disparate facts. He knew it had taken him a lot longer to develop in those areas. From a sailing perspective, however, Jazz was pure landlubber. But by the end of the summer he could handle the tiller with either hand, and talk at length about sail shape, lift, and appropriate docking procedure given current, wind, and sea states. He also realized during some of the onshore navigation classes that Jazz had a serious math aptitude.

The first week of business school that fall was a ball-buster, as he anticipated. He scrambled to get off to a fast start, determined not to fall back into old patterns. He knew that keeping pace with his classmates was both entirely possible and essential. He first learned that in junior high school, where he spent much of his first year after school with tutors coming up to speed. It showed him that despite a subpar start and lack of rigor in his earlier grade school curricula, he could compete with the best of them in time. College had reinforced his confidence.

He also learned during the first few days of classes that the big step up from college to business school involved the quantitative elements that underscored every aspect of each class and homework assignment. He saw that it was all about demonstration verses remonstration. If it couldn't be quantified mathematically or financially, then from a business problem point of view, it was irrelevant to the analysis. He saw the logic in it and became comfortable with the approach.

He decided to see Jazz soon after the school year started, and before things got too crazy. He figured he could build on the summer relationship and also provide a little motivation for him by bringing him up to the highly acclaimed university.

He called him to see if they could meet up for lunch the following Saturday afternoon. Jazz agreed, and let him know that he would be bringing a friend. "Not a guy friend," he said as he ended the call.

They all met at the big statute on the main quad, the easiest gathering point on campus and the location where the L street bus from Jazz's neighborhood would drop him. Brett picked up three boxed lunches before heading over for the rendezvous. He assumed Jazz would go for the roast beef, but he was unclear what the *lady friend* would opt for, so he grabbed a tuna fish sandwich and a vegetarian, both on multi-grain. He could go for either one, so he figured he was safe. They were on time and he spotted them as he approached from the mid-campus dining hall.

"Thanks for coming by, Jazz. I know it's a pretty long ride from home to this stop at the end of the line."

"No problem, thanks for inviting us." Jazz turned to his lady friend quickly, then to him. "Mr. Brett Howard, I would like you to meet Val Richards. Val, this is Mr. Brett Howard, the sailing instructor that I told you about."

"Pleased to meet you, Val. Call me Brett, please."

"Nice meeting you, Brett. Jazz told me a lot about the summer experiences you all had together."

As Brett offered up the sandwiches, he was surprised that Jazz went for the vegetarian choice and Val dug into the roast beef. The tuna fish turned out to be pretty good, and he made a mental note to try it again. Jazz mentioned that Val helped him in organizing efforts, and he wondered to himself what that could mean.

As they were digging into lunch, he realized that Jazz must have practiced his introduction of Val, because it followed all the rules of protocol. He suspected it was the first formal introduction that Jazz had made. He must have remembered one of the classroom sessions from the summer program, he realized. The lesson was about unfamiliar waters and unfamiliar places. The point was that you never had to remain uncomfortable in unfamiliar circumstances, and the solution was to think like a skipper: research the course, speak with local folks that have insider knowledge, and bring yourself up to speed. That got better results on a boat, and better results in life. Jazz had obviously taken that lesson to heart in planning his introduction.

"We had some good times at the dock and on the water, Val. I didn't see you there."

As he smiled at Val to put her at ease, he noticed her startling blue-green eyes. She also wore her hair in a large afro style that reminded him of some of the firebrand political activists who came to prominence in the sixties.

Her response reminded him even more of those old-time radicals.

"Well, to be frank about it, I debated with Jazz the whole concept of sailing and spending endless hours floating around on the water. My point of view is that sailing is a bourgeois pastime for those who are removed from the everyday struggle of the people. Besides, I personally don't like water, really, even baths."

He decided not to take all that on at one time, and instead replied that her point of view was an interesting one with some truth to it. He figured he would mention later the several people that he knew personally who were avid sailors, and also generous backers of efforts to bring opportunity to those without it.

"You know what, let's take these box lunches over to the east end, which is just a short walk from here. I thought we could enjoy them there while taking in the view of the lower campus that stretches out in the direction of the Bay."

Once there, they talked about the school year and how they were each faring in the early days after the long summer off. But he could tell that Val was a bit distracted. She clearly had something else on her mind. It was almost as if she was physically rejecting the peaceful scene around them, rather than taking it in and savoring the view. She would furtively glance down toward the Bay and, rather than drinking it in, she would practically yank her gaze away. He thought that maybe she was growing irritated with herself because the amazing view would grab her attention again and again.

Then she turned her blue-green gaze on him and asked the question that had apparently been sticking in her craw for quite some time.

"Mr. Howard, Brett, how can you invest all of your energy into this lily-white institution when there are serious struggles going on just a few blocks from here, where our folks are trying hard just to put food on the table and receive quality medical care?"

He imagined, but could not be certain, that he saw Jazz kick Val's foot with his own after that question.

"Val, that's a very good question. In fact it's an excellent question, one I have asked myself on several occasions when I was chasing a high school degree, a college degree, and now as I go after a graduate degree in business. The question, though, is usually only asked by those of us who know some level of deprivation and have a desire to give back."

Perhaps being guilty of having already classified Val into a certain box, he added more.

"The question, strangely enough, is also asked by those within our race who are from the privileged tier of society, either by money, skin color, or both." Brett could see from her slight blush that he had flushed her hole card—she was a child of privilege, carrying a radical political shield to deflect attention.

He adjusted the next part to address the inner conflict that she was very likely struggling with.

"I know for sure, Val, that the needs outside of these walls, and outside of all the walls of power, are very pressing. Many folks are struggling to maintain a roof over the heads of their families. But there are folks who are determined to make a difference in those struggles. How that happens, and what they choose to do, is a profoundly personal choice. For me, that choice was to complete my professional training and to establish an economic foothold in this society. From there I believe I can influence a broader type of change; one that's more impactful than if I never completed my education."

Jazz seemed intrigued by that answer and chimed in with a question.

"But don't a lot of those who get that education you spoke about get the big jobs and the money, and don't they sell out in the end?"

"Some do, indeed," he had no hesitancy admitting. "Whether we keep our commitments comes down to personal integrity. There are many highly educated and affluent folks who do give back, and who have influenced the path of change for many over the years. I'm sure you have read about some of them in your classes. And those folks come from all races and all strata of society."

Val was silent, but she had a hugely skeptical expression on her face. He noticed how light-skinned she was in the bright afternoon California sun. Her features were largely European, even though her complexion had too much pigmentation for her to be from a single European race. At first glance she might be mistaken for a Native American. He suspected when they first met, however, that she was of mixed African American and European stock.

He remembered first running into her manner of far left-leaning opinion in college. He didn't know whether it was pure coincidence or not, but often times in his experience, the most radical opinions seemed to emanate from the mixed-race kids. Or maybe, as he had later realized after a lot more experience, their position of relative privilege gave some of them more time to think deeply about the political and racial issues affecting the country.

Unable to restrain herself any longer, Val blurted out, "I think it's selling out. Mostly uppity folks who want to keep on getting theirs. They write a small check here and there to take care of their conscience."

He wondered in that moment if she was reacting to the reality of her own family's approach to giving back.

Jazz politely interceded to get the lunch back on track.

"Brett's a good guy, Val. He worked with us all summer and started the whole program for us at the marina. Nobody else ever did that around here. I think he's going to double down once he gets out and makes some big bucks."

Jazz's opinion was clearly important to her, and she relaxed and put her claws away while they all enjoyed the rest of the lunch.

Later that night, after ten-thirty, his phone rang. It was Jazz, but he was speaking in some kind of code and also attempting to disguise his voice. Jazz spelled out to him the last part of his message.

Tkn Quad UCB tonht Sty Awy

Before Brett could ask him what was going on, he hung up. Perplexed, he turned back to his thick business finance text, where he was committed to remain until one in the morning.

On the way over to his eight o'clock class the following morning, the meaning of Jazz's coded message became clear. The main quad of the campus was under occupation. At least thirty tents had been pitched over the large, open space. Tables and makeshift information areas were set up and piled high with literature. Signs were staked into the ground, pointing outward to send the message and reason for the occupation. In some areas, live cooking fires were burning and groups of occupiers were huddled around them. The quad had the woodsy odor of the campfire.

On the perimeter of the makeshift camp, the curious had started to linger as the university came awake. Many were shift-change workers passing to or away from work, but a substantial number were students and faculty.

He could hear the loud din of bullhorns that seemed like they were competing with each other. He moved closer to one of the staked signs and read a headline that meant nothing to him. It decried the university's recent theft of land belonging to the MLK High School.

As he wondered what it was all about, he heard a shrill voice that he recognized shouting into a nearby bullhorn. It was Val. Her head was covered with a closely drawn hoodie, and she wore a bandanna over her mouth to conceal most of her face, but he immediately knew it was her from the unmistakable blue-green eyes. Her words carried a hard edge and the undertone of threat.

"This racist school has sold the black community out," she shouted. "They have seized the land that was promised to us for MLK High School. Now they want to put a spice garden up there. That ain't going to happen. We've got their land, and we won't leave until the ground is broken on OUR land for the new MLK High School. Power to the people!"

Scattered applause followed.

She put down the bullhorn and took a long drink from a bottle of water provided by a fellow occupier. Brett recognized him immediately despite the drawn hoodie, bandanna disguise, and the additional black sunglasses. He moved over to the perimeter of the camp near the banner flags and called out to Jazz, who had moved inside to one of the food stations. Over the mounting clamor of the crowd and various bullhorn shouters, he called out Jazz's name in a low voice. Jazz looked up, recognized him, and made his way casually over to the edge.

"Are you kids out of your mind?" he asked him without any greeting. "Don't you know how these occupy things end? You can't afford that kind of mark on your record if you want to get into the colleges that we talked about."

Jazz loosened his hoodie and pulled it slightly off his head. After glancing around, he took off his sunglasses. Brett could see anxiety and nervousness on his face, some of which likely resulted from the lack of sleep last evening when they pulled off the stunt.

"This was the only choice we had. Last week the university bigwigs voted to reject the promise made to the community five years ago. They had been stalling and dragging their feet on that promise for years, but they officially voted to welch on it. They would rather see our school crumble, as it's been doing, than lift a finger. And they voted to grow spices on the land, Brett, when what we need is a school where the windows aren't busted out and the walls aren't falling in from old age. That's just plain wrong. We had to do something."

Brett was completely unaware of the issue.

'Look, Jazz, if I'd known anything about this, I would've tried to do something, tried to pull together some support for you all. You know me well enough to believe me, I hope. I'm new to the area, and this just wasn't on my radar. But I can tell you this—the school won't react well to this kind of pressure. They can't allow campus life to be disrupted, no matter what the issue. Who's behind this protest, Jazz?"

"You've got to promise me you'll keep this to yourself. " He waited for a nod from Brett that never came, but he continued anyway, as if telling him would ease the mounting stress he was feeling.

"It's the Urban Strikers. They've been backing the community for years. They had it right. There's been talk and empty words about the need for a new high school for five years. Now it's time for action."

Brett had no idea who the Urban Strikers were, but one thing he did know was that a lot of these kids could get hurt real soon. And an arrest record could sink their chances for admission to any college in the nation worth attending.

"Jazz, do me a favor and ask them to come over. I really need to talk to with them for a few minutes."

'They're not here. They run the operation from off site. They said if they stay in the background, the University would back down quicker."

That admission really worried him. They'd put the kids in harm's way and weren't even on the front lines with them.

"Jazz, listen, this is critical. You've got to set up a meeting for me as soon as possible with that group. You can vouch for me. Tell them I need to talk, and that I have some ideas to get to the goal—building the school on that land."

"Okay, I'll call you tonight"

As Brett continued on to his class, he heard the shrill voice of Val behind him repeating the same message.

Lieutenant James W. Dorn was the ranking SWAT commander in the San Francisco and Berkeley communities. He was equal in rank to Detective Walter Perry, who was in charge of containment and removal of the occupiers on the university quad. They both reported to the Berkeley Chief of Police.

At the initial response meeting, called together 90 minutes after the occupiers pitched their camp, Dorn was insistent that monitoring and perimeter containment had to be in place by 12 noon that day. The illusion of control had to be removed from the occupiers as soon as possible, he stressed. That was the first step in the reestablishment of order. Monitoring included 24-hour video surveillance and infiltration using deep cover officers from San Francisco's black ops unit. Facial recognition software would also be deployed as part of the mix to identify known radicals for takedown shots if the peace was breached.

Finally, Dorn was set to deploy full perimeter encapsulation consisting of a double exterior seal around the site that prevented media and other access, and that interdicted retreat by the occupiers. Largely consisting of checkpoints, the goal was search and interrogation to make media, bystanders, and resupply difficult, if not impossible. Dorn also noted that standard asset deployment would include rooftop snipers with night vision capability, as well as armored vehicle command and SWAT assault team deployment.

Detective Perry leaned back in his chair at the end of Dorn's crisp, military-style presentation and released a barely audible whistle that offered false praise for the detailed plan. Dorn looked supremely confident as he took his seat.

"With all due respect, Lieutenant," Perry began with a folksy tone and manner. "I reconnoitered the occupiers this morning, along with members of my command staff. Unless we missed something, I didn't conclude that we were dealing with Sandinista terrorists or some other paramilitary unit out there. Frankly, despite the bandanna getups and the hoodies, we think most of them are fresh-faced high school kids."

Dorn seemed to completely misread the comment and responded as if he was tone deaf.

"Our tactical options also include control of the media through compromise of their broadcast assets. We're also prepared to deploy interdiction of media and by-stander camera angles. Limiting biased imagery is essential during mop-up."

This time Perry leaned forward in his seat and turned to face the chief of university security at the head of the large oval table. "Bob," he said quietly, "please video conference in the chief and use this private number." He passed down a business card.

Dorn came out of the early morning video conference call with just about everything he recommended. The one exception that stuck in his craw was the need to clear any sniper fire on a threat target with Detective Perry. But he did win the concession that any imminent threat to life could be taken down without that authorization, so long as current rules of engagement were followed to the letter. No way to run an army, Dorn groused.

On the video call with the chief, Perry soon realized he had been set up and outwitted. Both outcomes he blamed on himself. Dorn had acquired superior intelligence that he didn't share before the video conference. Standing at parade rest in front of the room and down angle from the output camera, Dorn crisply presented his strategic and tactical recommendations to the chief.

Not at all happy to be rousted out of bed by this occupier business, the chief was in a crusty mood.

"Dorn, why do we need all these assets to contain a group of disgruntled kids?"

"Chief, I delivered a manila envelope by courier to your home earlier to answer that question. You have the same information now that we have here."

The chief reached for the parcel whose earlier delivery had disturbed his sleep and impatiently tore it open.

"Chief, I am going to roll through digital photo images and transcripts of recorded phone calls on your screen for the next few minutes, so you will not see me on your monitor. These images and recorded calls are captured in your hard copy material as well."

Dorn continued, closing the noose of his trap.

"Chief, the first facial image was captured at 3:16 A.M. this morning using our Nikon facial recognition technology from a fixed campus location."

"Next to the image is a printout feed from the national terrorist database, and several domestic and FBI watch list files."

"The individual is known by the street name Thunder, AKA Jason Washington. He's the leader of the Urban Strikers protest group. He left the occupy perimeter fifteen minutes after this image was captured. You can see the old run-ins with the law and the more recent arrests for protesting that populate his rap sheet on the column to the right. His past membership in other anti-democratic organizations is highlighted in red."

"The other two images belong to his second and third in command. They were also onsite at the university quad this morning. Their sheets are too long for the video feed, so they are only in your package."

Dorn paused to let the full import of his messages and the threat they posed to the peace sink in.

"Thunder first established command and control over the occupation at 2:35 A.M., when he issued his first pager message to all occupiers after they arrived at the campus. The message issued from a burn pager that we compromised six months ago as part of an unrelated investigation."

Dorn continued to document the extent of control through subsequent intercept transcripts.

Perry knew then that any appeal to the chief for a low-key approach to the occupation was pointless. He was certain that a violent end to the occupation was now the most likely outcome.

Perry was a quintessential California liberal. He was troubled by the actions of the university, which were largely responsible for the boil-over of frustration. Since the old MLK high school was in his precinct, he was familiar with its history and its present deplorable condition.

But twenty-five years ago, the school was a proud symbol of what public education could achieve in the country. Back then it had graduated a senator, and three or four current Assembly members who continued to serve in Sacramento. At least three Nobel Prize winners also attended the school. Yet that was a generation ago, and the demographics of the neighborhood had shifted radically. As the voter population increasingly diminished in the areas surrounding the school, political attention went elsewhere, along with what would have been the school's fair share of city dollars. Political neglect slowly evolved into a deteriorating and crumbling physical infrastructure.

That's why the grand bargain was reached five years ago, he recalled. The former chancellor of the university was a visionary who believed that his campus should lead the urban renewal effort and partner with other stakeholders. Back then the buzzword was public-private partnership, and the university seemed to be a shining beacon on a hill. The purchase of that abandoned parcel came with the university's commitment to develop the land to serve the community. Perry knew that no specific agreement to build a high school was ever hammered out, but that had been the going assumption back then. How could a spice garden become the grand vision now? He shook his head. It was a sign of the times, he figured. Budget-cutting bean counters had replaced big ideas and commitment to a cause.

Jazz called Brett later in the morning, using the same disguised voice. The meeting was set for eleven-thirty that night with an individual called Thunder. He could tell by looking at the address that the meeting was going to happen deep within the so-called *hood*.

Given the time and location, he bemoaned the fact that at best he would get four, maybe five hours of rest before his early class. But he knew the reality was that he had to get motivated and get to that meeting with a message that would make a difference. Tensions had escalated at the occupy site after midday when the police and SWAT teams appeared in force, deploying heavy weapons and aggressive security tactics.

Checkpoints, interrogation of visitors, cameras, and combat-dressed troops had chilled the spirits of the students and left a pall of fear over the camp. After the noon counter-invasion by police, the students were largely left to huddle among themselves, cut off from supporters and news coverage. But his most urgent motivation was the ring of sharpshooters that occupied several rooftops overlooking the quad. Their weapons were continually aimed down.

The situation was a powder keg that had to be diffused. He worked the phone lines hard that day, reaching out to all his contacts in an effort to put something together.

As the L route bus approached Center Street and the shadows and dark store fronts in the neighborhood seemed to envelop the bus, he had a flashback to the Chicago gang encounter—and although he knew it had to be psychosomatic, he felt a sharp pain in his lower back. It quickly dissipated as his rational mind calibrated that the assault occurred almost three years ago.

Nineteen fifty-seven Center Street turned out to be a step-down storefront with two large windows on either side of a central door. The windows were backed with black privacy curtains that were drawn completely shut. A variety of small banners and photographs were adhered to the inside glass, covering most of the surface area of each pane. The door was heavy reinforced steel, painted gunmetal gray. At the top was a six-inch square, opaque glass look-through. A faint light beyond the thick glass was visible that highlighted the black steel support wire behind the glass. On the lower part of the door, adhered on the outside, was a small 3x5 African American flag in the traditional red, black, and green colors. The flag looked new compared to the rest of the entrance way, and he wondered if it was purchased for his arrival.

He looked at his watch. Despite being five minutes early, he stepped down the two small stairs and knocked hard on the door with the heel of his hand. A shadow moved behind the glass-look through and he assumed he was being watched. Soon he could hear locks being opened. He counted six.

When the door pulled back, a tall, gaunt, dark-skinned man with wire-framed glasses and a goatee faced him, looking calmly back into his eyes. He had a curved mustache that fell below the sides of his mouth. His appearance was almost oriental, and anything but the threatening figure he had expected, given the name Jazz mentioned to him earlier. He relaxed a bit as Thunder gestured for him to enter.

"My brother," Thunder said after he completed relocking the door and approached him, extending his hand. Thunder moved through a ritualized handshake that Brett recognized from his Africa trip. But Thunder had added several twists and turns that weren't in the African version he remembered.

"Come in, come in," he said while pointing at two pillows on the floor, gathered near a small, squat candle that provided low light throughout the room. Beyond its reach were shadows and darkness. Brett sensed they were not alone. He started anyway.

"Thank you for agreeing to talk to me at such a late hour."

"Ah, my brother, it may be night here, but in the Motherland, the sun is soon to rise."

Of course he knew that to be true from personal experience, so he responded in kind.

"Deep within the Volta region of Ghana, the water carriers have already left for the fresh streams, and the gatherers of wood will soon depart."

Thunder hesitated before responding to the references, and then he nodded and smiled, as he appeared to know the exact region to which Brett referred.

"And so it has been, from time immemorial." Thunder nodded slightly forward in a gesture of respect.

"As oral tradition assures us it has," he said, returning the nod.

Whatever distance between them that may have prevented their ability to conduct business was lifted in that instant. Thunder appeared to accept him as a partner with whom he might be able to work out a solution.

"From whom do you come?" Thunder asked, seeking to establish the authority level that he represented.

"I have no official post or standing with the college. I come on behalf of the students who are in the gun sights of the snipers."

"The response by the university to the occupation was heavy-handed and crude."

"Yes, it was. I think the removal phase might start as early as tomorrow morning. Jazz, Val, and the rest of them will get thrown in jail, if they're lucky. If unlucky, it will be much worse."

"The struggle has always claimed its victims, my brother, and we must always hold their sacrifice high. *A luta continua!*" He watched Thunder's hands clench into fists as he loudly shouted the revolutionary slogan.

"Without struggle, there will be no change, my brother. We are part of the great diaspora, displaced five centuries ago. Yet we have not disappeared. As African people we strive together, give blood in the cause together, and pull our race forward together!"

Brett decided against expressing his strong opposition to the pan-African umbrella under which Thunder envisioned a global struggle. But he knew he had to quickly move the discussion away from sacrifice and martyrdom if Jazz, Val, and the others were to have any chance of leaving the quad unhurt.

Stay focused.

So he kept his mouth shut as he waited for Thunder to cool off, and for the opening that finally came.

'You and I must fashion a solution, my brother. Shall we begin with your thoughts?"

As he began to explain a possible plan, Thunder leaned slightly back in a lotus position on the pillow, stroking his short beard. He seemed to be gauging the intonations in Brett's voice as much as he was listening to the actual words.

"We need to build that school on the vacant land that sits in the middle of the community."

"To do that will take money, organization, and allies from the business community, the academic community, and the neighborhood associations who have long advocated for that result. But what has been missing, based on my review of things so far, is a spark. By spark, I mean a doer who by their own actions can pull the other parties along. A doer can put up big money, and challenge the university and the city to follow suit. I may have that person, but they will not move forward until the occupation is ended peacefully."

Judging by his facial expression, Thunder seemed far less interested than he expected. But his eventual response was one he had anticipated.

"Promises have been heard for five years here, and they have been broken. Why would this round of promises be any different?"

In his answer, he mentioned Bob Baum and his national foundation. Bob was a guest instructor at the business school, lecturing this semester on entrepreneurship. They met during one of the after-class Q&A sessions, where Bob had individual time with smaller groups of students. Bob was one of the calls he'd completed earlier in the day. He asked him about his charitable foundation that had seeded inner-city projects all over the nation. He had bluntly asked him, why not here at home?

Before continuing, he leaned forward on his pillow cushion, partly to ease a cramp that was taking hold of his left hamstring muscle and buttock. He realized then that his pillow-sitting muscles were way out of shape.

"Bob said he would be interested in taking on the task of getting the school done. He saw the need, and that's it. He doesn't need a committee to spend months and years writing reports. He is a doer, and he's now on our side. But the peaceful lifting of the occupation would have to occur first. This would allow the university to save face. The following day, an announcement would be made about the foundation, the university, and the city working with residents to build the school in record time."

"This may be the solution to get the university out of the vegetable garden business and back into supporting education for our kids," Thunder said. "But I'll have to check out this Bob Baum independently and determine his trustworthiness before I sign on. I will call you in the early hours this morning, my brother."

Brett groaned inwardly at the thought of a late-night call interrupting his sleep. But on the other hand, he felt a lot better, because he knew that Thunder's research would confirm Bob's credentials.

The call came in at one forty-five in the morning. Thunder expressed qualified support for the plan, even as he derided Baum as the ultimate new age capitalist. He demanded to know how Brett would ensure that Baum and the others wouldn't back out after the occupation lifted. He had anticipated that objection, and had traded emails with Bob throughout the day to get the best answer. Bob was an alumna of the business school, and had figured out that his financial support should flow from his foundation to the alumni association as a matching gift. This would sell the fund to other alumni, drawing in far more money than his contribution alone. The approach would also extend the reach of the school's fundraising apparatus, providing an additional group of graduates to appeal to for money in the future.

According to Bob, it was precisely the capitalist self-interest motive that ensured the university would be all over this one and not back out.

After the explanation, Brett could almost see Thunder stroking his beard on the other end of the line as he contemplated his next move.

"How soon before they are ready to publically make the announcement?"

"They're ready to go as early as tomorrow morning, once they get word and see the peaceful dispersal happening."

"Tell them, my brother, that the occupation will end this morning between 2:30 and 3:30 A.M. We came in the morning, and we will depart in the morning. No arrests and no harassment. Deal?"

"I'll get that word out to the university police, and to the president, after we hang up. No one will have a problem with the peaceful end to this. It will happen."

Sniper position seventeen was the first to observe unusual activity in the camp. Then he heard Dorn bark into his earpiece.

"Word received that camp will voluntarily disassemble within next hour. All transport vehicles will be inspected before access to site. Keep sharp eye out for any suspicious activity. Rules of engagement Alpha still operative."

Similar information had been passed on to the police and other perimeter units. Detective Perry received an early morning call at his house from his night shift commander, and he was relieved despite having his sleep broken. A deal was being brokered to save face on all sides. For once, he said to himself, cooler heads had prevailed. Building the high school would be a big deal for the community, and it might inject some badly needed optimism out there in the streets, making his job a whole lot easier.

Jazz and Val were amped when they heard from Thunder. Jazz figured that some deal had been worked out with the university, and that Brett had been involved in it somehow. Val was also in a rare celebratory mood as she set about packing things up. Then she remembered that they'd all agreed during the early planning stages of the occupation that victory would be symbolized by setting off a red, black, and green fireworks display. They had packed fireworks just for that occasion. She looked around for Jazz to help her assemble the stuff, but he was nowhere to be seen.

Undeterred, she pulled out the box of shells that would be launched from the three tube mortars. Without his help, she had to place them in a small wagon and drag them over to the far end of the field for a good shot at the night sky.

Sergeant Timothy Murphy was hunkered down in his position, facing N.W. He was really happy about the end of this deployment, as he could now get back on day duty and play with his new baby girl in the sunshine for a change. Only nineteen years old, he had completed all of his advanced marksman certifications and led his team in each of the practice range competitions, as well as in money made from bets. Having handled guns since he was three years old, the competition with his buddies was stacked in his favor.

Murphy stiffened in his crouch position, having seen at 300 degrees a slight movement in his night vision eyepiece. At first it was just a green arc, but as he calibrated the lens, the image stabilized. Combined with his heat signature software, he focused on an eerily glowing figure moving slowly at a tangent from the occupy site. The human image pulled a flat object without heat signature. Murphy increased his field magnification on the flat object and observed at least three faint heat images that seemed to be in vertical position, floating just above the horizontal object.

He clicked on his microphone and radioed base, reporting the observation in detail.

"Copy 19, hold for reply."

"Target now stationary, copy," Murphy said quietly. "Target kneeling down to vertical devices, copy."

Because it was a windy night, Val soon learned after several attempts that she couldn't keep the stick matches lit long enough to ignite the mortars, so she decided to improvise.

"Target activating vertical devices. Confirm rules of engagement, copy."

"Sniper 19, this is base, Alpha Rules of Engagement continue to apply."

Murphy lowered the inset-mounted braces and adjusted his digital wind gauge on the scope of his .308 caliber rifle. He assumed a well-practiced shooting stance and sighted the target through the night scope. Multiple flashes from an ignition source were now burning, and the target was bending forward to the vertical devices.

Murphy stopped his breathing and added increasing pressure to the trigger.

Val's eyes gazed lifelessly as she pitched suddenly forward and toppled into the bed of the wagon, her hands reflexively clutching the lighted wick. She had improvised, making the wick using a broken tree branch and a ripped-off strip of her tee shirt. Her last thought was that they would do the trick.

Jazz and the entire occupy camp, along with the police and the media, looked skyward after the crack of the rifle shot from the roof. Fear was replaced with relief as the red, black, and green colors burst forth in a pyrotechnic display high over the quad. Jazz smiled.

I'll bet Val remembered to pull that off.

Brett would always carry with him the uncertainty of whether he could have done anything differently that night. One easy answer, which he refused to accept, was that he had done everything possible to broker the deal, and because of that a school had been constructed. There were other answers, though, and he refused to avoid confronting them. He finally concluded that big operations required a huge focus on detail and loose ends. The end of the campus occupation had been left to the police and the SWAT team. Civilians, including him, were home safely in bed, for the most part. No one asked the tough questions about what the rules of engagement would be during the final moments of the camp breakup. No one bird-dogged the issue to the end to make sure that mistakes were avoided. While he didn't put all the blame on his own shoulders, he learned a valuable and painful lesson.

When he returned for the first graduation from the new school, he had mixed emotions about the changes that had taken place. The school was graduating its first class, which included Jazz, even though they were only able to spend the last three months of their senior year in the building after its completion.

Jazz had buckled down and lived up to his academic potential. He was heading to USC in August as a freshman on a full scholarship. He gave the valedictorian address, and it was a pretty good speech. He spoke to his classmates about struggle and promise and fulfillment.

Brett worked closely during that previous year on the planning and initial construction phases for the new school with Bob and his team. It provided him both hands-on and strategic experience in business development and real estate. And while he didn't know it, Bob was keeping an eye on his progress through his site managers, who gave him high marks. Months before his own graduation, Bob offered him a job at his Palo Alto headquarters, and waived the application and interview process. Now with his own apartment, a steady paycheck, and a new sporty German car, he believed he was entering a new phase of his life.

Yet despite all of the positive changes, in his mind their value would always remain diminished, because there would never be a Val in the graduating class.

Chapter Nine
Palo Alto

Bob Baum made sure Brett was not lost in the shuffle of all the newly minted MBAs that started with him at the company. He assigned him to work as his second to push the Chipwell Development project through the City Council. It was a three billion dollar project that Bob believed would be central to unleashing the potential of the east end urban renewal area. Funded by private money to the tune of sixty-five percent, and public bonds covering the balance, Chipwell was a four hundred acre parcel in a location with ready access to rail, highway, and bus modes of transportation. It promised to be the next micro and nano technology mecca that would bring grassroots innovation back to Northern California. It would stem the rising tide of defections to Taiwan, India and Eastern Europe, where some of the best and brightest entrepreneurs were heading simply because they couldn't afford to lease space at astronomical Palo Alto prices. Chipwell would not only address that problem, it also promised entrepreneurs access to seed capital at subprime rates.

Bob asked Brett to meet him on the roof deck in the beach area that was part of his new green roof design. The roof looked like any street-level green leafy park and beach venue, except that it was forty stories above the city. As he approached the area that was set to the east quadrant of the green space, he walked along side a thirty-yard wide sandy beach that slopped gently down to an artificial saltwater sea. In the shallow water were two white beach chairs that faced one another. Bob was lounging in one of the chairs.

Bob spotted him as he approached and waved him over. He left his shoes and socks on the beach, rolled up his pant legs and went over to sit across from his boss.

"Thanks for joining me," Bob said as he notched the chair back a peg and relaxed. "We do some of our best thinking up here on the green roof. Feel free to use it any time, Brett."

"Thanks, I will. It seems like a real island of peace in the middle of a fairly hectic part of the city. The street noise up here is virtually nonexistent."

"That's due to 15 hidden attenuator units we installed last year to dampen the noise updraft. But they're all solar powered. This roof and the building together provide substantial carbon offsets, to help with some of the less efficient buildings that we own."

"Tell me, Brett, how was the graduation ceremony at the new school last June? I've been meaning to ask you that for a while, but things have been hectic lately and I've spent most of my time on airplanes the past two months."

"It was really something else, Bob, something special. The parents and guardians were just so proud of their kids. I admired all of them for buckling down and striving to be the first class in a long time to make a mark. I think fifteen percent entered a two- or four-year college, a record number. And the vocational and technical numbers were also substantially higher. Still a long way to go, but the momentum is now in the right direction."

"Maybe they'll build on that record now that crumbling plaster and cement aren't part of every classroom lesson."

"I think you're right. The physical space, particularly the common areas and labs, is really state of the art. It has helped attract a whole new crop of motivated teachers for the upcoming term. Along with those that stuck it out through the bad years, they'll make a difference. You know, I don't think you ever met him, but the valedictorian at the graduation, a student named Jazz, is a mentee and a friend of mine. He delivered quite a speech that day."

"That sounds like the plan we envisioned. I owe it to you for bringing that opportunity to my attention."

"Well, I think you've repaid any debt that was owed many times over, Bob. Thanks again for this opportunity."

"Good. I'm glad we're even. Now, let's discuss a bear of a project that I plan to put you smack in the middle of. It's not a huge deal, but it is a strategic deal for the company, and thus one that will open growth opportunities for us down the road. I'll send you a detailed brief this afternoon, but let me give you the inside skinny in the next thirty minutes. Ease back your seat, Brett, and let me tell you a story."

What Bob described was a real estate development project that was entirely new thinking. Other projects were either massively large, attracting the well-established and the well-heeled, or they were micro startup efforts that allowed dozens of small tech operators to open their doors, and then close them within eighteen months when financing and markets denied them expansion opportunities. Chipwell would serve the middle market, however, where entrepreneurial companies with intellectual property, strong management, and some track record of success could build their business on a launch pad that had low infrastructure costs and low costs of capital.

But two big problems remained in the next six months. One of them was permitting and infrastructure build-out at the site. The second was named Trent Johnson, a rival developer who was going to propose an entirely different use for the parcel at the upcoming City Council meeting. That meeting would select one of the competing proposals. It was winner take all.

Back in his office that afternoon, Brett unsealed the heavy briefing package that Bob's team had prepared. For the time being, he put aside the separate manila sleeve that was labeled *T. Johnson Background,* and opened the big binder clip with a cover tab ominously labeled "**Confidential Ground Water Remediation Chipwell Site EPA no. 347-CA 15578**".

As he plowed through the voluminous reports during the next three hours, it was clear that the new development parcel sat atop a former industrial site that had been remediated, pumped, and treated for safe development. Yet he recalled that lesson number one in his real estate development classes in business school always stressed staying far away from remediated land. The indemnities were worthless, and buyers picked up joint and several liabilities, even if they never disposed of anything at the site.

Why in hell was Bob getting involved in this kind of snake pit?

As he read the parcel valuation surveys, the answer to that question became clear. Per-acre land values had been depressed by 90 percent from pre-pollution levels. The City, desperate to snare its share of the next generation high tech bubble, was asking 15 percent over those cratered levels. Any developer would reap a fortune in land appreciation value and leasehold values. The tax incentives and construction allowances that were part of the package also made the project extremely desirable.

The final section, containing detailed financials, confirmed the wisdom of the investment. It concluded with a narrative section providing assurances that neighboring communities would benefit from the project.

After a short break, he turned to the manila envelope to get up to speed on Trent Johnson. It was soon apparent that Johnson would be the major obstacle to success. The Johnsons were descendants from the Mayflower voyagers who settled in New England. The background report contained a detailed genealogy chart, showing the long lineage of a family that originally received a large land grant from King George. Through the generations, the family had vastly expanded their holdings, owning other large tracts of land in New England and the Middle Atlantic states, as well as in Virginia and Georgia.

Something odd about the description of the Georgia property purchases drew his eye. They were all located in and around Valdosta. He remembered that his mother, Clara, and her family were originally from that area, and that they were forced to leave for some reason when she was young. Old family stories had always been told that mentioned a theft of property from his maternal grandfather, or maybe his great grandfather. But the stories were murky and vague.

He read more about the impressive history of entrepreneurship in the Johnson clan. They had financed the development of water systems in the early 1900s that helped give birth to Los Angeles. They would buy up cheap land along the planned pipelines and reservoirs all the way from the mountains to the city, and then, after the aqueducts were built and the pipelines and reservoirs were constructed, they reaped enormous wealth by controlling the sale and lease of that very same land that was bought for a song. He wondered as he looked over the California pattern of purchase and resale whether the Johnsons were just lucky, or whether they had a private pipeline to valuable insider information.

On the other side of the table opposing his boss would be Trent Johnson, head of the west coast branch of the family. From the brief bio about him, Johnson seemed to believe that whatever he touched in California was his birthright, his by right of pedigree alone. Judging from some of the newspaper quotes, it seemed as if he looked at Bob Baum's millions and his third-generation heritage from immigrant Eastern European Jews as more of a pestilence, something that needed to be eradicated and removed from his path. The more he read, the more he realized that this fight to win the bid would be personal and bitter.

Preparation for the City Council hearing consumed his days, and a good chunk of most evenings. Even with the recent financial analysis showing the City would benefit by a factor of three from Bob's development plan, he worried that Johnson had some secret plan to trump those numbers. The Johnson proposal, so far at least, was elegantly simple—develop the space as a high-capacity solar generator that would power 20 percent of the region and incubate next generation technologies. Oddly, he thought, the proposal ended with a paragraph promising that the plan would not endanger abutters to the site, because no digging and excavation was required. It emphasized that the solar infrastructure was completely above ground. He reread the ending, and it raised a small red flag that he noted but could not yet classify.

Two days before the City Council meeting, Bob called his team together at his executive conference center in northern Marin County. The goal was to isolate them from other responsibilities, game theory any possible weaknesses in their approach, and anticipate and plan for any surprise Trent Johnson strategy at the hearing.

The independent consulting engineers went first, and they assured Bob again that the site was in good shape. That assurance took two long hours as they detailed the history of pollution and remediation, including the long-term pump and treat remedy that ultimately led to the return of neighborhood abutters, whose wells had been poisoned. Most of his colleagues zoned out during this technical phase of the meeting, checking email, scribbling, or secretly playing computer games while appearing to listen intently. Bob was completely oblivious to the latest hi-tech distractions, but even he checked emails and responded to notes from his executive assistant during the long presentation.

But Brett stayed focused, because of that bug in his ear.

Why would the Johnson presentation conclude with a paragraph about safety, when safety wasn't an issue?

Part of the answer came in the headlines the following morning that shouted from the front page of the Palo Alto Daily.

MONITORING WELLS AT CHIPWELL SITE RECORD HIGH LEVELS OF DEADLY BENZENE

This was a game changer, and all of the bright young men and women on Bob's team realized it. How could they go into the City Council meeting with a development plan that proposed excavation and construction, when containment at the site had been compromised?

The mood at headquarters was bleak when they returned to the office. They met in emergency session to develop a possible saving position, but the most they could come up with was delay and waiting for the EPA to recertify safety at the site. Bob realized that was no game plan at all, since the solution could take years of drilling, monitoring, and chemical analysis. His plan was sunk, and the Johnson plan would be approved, because it generated revenues during the EPA's long underground investigation. In his office after the meeting, Bob kicked off his shoes, leaned back in his chair and let out a slow, quiet breath of air.

We're screwed, he said aloud.

That's when his assistant buzzed the intercom and announced that Brett would like to speak with him. Bob really liked the kid. He admitted to himself that Brett added zero value to the current project, kind of like a duck out of water, but after all, he was thrown into the deep end of the pool on this one without a lot of guidance. He continued to believe that Brett would be a fine addition to the company in the next few years.

But he knew that the coming years would be radically different than the company Brett had signed up for, because he had been formulating change of control plans with his small circle of financial advisors for the past several months.

Got to get free from this public company reporting crap and do my own thing again.

"Come on in, Brett. Sorry that the air has left the balloon on the Chipwell deal. It would've been a great thing for the region, and for us."

"It still may be, Bob. I wanted to take fifteen minutes of your time to run a theory by you that might explain what we're seeing."

"Take all the time you need," he said out of respect. But his mind was elsewhere.

"You remember the strange conclusion at the end of the Johnson presentation that talked about not endangering abutters, and the safety of his above-ground solutions?"

"Yeah, I remember it, and I wondered what the hell that had to do with the high price of fish. That site's been certified as safe, for crying out loud. Johnson's proposal writers obviously got carried away with their own rhetoric."

"That's what I was thinking, until the headlines this morning. Suddenly out of nowhere, and despite all of the years of remediation, we have a chemical leachate problem in the groundwater. What an incredible coincidence that Johnson's team would highlight that same safety issue just before the Council meeting. Particularly when the last poisoned wells at Chipwell occurred more than ten years ago."

Bob eased his chair up from the recliner position and looked at him. His mind rapidly tumbled through the alternatives. Then, looking dead into Brett's eyes, he asked him if he thought the wells had been sabotaged.

"I'm no engineer, Bob, but I did stay awake through the tedious engineering report from our consultants yesterday. Well, mostly I stayed awake. According to them, any contamination plume would move southwest through the site, following the underground topography. Southwest through the monitoring wells cited in areas 6,7, and 8." Brett handed Bob a site map that showed the location of all test wells. They were sequentially numbered and set in a spiral pattern.

"According to the newspaper reports this morning, benzene contamination was recorded at wells 17 and 18, located here." He indicated the position as he looked over Bob's shoulder. "Each monitoring well broadcasts automatic warnings to both the EPA and Cal EPA. There's no manual intervention before a warning issues."

"Funny thing, though, the manufacturing facilities that generated the pollution were located here." He pointed to the hatched area on the map.

"If the plume was contaminated, wouldn't that be detected by wells 6, 7, and 8, downstream from the contamination sources? The benzene couldn't have gone below ground and avoided the wells, because testing done during the early stages confirmed bedrock at those depths. It forms the bottom seal under the site."

"Then the wells were deliberately poisoned."

"I think so."

"We've got to get our engineers in there to confirm that," Bob said with energy, already feeling like he was back in the game.

"We definitely need to go through the tedious process of gaining access and getting agreement for a test plan," he agreed.

"But I think there may be a shortcut that could help us at the hearing tomorrow," Brett said. "Benzene is a colorless, sweet-smelling chemical that is soluble in water. And it's highly flammable. Benzene isn't found naturally in the Palo Alto area, based on what I read. If it were, our normal fire season would be far more combustible.

"Funny thing yet again, Bob. When I pulled the original list of companies that were sued by the EPA and the state, benzene producers were not identified on the list.

"Finally, I reviewed the official chemical inventory manifest published by the EPA. That list is easy to access. As you know, it includes all chemicals used in manufacturing, and those found in the contamination. No benzene was identified. So if no business produced benzene byproducts, and it's not found naturally in this region, where did it come from?"

"I know one thing," Bob said. "The angels didn't place it there—at least not the ones working with us."

Bob reached over to his desk phone and punched the intercom.

"Liz, get Robert Stricker and his chief engineer on a conference call with me in ten minutes. The reason is *highest priority.*"

He looked at Brett and smiled.

"I knew there was a very good reason why we recruited you into the company."

Then Bob got serious again.

"I need you to pull together the team and rewrite the entire presentation. New slides, new order, new handouts have to be produced. Your assumption is that fraud has been committed. Leave the evidentiary sections blank for now. Stricker and his team will feed you the detail for inclusion real time. He has a buddy at Cal EPA who just might be persuaded to allow him limited access to sniff out possible fraud. This is going be an old school all-nighter for the entire team."

The all-nighter was well worth the lack of sleep and occasional yawns at the Council meeting the following day. The engineers were able to document injection drill holes that were recently bored, and then sealed over by sophisticated machinery. Traces of benzene were found at surface level near the injection holes, negating any plausible theory of leachate flow through the ground water. Trent Johnson's team vehemently denied any involvement, but the facts put them on their heels throughout the meeting. It was clear from the order of their presentation that they didn't anticipate Bob's team would see through the ploy.

Bob's company was awarded the development deal. Brett received his first significant promotion.

The last thing Brett expected to be dealing with during his first six months on the job was crossing daily picket lines to get into his office. And these weren't union picket lines. They were from the NAACP and other local advocacy groups. Forty to fifty loud, energetic, and occasionally foul-mouthed picketers manned the lines from sunup to sundown. This meant that at least twice a day he was called a sellout, an Uncle Tom, or an Oreo. The latter term was particularly galling, since he wasn't black on the outside or white on the inside. At times the shouting and accusations came very close to prompting physical confrontations, as some employees felt intimidated by the close physical proximity of the picketers. It was a tense situation.

He limited his own stress by cutting out virtually all mid-day meetings or lunches that required him to leave the company and thereby double the time that he endured the heckling. Conference calls and video calls became survival tools.

He also found it hard to understand why a guy with a good heart like his boss would end up the target of scorn. But his was just one of a dozen companies that were targets in the high tech belt. He couldn't help but wonder whether the picketers had applied the litmus test he found to be most relevant—the doer rather than talker test.

But as he researched more into the issue that was central to the protests—falling numbers of women and minorities in Palo Alto's high tech businesses—he started to better understand some of the picketers' frustration. Everyone was aware, of course, that high tech companies employed a huge number of J-1 visa foreigners. Most folks understood that without that foreign brainpower, the American high tech industry would grind to a halt. The real issue was the rapidly declining numbers of women and minorities that were recruited and retained by the industry. What he read confirmed that if present trends continued, those numbers would fall very close to zero by the end of the decade.

After his research, he looked around his company with a different level of awareness. He realized, of course, that as a newly minted MBA he was alone as an African American among the eleven others. The others included four Japanese and four Indian men, and two Chinese women. He made it a point after that to get away from his office more often and walk through some of the other floors in the gleaming high tech building. He saw very few people like himself, and very few women at the higher levels. As a final check, he contacted HR and scheduled a presentation to the college juniors and seniors that the company had proudly touted as a cornerstone for their diversity efforts. While the representation of women and minorities was higher, he wondered what the actual sign-on numbers would be. At lunch with a colleague later, he learned and that both the offer and the retention numbers were falling through the floor, and the trend was accelerating. The protestors were clearly on to something, he concluded.

On the other hand, he knew that he was recruited and hired by Bob, who had waived both his interview and his background check. And Bob's national work to provide opportunities for those without it also factored into his assessment.

And of course, MLK High School would be a spice garden without his boss's efforts. Beyond simply hiring him, Bob encouraged him to participate in local community organizations, and had supported his effort to become a board member at the Urban League. That included a budget that he used to support programs in several inner-city communities.

The League was always attractive to him, and he was honored to serve. Its emphasis on programs, combined with the capacity to partner with business in proactive ventures, suited his approach.

So while he was deeply concerned about the issues raised by the protestors, he could see a dimension of complexity that was invisible to them, at least at his own company. He also wasn't convinced that the current confrontational tactics would be effective in driving real change. Something else was needed.

On that third Thursday of the month, as always, he left the company for his two o'clock board meeting at the League in downtown Palo Alto. He braced through another round of heckling on his way to the parking lot. When he arrived, the usual seven out of fifteen board members were present. Most were distinguished members of the local community who had served for more than ten years. On the agenda was the upcoming annual meeting next month, as well as elections for board members and officers. As he approached his usual seat at the table, he realized that the future of the League didn't reside with some of the board members in attendance, or with those that made a habit of missing meetings. He believed they were from an era where status was more important than action and new ideas.

Several, of course, didn't share his view that major change was needed. New ideas like rotational terms, minimum board member financial contributions, and mandatory committee service seemed like intrusions to some of the old warriors. They had always been there when the shit hit the fan, they said. Why change for the sake of changing? Willie Helms, chairman of the board, was from the old school. He was a Guardsman, one of the oldest black private clubs. He was a Free Mason and chaplain of his local Grand Lodge. He was also a deacon at the Mount Royal Episcopalian church. From his high vantage point, things at the League were moving along fine, and he assumed that the occasional blather about new ways of doing things and board rotation and the like would fail to pass at the annual meeting. He believed it was as sure a thing as his own reelection to chairman.

Brett sat down next to one board member who to him represented the future. Ms. Beverly Hill was exceptionally bright, and also dressed to the nines. Bev was his own age, and a very important reason why he had never missed a board or committee meeting. She was also stunning, poised, and engaging. She had the whole package and seemed to know it, but not flaunt it. She turned to him as he took his seat, and her face lit up in greeting.

"Well hello, Brett! I'm so tickled that you braved those fierce lines of picketers and made it here safely."

She smiled and made his day bright right then and there. She had hazel eyes that were large and engaging. Her completion was cinnamon brown, and she wore her hair long down her back. He loved her high cheekbones and the way her tight, shapely figure seemed to move her clothing slightly back and forth around her at the waist and hips, commanding all of her lovely parts in unison as she walked.

"It's always a pleasure to be wherever you are, Bev. Elbowing my way through that gauntlet of picketers was the least I could do. That allowed me to arrive a few minutes early to chat you up."

She seemed to blush, but he wasn't sure. He wondered if she really was genuinely pleased to see him personally, and not just as a fellow board member.

"Truth is, it's not a lot of fun being heckled twice a day, four times today, by folks that seem to make a whole lot of wrong assumptions about who you are and what you stand for."

She was genuinely concerned and turned her chair to face him.

"I can understand how that must feel. Those people don't know anything about you and your values. And they don't care to learn. I wouldn't be surprised if they soon started picketing us downtown at the DHS. After all, we could be accused of parceling out welfare benefits and programs on the unfair basis of need rather than ideology."

They both chuckled at that.

Even when Bev was serious, he admired how she maintained her almost angelic composure. Only her eyes seemed to narrow slightly as she made her points with emphasis. He thought she really was something.

The meeting was about to get going, and he regretted that. It meant the end of any personal interaction with her. Those moments were always pleasant, and he often wondered how she would react if he asked her out on a date. Unfortunately when the meeting was concluded in an hour, they and everyone else had to hustle out and get back to their day jobs.

"Brett?"

Bev turned back to ask him just before opening remarks and rested her hand lightly on her arm.

"I don't know if you are much of a churchgoer, but my pastor, Reverend Sipes, is giving a sermon this Sunday entitled Ending Boycotts and Working Together for Change. It's a televised citywide event, drawing together most of the major churches, as well as political and social leaders. I'd love for you to be my guest. We may even get some insights into how the League can play a more influential role in conflict resolution with the other organizations."

He thought he felt his heart skip a beat, but on the outside he remained calm. While he hadn't been much of a churchgoer since he left home for college, the idea of spending more time with her was extremely appealing.

"You know, Bev, I would love to attend."

The meeting was called to order, and the treasurer began her review of League finances.

Bev soon passed him her business card with the name and address of the church scribbled on the back. She placed a smiley face after the address and wrote that she would see him in front, Sunday morning at 10:45.

He was not at all sure what passed for proper church attire, so when Sunday finally arrived he opted for the safe blue blazer look, leaving the tie at home. He learned that Third Baptist was one of the oldest black churches in Palo Alto, and that Reverend Sipes had transformed the membership into a communal rainbow, welcoming families and individuals of all races and walks of life. That picture began to emerge as he strolled from the parking lot to the front of the church. One thing everyone seemed to have in common was a pleasant facial expression that said they were happy to be there. Nowhere among this congregation were the workplace sourpusses that walked the corridors of many companies. And to his further surprise, folks actually greeted one another and made eye contact.

Bev was waiting for him in front of the church, despite his early arrival. She greeted him with a polite hug. She looked stunning in her usual restrained way, her clothing neat and trimmed and cut to her body.

"Thanks so much for joining me, Brett. Let's go in and be seated. The church is filling up fast."

She firmly clasped his hand, and he followed her into the enormous sanctuary. She kept a small lead in front as she looked for space for two in the closer pews. Spotting a couple of seats together about fifteen rows from the pulpit, and with him in tow, they politely moved past the folks who were already seated. He noticed a few curious glances and saw one or two whispers among the onlookers as they passed by. He was sure it was the blazer that drew the curious attention, so he quickly removed it after they were seated.

The first part of the service consisted of songs that were sung by an enormous choir. Everyone in the church joined in. The words to each song were projected on a large screen in the front that lowered from the ceiling. Sort of removed the excuses that he had as a kid not to sing in church, he thought. The emotional power grew in intensity as the choir led them through a series of communal praise and worship songs.

Some of them were familiar and touched a deep chord, taking him back to his first remembrance of church, when he and his sister and brother were commanded by their grandmother to attend every Sunday. And they obeyed, while she stayed home. As they grew older, their odd circumstances having no parent or grandparent present seemed to push them away from the church, or maybe they were pushed away by the church.

He felt a light brush of something against his head during the singing. Bev was next to him, her arms above her head as she waved them slowly back and forth. She would gaze toward the choir at times, singing and swaying in unison with them, and sometimes close her eyes. She had no idea that she had brushed him, and she continued in the spirit of the singing.

As it slowly wound down and the volume waned to a near whisper, Reverend Sipes mounted the pulpit, dressed in a long black robe trimmed in velvet purple. He was a barrel-chested man, perhaps six foot four and well over two hundred and fifty pounds. But it was his moral authority alone in the Palo Alto community that commanded the church. When he raised his broad arms, the entire assembly quieted as he intoned the opening prayer.

Then he wasted no time getting right to the point, and he asked a straightforward question early on in his sermon.

How can we work together for lasting change without tearing each other down in confrontation?

To Brett, having run the gauntlet of picket lines and insults for days, it was the exact right question to ask. But of course, Reverend Sipes also had the answer, and in the next thirty minutes he meticulously delivered his biblical prescriptions, along with issuing a moral challenge to men and women of faith to follow him.

He knew that the Reverend was appealing to a vastly diverse leadership group. That was apparent from his walk over to the entrance of the church. He had first noticed them as he passed the parking lots. They were highly segmented. There were printed signs declaring regular parking, valet parking, and VIP valet parking. The upper echelon religious leaders were clustered in discreet sections of the VIP lot that was dotted with burly security guards. There were Methodists, Catholics, and Episcopalians as well as the Lutherans and the Pentecostals, each group under their own flags that adorned the hoods of black limos or sedans. From the garishness of other cars, he assumed the super wealthy were also in the same lot. The political and other secular leaders, along with the merely wealthy, sheltered nearby in the regular valet lot, and many of them flew their own colors or flashed other shiny symbols. No wonder there was such a large VIP reserved section near the front of the church.

Seeing that display of segmented allegiances among the leaders of the community made him highly doubtful that any type of reconciliation would be reached during the service.

But he was wrong.

Several of the factions rose in the middle of the sermon and voiced open agreement with the Reverend's invitation for peace and unity. Others shouted loudly that they would work together and end the confrontations and squabbling. The tide of agreement spontaneously rolled back throughout the vast hall, and the Reverend responded. He called to the front of the church all of the religious and secular leaders. He came off the pulpit and engaged in long prayer with each of them, both individually and collectively. While this was happening, the choir started up a different repertoire of songs.

That couldn't be it, he thought, agreement gained so unanimously with a basic message of love and respect. But to his astonishment, that seemed to be it completely.

He looked at Bev for the first time since she accidently brushed against him. She was less energetic now, but she still looked toward the choir and waved her hands slowly back and forth as they sang.

When the extraordinary experience finally wound down and ended with the Lord's Prayer, he left the sanctuary with Bev at his side. He vowed to himself that once he was outside, he would ask her to join him for dinner.

When they finally steered past the vast crowd, he slowed and turned to face her, holding her hand gently in his own.

"Thanks for inviting me to this remarkable service, Bev. I reconnected in there to a part of me that I believed had been left behind in childhood, and to a part of my faith that had long been dormant. Can't promise that you'll see me in church every week, of course, but I will attend more often."

"God is good, Brett."

"Bev, there's something else I want to share with you. I would like to get to know you better, outside of our work-related activities, and even church. Would you join me for dinner this evening, or perhaps later in the week? I would be honored."

Her lovely hazel eyes met his, and she smiled.

"Brett, you are so dear to me, in just these brief months that I've known you. I hope we'll remain close. But I can never be your lover, Brett, only your dear friend. My true heart and life's partner was singing in the choir today. She's been in my life for five years, and we've become one."

Unlike most of the community leaders and parishioners who left Third Baptist that day with a genuine sense of renewal and commitment to change, Willie Helms left feeling completely unmoved by the sermon. He wanted to know why the League should engage with those who spouted polemics and slogans, but never fielded any real operational programs that changed people's lives.

He was also resentful of the tactics used during the service that were aimed at stirring emotions rather than reason. He chafed at the recollection of standing for more than an hour, singing songs projected onto a movie screen. Next thing you know Sipes will allow the holy rollers to run around the church shouting at the top of their lungs.

As a devout Episcopalian, Willie was accustomed to order, timeliness, and discipline. He couldn't get by the fact that the Pentecostals, with all their noise and bluster, had actually been invited to the service. If it was an outdoor tent revival meeting, he might have understood why they were needed. And why were the radical left ideologues needed at all, since most of them would rather just dismantle the country and hand it over to the communists and socialists?

His antipathy to the sharper-tongued advocacy groups was as old as his own pedigree. His father and his father's father always believed they were apart from the common everyday squabbles that involved racial politics in America. His father had been a leader of men during WWII, he met Eleanor Roosevelt personally, and was on her mind when she publically declared that black soldiers and pilots were prepared to enter the European war theater and help turn the tide of battle. His father had helped turn that tide through personal heroism when his all-black fighter group over Europe became the escort group of choice among white bomber captains. They would not fly without Helms on the wing. His father's group never lost a bomber to the Germans in aerial combat.

Willie knew his family history well, and knew that his blood relations had always helped turn the tide of battle since the Revolutionary War, and even before. A distant male relative had fought with Washington against the British, and thanks to the generosity of the First President received land and a stake, later moving his family to Canada, where they prospered until slavery finally fell. Other relatives battled alongside U.S. soldiers to defeat the Native Americans. His distant uncles and cousins were the officers among the buffalo soldiers of lore, just doing their job. Willie paid his own dues in Vietnam. He wasn't drafted into the war—he enlisted, as Helms men always did. And his Medal of Honor said all that needed saying about his valor.

So he refused to call a special meeting of the League as Sipes' plan required. His strategy was to do nothing and to wait them out. If they really wanted his help, and a clear picture of what path to take forward, then they could find him in his bunker.

His obstinacy was exactly the spark needed by his opponents on the board, who had grown weary of his regal management style. They respected his military record and knew that he was at his core a decent man. But he was out of touch with the thinking and needs of the younger generation, and the future of the League.

Brett's phone rang at nine in the evening. The number was blocked, but he answered anyway.

"Hello, Brett. I hope I'm not calling you too late."

Hearing Bev's voice was a pleasant diversion from the three thick financing bids he was reviewing for the Chipwell electrical conduit installation.

"Oh no, Bev. Believe me, I always appreciate hearing your voice. And how are you this fine Palo Alto evening?"

"Things are great on this end. I hope we're still on good terms after my...revelation last Sunday."

'Truth is, I was pretty crushed from a personal standpoint. But you know what? I'm very happy for you, that you've found your life's partner. I'll comfort myself by thinking that things might have been different between us if we'd met earlier."

"That's so sweet. But we would have had to meet when I was about eight years old, you know."

They had a good chuckle together, and then they turned back to business.

"Brett, I know Tony called you a few days ago, as he did several board members. He has now completed an exhaustive and confidential survey. Other than the five Helms loyalists who would follow him over a cliff, the outcome of the upcoming vote is clear. Board membership cannot be trophies any longer. Members who aren't pulling their weight have to go. That's the only way the League will meet the current challenges, let alone plan for and anticipate the future."

Listening to her soft voice almost made him ask her to meet him for a nightcap later that evening. Then he quickly remembered why that idea was a nonstarter.

"But one big problem remains."

"What problem, Bev? It looks like the future, rather than the past, will soon be in the driver's seat at the League."

"Willie Helms is the problem. If he remains as chair, he'll undermine and pocket veto every step forward that we might gain from the other changes."

"Then he needs to go."

"A majority of the board is willing to vote for his removal. He'll be voted out of office on Thursday, and we believe you are the right person to replace him."

He was genuinely surprised. He had been nose to the grindstone on the Chipwell deal for the past several months. Other that the board meetings and an occasional committee meeting, he had shut out the world completely. His mom even chided him on a call recently that she was going to put out an APB out for him if he continued to stay out of touch.

But chairman…could he be chairman of the League. He started to feel a little bit of panic rising in his chest.

"Brett, we all know you're a busy young executive at the start of your career. I made it crystal clear to Tom and the others that you couldn't afford the time to be a one-man show. Unlike Willie, you'll need committed and involved fellow officers and active committee chairpersons. I agreed to be there with you as vice chair, and Tom would take the treasurer's role. Stephanie would be recording secretary. Together, we can balance for each other and get the job done. What do you think?"

"Bev, you know I strongly agree with the mission of the League. I want to see us thrive and impact current problems. We certainly could be a better at working with other groups to affect change. And maybe I can help us get there. We should be okay if you and the team can work together, and we can all pull on the oars at the same time to move the League forward. I'm in, Bev. I'll stand for chair. Sorry for the long windup, but I suppose I was convincing myself."

"That's perfectly okay. Most of the time we have to convince ourselves first. I know you'll make a great chairman."

Willie arrived at the Masonic lodge ninety minutes before the regularly scheduled meeting. As Chaplain, his role was significant and laden in centuries of tradition. There were prayers and incantations to perform, as well as rewards to bestow for loyal member service extending the lodge's influence. And finally, there was metered condemnation for those who fell short of specific missions and undertakings. Today's gathering held a little bit of everything, thus his early arrival to prepare.

His grandfather first exposed him to the Masonic secret book, revealing it to him when he was only five years old. Pops unwrapped it from within folds of blue velvet cloth and placed it carefully on the dining room table. Willie, who was barely able to see above the table, sat back with his hands under his legs as Pops lit candles around the book and moaned ancient prayers and incantations from memory. Since that time, joining had always been his dream.

But the magic and mysticism had long faded, and he understood that contacts, connections, and power were the real cohesion. Most of the new recruits could be influenced by the hocus-pocus for a short time. Yet before long, and after advancing through a few degrees, the hard practicality of the business side became clear, along with their own role.

"Willie, greetings," said the Master of the Lodge, who had silently entered the Chaplain room through the secret door. On his head, the Master wore the hat of authority.

"Master," Willie responded, bowing his head in the ancient sign of veneration.

"The wind of change is coming to the League, Willie. You will not be part of that change, though you have served well there for many years. You must continue to serve by standing aside and allowing the new board slate that will reveal itself to hold sway."

Willie contained his surprise, as he had expected to be easily reelected at the annual meeting. But he knew that the Master's information was unimpeachable, as it had always been.

"I will stand aside," he said, bowing once again.

"Thank you, Willie." The Master silently left the room.

Chapter Ten
Bankers and Activists

Shaka walked purposely to the front of the room to deliver his verdict on the speech they'd all just received from the trim, well-dressed New York banker. He was a tall, burly man with a shaved head and dark brown skin. His beard was black and full, and his bearing was ramrod straight over long, muscular legs.

He felt his anger growing as he neared the front of the hall. He didn't stand behind the speaker's podium, and he didn't have a PowerPoint presentation like the banker. But what he did have was presence and leadership experience.

Standing before them without fancy props, he looked out at the forty or so folks who gathered that morning in the Arbor Hill Neighborhood Development Center. He recognized most faces. There was the small group of community activists who cared about local issues, current neighborhood politicians, elderly folks—mostly women—and four of five others representing different types of social causes. And there were a few curious onlookers sprinkled in who came to see a good verbal fighting match. They had nothing to add on their own during the meeting, but would wag their tongues furiously once they left. The other attendees were drifters who'd wandered in the front door, hoping to enjoy any food that may be served after the meeting. He also noticed a couple of new faces in the small crowd, including a black man in a suit and a well-dressed young woman who accompanied the banker.

Instinctively he assumed a wide stance, and then cleared his throat before beginning his baritone-throated rebuttal.

"Brothers and sisters, don't be fooled by the color of this banker's skin," he said as he pointed his large index finger at Ned Jensen. "This banker may look black, but I'm here to tell you that he ain't thinking about what's good for black folks in Arbor Hill. He's only thinking about how much green he can make after he destroys a good chunk of our community over on Broadway."

He heard a few murmurs of approval from the activists in the back of the room. But he was just warming up.

"Y'all know me well. I've been in this neighborhood workin' for our interests for twenty years. I helped organize the health screening clinics. I was with y'all when we put the free breakfast program in place for our kids. And we set up the blood pressure monitoring program that comes in every year. You see me at Franklin Park, working with the young ones during the day camp programs. And I work with some of those that everyone else has given up on, 'cause I believe they can make it if they get a break."

His remarks struck a chord with several in the audience, who nodded and voiced loud approval and encouragement.

Feeling that energy, he paused, and then raised his voice.

"I care about this community, and I care about the kids on these streets. I live here, and I work here! And you know what? I will die here. This black banker lives in a fancy house downstate in Manhattan. Yet he had the nerve to stand up here with his suit and lighted up presentation, and tell you that he was here to help Arbor Hill. We don't need his kind of help!"

Some in the audience stood up and gestured at Shaka, showing their support. Others turned to their neighbor on the right or left, and nodded their heads in apparent agreement.

But to Brett, seated in the middle of the room, this was no time for celebration. He sensed that the meeting was slipping away from those like himself, who saw the promise of investment in Arbor Hill as a very positive and sorely needed thing.

He raised his hand and stood, knowing that by standing he'd made an aggressive move for attention. But after Shaka's powerful opening remarks, he knew that something drastic needed to happen to recapture audience support.

Shaka was not at all pleased to see him standing, but he had to take the question or risk alienating several onlookers who seemed to know this man.

"Yes, brother, what's your question?" he asked, trying hard to mask the anger.

"Thank you," Brett replied as he moved out into the aisle, facing the room to make eye contact with just about everyone.

"My name is Brett Howard, and it's a pleasure to be here. I look forward to shaking hands with many of you that I don't know personally when we break bread together after the official part of the meeting."

"Those of you who know me will recall that I spent several years of my youth in Albany. They were the best years of my life. They were the formative years. You know what I'm talking about. I mean those that shape you and provide a foundation for later success or failure. The years in Albany helped prepare me for success. But that was a different time. Our kids face bigger challenges today, and they need more help."

"I've been a lot of places since those days, and I've seen a lot of the world. I made my way in the business world for many years. Most recently, I was with Taurus Corporation in New York City. I started my business career in Palo Alto, California, where I chaired the Urban League board there for several years. You all are familiar with the programs they run, and you have a very good League right here in Albany. So I've always remembered our needs and my roots, no matter where I've been. I moved back to Albany last year to try to make a difference."

He could see that his opening had established a connection with many, and that the whole crowd was looking at him now and expecting something to be said that was meaningful.

"Some who know me asked why did I come back. Why would I return to a neighborhood like Arbor Hill, when I was living in California or New York City? Well, I came back for two reasons—to build a life here with my family in the neighborhood that I love, and to build up the lives of the youth in Arbor Hill by investing in the things that will help make that happen."

He knew he had already made an enemy of Shaka, who might cut him off at any time. He also knew, as an experienced speaker, that Shaka would lose support from the audience if he shut him down after such a smooth opening.

Shaka shifted his stance in frustration at the front of the room, but said nothing.

"One of those very positive things that may soon happen is the proposal for investing millions of dollars in Arbor Hill, which you just heard Mr. Jensen describe."

"Look around you," he continued, fully into his speech at this point. "When is the last time in your memory that a business opened a store in Arbor Hill, on your block? But I bet you all know how many businesses have closed. When is the last time you saw one of your neighbors putting some new shingles on their home, or repairing roof drains, because they received a bank loan to do so? Have you asked yourself why we pay thirty percent more than most other areas in Albany for basic food supplies and pharmaceuticals?"

Brett looked around the room. It was clear that he had struck a responsive chord with most.

He kept going.

"And we know there are the rows and rows of abandoned residential and commercial properties. These are a danger to all of us who live here, and to our children. But recently, growing pockets of development in Arbor Hill are taking hold. This has happened because neighborhood associations like this one have realized that modern development is a way forward. It will bring in jobs, housing, residential loans, and hope to this community. We can't afford to be shut out of progress. We need to get our fair share of investment, just like other neighborhoods in Albany are doing."

Bringing as much energy to his long frame as he could muster, he loudly concluded.

"That's why I support Mr. Jensen's plan, and I hope you will as well. Thank you."

He sat down and could see that many folks were speaking to their neighbors in the seats around them. He knew that he had at least neutralized the negative message from Shaka.

Avoiding any direct attack against him, Shaka resumed his emotion-laden message against the planned development.

After the meeting, Brett tried to approach Shaka, extending his hand in greeting, but his gesture was ignored.

Seeing Ned Jensen across the room, he made his way over to the banker who turned to him and extended his hand. "Mr. Howard, thank you."

"Please, call me Brett."

"Well thank you, Brett, for that support. It was tough going there for a few minutes."

"That is was. This is the kind of emotional opposition you'll face at the three remaining community meetings, before your plan is approved or rejected. Believe me, they will be better organized than they were today. How do plan to meet it?"

The banker looked at him with a small grin on his face.

"That's exactly why I would like to meet you for dinner this evening, as my guest. I think I can learn a great deal from talking to you. I'm staying downtown at the State Street Hotel. Can you meet me at eight tonight?"

"Yes, I can. I'll be there at 8:00 sharp."

"See you in the lobby."

Chapter Eleven
Fire

Several weeks later, Brett was on his way over to Ned's Broadway Street office to leave some documents for him to review. Ned had taken out a short-term storefront office lease. The hope was that during the last few months of his push for approval, a brick-and-mortar presence in the community might prove to be crucial to that acceptance. This was one of the concrete suggestions he had offered Ned at their dinner weeks ago.

Recently, after he mentioned the gaping youth services deficit in Albany, Ned also agreed to take a look at some early ideas he had sketched out for a high-impact summer program targeted at neighborhood kids. Brett told him that summer was a time when many children lost discipline, lost interest, and lost academic ground.

He also shared his belief that idle time and lack of motivation were twin anvils for failure, weighing down or completely crushing many opportunities. He cited his own personal experience in the same Albany neighborhoods as proof that the phenomenon was true, even for those kids who had many of the other ingredients around them for success. Ned gradually started to understand his passion as well as his point of view, even though Ned's own background as a child of privilege had been vastly different.

They had become more than just advisor and advisee during the past few months. A genuine friendship developed between them, one grounded in the experiences that they shared with each other about battling their way up the corporate ladder in the wealthy businesses of America.

Ned talked about his challenges in the New York City investment-banking arena. He jokingly referred to it as the cutthroat, high wire, highly compensated business of using other people's money to lavishly enrich the bankers, while on most occasions managing to satisfy client needs.

But he also said that he'd always had a dream to strike out on his own. So he had saved and invested wisely, and then pooled together sufficient capital using business connections, family, and friends to start his own bank. He finally entered the inner circle of capitalism as the head of his own shop. Ned's willingness to invest capital in the inner city of Albany was part of an evolving personal journey that Brett understood and valued.

Sharing some of his own experiences, Brett mentioned that he'd paid his dues in real estate investment firms, as well as in high tech and consumer products businesses. He also conveyed to Ned his long-held belief that there was an apparent paradox as he climbed higher up the rungs of the ladder. It was that after a certain point, the gravity of falling back down usually associated with dislocation or failure stopped being a force to fear. Ned was perplexed when he heard that, until Brett explained that the very same leveraged investment schemes engineered by Ned's creative colleagues on the banking side often ended up enabling business executives to cash it all in and buy the freedom that they had been seeking all along. He cited himself as a case in point.

As he approached Ned's office, he smiled as he looked around at the familiar neighborhood streets. Even though they looked a lot smaller now, he could still remember the times back when he was a kid passing through this particular stretch of Arbor Hill. In those days it seemed like he and his friends never walked at all, but actually ran everywhere.

He had just crossed over to Broadway and was twenty yards from the office when he saw a growing red and orange wall of color coming from the front of the storefront. His mind had not finished processing it before the strong wave of heat and pressure sent him backwards and sprawling into the curbside, just as the whooshing grumble of expanding dynamite jammed his ears.

Facedown and staring into the foul-smelling curbside drain, he finally comprehended the extent of the tragedy around him as flames and acrid smoke mixed with the screams of the injured and dying.

Captain Williams took off his glasses and rubbed his tired eyes. He had been in his precinct office for thirty-six straight hours since the explosion. The statistics were grim—five killed, sixteen hurt, and of those nine were critically wounded and being held in ICU. The forensic reports from the scene were providing anything but clear-cut leads.

The most unusual evidence so far was an untraceable telephone call that came into the development office fifteen minutes before the blast. The caller warned there was a bomb on the premises that would soon detonate. Because of that warning, no office personnel had been injured. But the real tragedy was that instead of calling in the threat to the police immediately, the staff walked the three blocks down to the police substation to report it in person. By the time the bomb squad could respond to the scene, it was too late.

The other interesting fact that he mulled over was the report on his desk about the bomb fragments, and the quality of the other bomb-making materials that were recovered. The data indicted a very amateur ignition device and material pack. Almost too much so, he thought as he reread the report. It seemed to him that the bomber used the simplest techniques and materials possible to construct the device, almost as if trying to avoid all traces of sophistication.

The problem was that virtually every do-it-yourself recipe for explosives available online or in underground pamphlets contained certain enhancements that incorporated advances in the bomb-making art over the years. Based on the most recent forensics, none of those workarounds were present in this device. Yet the bomb contained explosive power equal to or greater than any of the cookbook bombs of similar size. Only someone truly skilled could accomplish that, he figured.

Captain Williams started to formulate the early contours of the killer they hunted for. He only meant to warn, and not kill or injure. He was aware of police bomb prevention procedures and timing. But for the unanticipated decision of the office staff to walk to the police substation, he would have accomplished his objective. The killer was also very likely an expert in explosive devices. His only mistake was to construct a device of such simplicity and elegance that its power exceeded anything an amateur could achieve. Pride in his craft had undermined the attempt to deceive.

Williams grabbed for his desk phone and placed a call to his lead investigator.

Chapter Twelve
Collaboration

The destruction of Ned's office had the opposite effect of what was apparently intended from the bombing. The gruesome tragedy galvanized community support for the development plan. Residents spoke supportively about the benefits that could flow into the neighborhood after the project was approved. Pastors gave encouraging sermons, and many neighborhood activists talked about Arbor Hill finally getting its fair share of resources. Yet because the killer had never been captured, an undercurrent of unease and fear remained. Many believed that another attack would occur at some point.

Brett spent less time supporting the project now that the Council had granted the needed permits. But his early involvement in researching and advocating the positive benefits it would yield left him with a stark sense of the enormous challenges that remained in meeting the many needs in the city. He realized that on its own, the development project was not nearly enough.

The numbers in Arbor Hill and surrounding inner-city neighborhoods were stark. Teenage pregnancy, gang violence, drug use, and school dropout rates had been rising for a decade or more. The recent economic downturn had accelerated those gloomy trends. It was clear to him that someone needed to plant a big stake in the ground that said *this is as far as we go toward the bottom!*

So, acting on his worst fears and greatest hopes, he set up a meeting with the Chairwoman of the Youth Council of Greater Albany to talk about specific program ideas to help change things.

Mrs. Gwendolyn Russell was a longtime advocate for underserved youth, both nationally and in the Albany area. Her experience was substantial. She had lead the Children's Defense Fund based in Seattle, and also served in senior executive roles for several major nonprofit organizations in the Midwest and Southeast. Recruited by the Youth Council last year to increase fundraising from the private sector, her ambitious target was to increase hard cash, unrestricted contributions to Council programs by thirty percent.

When she looked over the summary of Brett's background prepared by her staff, she immediately eyed him as a possible valuable future addition to the local Board of Directors. A substantial amount of money was generated directly from engaged board members, and they were one of the sources for increased revenue that she was targeting. But she was professional enough to mention that to him at a later time.

The meeting took place in her office at the downtown headquarters building.

After opening pleasantries, Brett got right down to business.

"Gwendolyn, we have a lot of dedicated professionals trying to make a difference in the lives of our kids in Albany. That has been made very clear to me in my brief time back in the city. But my research indicates that things are going backward, not forward. Look, I know that you have many more years of experience than I will ever have in this area, and I'm not making this personal. But looking at the numbers, I have to ask—what is missing? Why are we sliding back? What would it take to start reversing the trends?"

She was very surprised by his direct approach. So many of the folks that she worked with on a daily basis in the children's services community were afraid to call it like it was. They hesitated to acknowledge that their efforts were being swamped, in many cases by the new trends and the new needs. It was almost as if acknowledging the crisis would make it worse, or make their own efforts seem petty and unimportant. She found his candor refreshing, and so she decided to share with him her own personal assessment, arrived at after many challenging years working in the trenches.

"Brett, let me be as honest in my reply to you as you were with your question. And by the way, my answer is not a popular one in the children's services community. But I think it's the truth. And I know you are discrete enough not to attribute the quotes to me in local newspaper headlines." She said that with a sincere smile. He nodded.

She pushed her chair slightly back from her desk, folded her hands in front of her, and plunged ahead.

"We are here, in my view, because inner-city family values have been under major stress, and have in some cases broken down. Falling income and opportunity, a host of media that touch our children dozens of times every day exhorting freedom, buying, and wealth with no accountability, all can lead to failure in the long term.

But most of all, in my experience, there is no real value center in many homes that asserts strongly 'this is what we believe, and these are the principles that guide our actions."

Shifting a bit, she sat up while slowly rotating and stretching her shoulders together and apart to relieve some of the tension from a long day.

"It's not only the absence of men in the home that we always hear about. In fact, the wrong kind of man in the home is a much bigger problem. I believe instead that it's the absence of core values. And the inability to translate our historic and sustaining values to the new generation. Translation doesn't mean compromise. Single parents, many of them women, have the wherewithal to provide the basics. But what we are missing are those bedrock values that sustained families through difficult times for generations."

She reached behind her and opened a small fridge, removing two bottles of spring water, and offered one to him.

After enjoying the clean taste, she plunged ahead, filling in the end of the story at least so far as her own experience had allowed her to see it.

"That's why the church and faith formed the foundation for so much progress. Those missing values today are given secular labels like individual responsibility, accountability, and trust. But progress has to be made there, and it has to be infused into our children by repetition and example. Then, perhaps by the force of our youngsters, we can begin to enlist the support of many more parents and guardians. The Good Book says, *and the children shall lead them*. I think only the energy and fire of the coming generation can lead lasting change. But they need help to get to the front."

"In my opinion, Brett, the breakthrough is to find a way to champion those old-fashioned values in a big, visible way that can serve as an umbrella for many of the fractured efforts that are trying to get there by themselves. That will take a big vision, substantial money, and credible new leadership."

She had put it out there, her core beliefs, to someone she really didn't know at all.

I must be getting ready to retire.

Brett was surprised by the sincerity and starkness of her reply. No fancy words, no fancy phrases or slogans. She was just telling it like it was, as she saw it.

"Thank you for sharing that with me. I know it comes from deep within you and from a wealth of experience. I read a little bit about your background before this meeting. I know we both did our homework. You could have thrown the snow at me, and you chose not to."

He took a generous sip of the spring water before he started.

"My research so far indicates that one of the toughest challenges that undermines so many other efforts is dealing effectively with the so-called hard core youth issues. Gang members are one huge example, among two or three others. The gangs control the cloak of fear around the streets where everyone works and travels daily. It seems to me that progress and success in that arena, though difficult, could be leveraged to support initiatives in other areas. Turnaround in those kids' lives has a multiplier effect throughout the community. And believe me, I've had my own painful run-in with gang violence in the past, so I know firsthand how difficult a challenge it is."

"Well you know, Brett, right here in Albany there are a number of good programs that intervene to help young people reject the appeal of gangs. They're mostly small micro-programs that don't get a lot of publicity. Unfortunately, many of them shun the application processes and chafe at the oversight that comes along with receiving financial support from public or private sources."

"But you know what? There is one brother who's fighting the good fight right there in your neighborhood. I've known him for quite some time, even before he went into the army years ago. He runs a small gang intervention program. Unfortunately, he's also been reluctant to do the things needed to grow his resources and expand his footprint. But he has had some solid success. He might be a resource for you one day. Maybe you've met him. His name is Arthur Hill. Well, that was his name way back when. Shaka is the name he has used for many years now."

Brett was very surprised on two levels. First, he had no idea that Shaka was involved with gang intervention, and second, he had no idea that he was ex-military. As he continued his conversation with Gwendolyn and talked about other intervention ideas, his mind wandered, and he became profoundly curious about the precise nature of the specialized army training that Arthur Hill had received.

There were ways to find out, and he intended to follow up.

Chapter Thirteen
Trapped

Captain Williams had a gut feeling that the killer would soon strike again.

His experience was that they always made the mistake of thinking they were smarter than everyone else, particularly when they weren't caught. And in this case, all the leads had gone dry and they were no closer to catching the killer now than they were immediately after the explosion. He desperately needed a break, some decent clue, or any type of new intelligence to jumpstart the investigation.

But where and when would he strike again? The obvious targets had recently purchased extra private security help, and also tightened up their internal procedures. There simply were no other soft targets connected with the development around the neighborhood that could be attacked.

As he racked his brain for an answer, he glanced at an old neighborhood newsletter strewn open on his crowded desk. A headline grabbed his attention.

Groundbreaking Ceremony for Arbor Hill Mall Next Week

Staring at the headline, he realized that the killer would very likely read the same newsletter. One thing he believed for certain from the investigative findings was that the killer was someone from the local area. They had the ability to easily fit into the neighborhood without attracting attention. That was the only way they could have cased the development office before the attack without being noticed. While Williams remained unsure how the bomb was left at the premises, speculation was that someone posing as a delivery person might have dropped it off. Or according to another theory, the package may have been deliberately placed at the office during a concealed break-in.

One thing was certain, however. The bomb was detonated remotely, exploding in the small closet behind the receptionist station. To detonate the device, the killer had to be in the neighborhood, but not close enough to be impacted by the blast. Yet because he was a natural part of the background with the remote detonator concealed in his pocket, no one would notice or remember him.

As he read more in the newsletter, he became convinced that it was the red flag waving in front of the bull. Its content and editorial slant alone would very likely precipitate another deadly attack. It boasted about how opposition to the project had been swept aside by the strong hand of progress. At the end, it mentioned that dignitaries and local officials would dig the first shovels full of dirt at the groundbreaking, which he realized was only two days away.

He buzzed his assistant and asked her to assemble the bomb task force in his office at 0900 hours the following morning. He told her to once again invite FBI and Homeland Security to the meeting, but he doubted they would tear themselves away from other pressing national security issues to make an appearance in lowly Arbor Hill.

They met for breakfast before the groundbreaking ceremony scheduled for later that afternoon. Ned requested the meeting. Brett assumed that he would finally react to the preliminary ideas he had asked him to look over weeks ago. He'd recently supplemented that draft with an updated version, incorporating design versions that he had tested with Gwendolyn.

Maybe Ned just wants to tell me to stop drowning him in paper.

He really believed that his concepts formed the basis for a big idea that would impact summer learning programs and life skills for hundreds of city kids. So he was looking forward to convincing Ned that it was a worthwhile early draft of a plan, and also one that Ned's bank should be associated with.

But before leaving his home office, he took care of one outstanding matter. He faxed a summary sheet to Captain Williams at precinct headquarters. It contained his research on Arthur Hill. He knew that Hill's specialist training in demolition and explosives would be of great interest to the captain. He also described the vehement opposition that Shaka first expressed during one of the early neighborhood meetings about the mall and plaza development project. Curiously, that visible opposition had waned after the bombing, and he couldn't recall another forum where Shaka spoke out publically against the project.

Before they got down to business, Ned looked at him with a wry smile and offered a surprising comment about life.

"You know, Brett, I learned how small the world really is last night. It's no longer six degrees of separation. We are down to one degree."

Ned shifted in his seat and stretched his legs out on the side of the table.

"I was having dinner at my aunt's house down in White Plains a couple of days ago. My first cousin was also there, along with her fiancé. At one point we were talking about why I was spending so much time upstate in Albany, of all places. You know how it is—New Yorkers from downstate look at this part of the world as the provinces. Of course, I was probably a bit defensive, but I gave them a tutorial about all of the positive things that are happening. I happened to mention you by name, and how you are one of the prime movers in all of this."

"After hearing your name, my cousin literally dropped her fork on her china dinner plate and stared at me in disbelief. My elderly aunt, bless her heart, started carefully inspecting the plate for damage. We were all pretty surprised at her reaction. My cousin's name is Zena Melody Jensen."

Hearing the name of his long-ago girlfriend was a bit of a shock to him. She hadn't crossed his mind for several years. But he certainly recalled the circumstances that led to their break-up. It was a difficult, emotional time for both of them.

He looked back closely at Ned.

"I hope Zena is doing, well Ned. We were very tight for many years. She also helped me recover from a very serious spinal injury that I sustained during a cup race in Croatia. She practically moved into my Manhattan townhouse and became my recuperation specialist in chief. I'll always be grateful to her for that. The next time you see her, please tell her that I send my warm regards and best wishes."

Ned listened as he mentioned other highlights from that long-ago relationship. He looked over at Brett when he finished and nodded.

"She seemed to be happy as a clam to me, Brett. We were never really that close as cousins when we were young, largely due to the age difference. I could tell that she had some remaining warm feeling for you, though, since she didn't rip you to shreds at the dining room table. She also seems to have her fiancé totally in the palm of her hand, which is how she likes to operate."

"You know, I think I can see why you two might not have made it together. The truth is that the only serious thing my cousin consistently does, as long as I have known her, is shop. I really can't see her supporting you in the kinds of things we've been working on in Albany. It's just not her space. Anyway, very small world indeed."

Then he pulled out a dog-eared copy of the most recent proposal that Brett had sent to him.

"First off, I owe you an apology for my delay in getting back to you about this. It's important work, and I want to be a part of it. Let's talk about how the bank might be able to assist with this big idea. And I also have a few additional thoughts that may help leverage the initiative.

Captain Williams acted immediately on the tip. Arresting Arthur Hill was the easy part. The search of his apartment by the forensics team was very likely to produce evidence linking him to the first bombing. Yet because Hill had not cooperated during the interrogation so far, the possibility of another attack still loomed. With only three hours to go before the groundbreaking, his task force was pressuring him to cancel the event, clear the area, and allow robot detection vehicles to crawl all over the site.

But he viewed cancellation of the event as a defeat for the community and a win for the forces of chaos. He wanted to play one last hunch before calling it off. He punched his intercom button and asked his assistant to have Peterson from the canine unit and his dogs meet him at the development site in fifteen minutes. Then he rang up his second in command and ordered him to give him twenty minutes at the site alone. After that, he wanted the entire area evacuated and cordoned off.

When he arrived and looked over the vast acreage of the cleared lot, he let out a quiet sigh.

The bomb could be buried anywhere.

He could see that at each of the four corners bordering the lot, dozens of pedestrians, as well as a steady flow of traffic, could be impacted by an explosion equal in size to the last one.

Then, as he continued to stroll around the area, an inspiration hit him. He quickly radioed Peterson and told him to head over with the dogs to the southwest corner of the site, where by chance he had stumbled upon a small space with two concrete circular bases. They were cemented into the ground, roughly nine feet apart. Both of them had circular metal holding rings in the center.

Maybe it's a kind of makeshift stage.

He had a hunch that the metal rings might be the seating for standing poles that could hold a cordon of some kind between them. He'd seen similar setups at other official functions. That cordon would form the barrier between the dignitaries and the spectators. As he walked around the small area, he tried to physically orient himself to how the ceremony might unfold. Given the afternoon lighting conditions, he figured that the dignitaries would have to face to the west, into the sun, for a non-glare photograph to be taken.

That would mean they would stand about here.

He shifted his position to where they might pose with shovels during the typical groundbreaking photo shoot, but he kept a respectable distance away from the space. He called out loudly to Peterson as he approached with the big dogs that seemed to be towing him over.

"Make sure to hold them on a very tight leash. Don't let them dig!"

The three muscular animals moved in, straining forward. Peterson, a beefy officer, braced himself and allowed them to slowly inch closer. In a few minutes they had picked up a scent, and their excitement showed. When the noses of the dogs pointed vertically downward, Peterson ordered them back. They sat obediently as he handed them large treats.

Williams called his second in command.

"Eddie, we have the bomb located at the southwest corner of the lot. Deploy the extraction team when you arrive. You should be able to get it out and cleared well before the start of the ceremony."

Part Three
Origins

Chapter Fourteen
The Ask

In Brett's estimation, this was the biggest pitch of his life. Through the years he had made dozens of important presentations before his retirement. Unlike those occasions, however, the significance of this one was not in the amount of money and prestige he was promising to earn, or in the bold reorganization plan he was proposing.

It lay in the fact that he was appealing to this Board of Directors to help him save and transform lives. He had himself once been a young kid enrolled in a local Boys and Girls Clubs organization. Those programs helped give him a chance to live out his dreams. He wanted this board to understand that, and also know that he was the literal proof of what was possible when parenting, private philanthropy, and refusal to give in to bad breaks came together.

The good news was that they were already in the helping business in a big way. They ran the Greater New York State Clubs. The directors were each well-heeled philanthropists who helped support and influence the world of charitable giving in New York State. Many were CEOs or executives of large, profitable industries. Among their many other eleemosynary endeavors, the Clubs meant a lot to each of them on a very personal level. Over and above the normal contributions and fundraisers that they provided during the year, most of them also marshaled the internal resources from their businesses to support one or more local Clubs. They freely donated in kind services, various corporate resources, or human capital.

Soon he would ask them to do even more.

As the high-speed commuter train approached Grand Central Station, it slowed and began to weave and turn at a snail's pace, covering the last mile as if everyone on the train had time to spare. He looked at his watch and saw that he had very little extra time, if he was to arrive on schedule. Grabbing his briefcase, he moved to the closest exit door and waited. To his relief, after obtaining a taxi in the cue, his Eastern European driver did the rest—cutting the time of the ride in half after Brett showed him the fifty-dollar U.S. Grant note he could earn for his best effort.

When he walked into the 49th floor conference room, he felt his old surge of energy along with the usual slightly paralyzing tingle in the knuckles of his hands and the tips of his fingers. He knew it meant he was ready to go. It had been that way since he learned to embrace the strange feeling way back in high school, when he delivered his first dramatic performance in front of his classmates.

After he was introduced, he spoke passionately for the allotted thirty minutes. He talked without a microphone and without notes. Pausing before his final closing comments, he looked at each of the board members around the large conference room table. They had given him an enthusiastic welcome and their complete attention.

"It leaves me with a profound sense of gratitude to make this proposal to you. Thank you for the courtesy of allowing me to do so. I can only imagine the volume of grant requests that you must receive, and I'm pretty sure that this specially called meeting has cramped your schedule. But as I look around the table, I am also aware that several of you have been doing this for decades. You were at the table supporting many of the initiatives that helped impact me personally when I was a young, wild kid running around the streets of Albany. I learned to swim at the Club, and I participated in summer camps, and after-school learning programs. Your generosity and vision made that possible, and I wouldn't be standing here today without it."

"As a graduate and beneficiary of your past vision, I'm asking you join with me in a great new push to make a difference in the lives of this generation. Your financial support is an essential part. I will personally donate one hundred thousand dollars to kick off the campaign. In addition, I have a banker who is as passionate about this as I am, and he has committed to match every dollar that we raise. In eighteen months, if you provide the support that I know you can, I would like you to join me at the grand opening of the Arbor Hill Summer Sailing Camp."

"As the Executive Director of Sailing, I look forward to welcoming you there. And of course, that position will be a non-paid volunteer position for as long as I am able to serve in the role. Thank you again for your time. Are there any more questions?"

One board member spoke up. His name was Carleton Smith. As Brett recalled, he was a wealthy banker, or an industrialist. Then he remembered the exact context from which he knew the name. Smith was a central figure in the takeover attack against his company several years ago.

Smith wanted to know what were the ideal attributes and location for the sailing center that Brett envisioned, so he gave him a detailed description, including the ocean or lake frontage acreage that the facility would encompass.

The board Chairman then stood and turned to him.

"Brett, on behalf of this board, let me extend our thanks for your energy, time, and commitment to the cause that we all hold dear—broadening opportunity for all of our youth. I can say to you at this early stage, before the board retires to deliberate on the level of our involvement, that we are quite interested in your proposal. And I might add that we are not cowed by the size of the commitment that you ask of us. We intend to deliberate and reach a decision within the next two weeks. Without foreshadowing that decision, let me say on behalf of many of us here, that we believe you will not be disappointed. Thank you again, and God's speed to you and your family."

On his way back home to Albany, the fatigue from the early morning departure and the released stress from the presentation began to catch up with him. He took off his jacket and tie, and unbuttoned his collar before resting his tired body against the commuter train's hard vinyl seat. Crowded urban vistas moved past his window as he thought about the many changes in his life that had occurred during the last few years. The one he liked the most was leaving the shirt, tie, and suit in the closet, at least most of the time.

As he relaxed more, he began to reflect. He wondered whether he was discovering more of himself as he lived his early retirement lifestyle. His life so far certainly wasn't easy to define—city kid turned businessman, late-bloomer community activist, minor philanthropist, and aspiring writer. He knew that they each described some of who he was, and what he was becoming. Or he wondered, were they all merely part of a larger dimension, not yet fully defined?

So being honest with himself, he had to admit that it was only the thumbnail, Reader's Digest version of his life that he had just given to the board, devoid of the complexity and subtlety that comprised his real existence, his real voyage.

Did I oversimplify just to get the money?

Yes, he had to admit, he had oversimplified, and perhaps he had played deliberately to the liberal sympathies of several board members.

So do the ends justify the means?

He knew the answer was not always, not even most of the time. But what mattered now, and what he continued to feel passionately about, was what could be built and made permanent. That was tangible, and he was determined to make it happen.

The monotonous *click-clack-click* of the high-speed train helped to gradually ease him into a long-overdue sleep. He drifted through fragmented images of the son that he was long ago, and through images of the corporate soldier he had become. And once again, he returned to the sea.

Chapter Fifteen
Onset

"Ready about!" Brett yelled through the stiffening wind and drenching sea spray that surrounded them. He instinctively glanced up again, squinting through salt-stained goggles at the 70-foot aluminum mast and mainsail powering his 54-foot sloop.

So far so good

Onset crashed down hard into a rolling ten-foot wave that enveloped the forward section of the bow, but she kept stubbornly slicing close hauled into the 30-knot Sirocco wind. That famously strong blow was right on schedule for this racing season, and he was having the time of his life.

He and his five-man crew were beating north, well off the fabled Dalmatian Coast of Croatia. He was awash in several inches of roiling wine-blue seawater that sloshed heavily over his feet and ankles, which were protected by neoprene boots. Bracing low, he cranked the helm hard left, moving the bow across the wind.

"Hard alee!"

He balanced himself with a wide, low stance as the deck rose and fell under him. Onset responded as the rudder swung the bow through the wind and over to port side. At the right moment, based on many hours of racing and feel, he brought the wheel a full turn back to center position.

Grinders Jim Storm and Dave Firth, both well over 200 pounds, were in power squats, using their bulked up shoulders and powerful arms to rapidly crank the stout mainsail winches. As the large sail moved across the wind, the heavy boom beneath it swung hard over the deck in a violent and deadly arc above their heads, landing snugly at its port position with a jarring thump.

Two smaller grinders did similar duty, taming the furious flapping of the large genoa. With both cranked in tight, Onset pointed out smartly on a starboard tact, and they could all feel the building surge of acceleration. The navigator came up on deck from below and mounted the windward rails with the rest of the crew, hiking out to increase boat speed. They added another 300 meters to their half-mile lead on Invictus, the past two-time winner. He knew she was out there chasing hard, and that her skipper would try to match their most recent turn. But Invictus was no longer in visual sight.

Here you are again, he whispered to himself through the salty spray.

For some reason, and despite the challenging conditions, he recalled in that very moment his first introduction to sailing twenty-five years ago as a slightly built and lanky nine-year-old. His dream then was to win the America's Cup—why not? He also remembered the warm greeting from some of the regular kids when he showed up for his first sailing lesson. The upstate suburban boys had a clear opinion about his chances: *black kids can't sail, you can't even swim,* they opined on his first day. If they cared to ask, they would have learned that he was a very good swimmer.

Looks like they were also wrong about that sailing thing, he thought, while bending the helm hard right to absorb a stiff gust.

But the Clear Lake Club, with its historic free sailing program that bused a few lucky inner-city kids out from Albany, was a long way from the Cup level racing that he was now involved with. It had taken him years of additional training and racing to make it to this level. Though he had no idea at the time, in his younger days he had already fallen far behind the other racing skippers that he now led on the way to the finish line. Rather than the 13-foot beamy and slow centerboard boats that were his training ground for a number of years, most of his competition by the age of eleven had already raced 27-foot Solings or the J 24's. Later on, others learned to sail their fathers' much bigger yachts in and out of the storied ports on the East Coast.

With twenty-five nautical miles to the finish, he knew that a win was possible. But on this course, the path to the finish line meant at least six more hard turns into the increasing Sirocco. He glanced up at his wind gauge, which was now showing gusts up to 35 knots.

We'll need to get that genoa down and hoist a storm jib if these conditions deteriorate any further. How much of the lead will that cost us?

His unease about the stress the upcoming turns would inflict on Onset was increasing. It came from his knowledge that unlike many other racing yachts on the course, he hadn't been able to invest significant money to upgrade the wind spill technology that read building stress conditions on the rigging, and automatically made adjustments to reduce wind load. It had taken a big chunk of his available cash just to pack Onset up and have her shipped across the Atlantic on a freighter in time for the Regatta. Given that expense, he had decided to take a pass on spending even more.

But the wind and the sea were indifferent, and they continued to build.

Instinctively and without looking back, he reached behind him for his backstay winch, manually yanking it in tight to spill some of the wind load. Without warning, the steel backstay halyard started to shred vertically toward the top of the mast. The mast jerked forward and yanked the rest of the line through the small winch, until it ran out of the chocking cleat. He knew that any hope of decreasing wind pressure was now gone. Worse still, with the mast in its full upright position, the mainsail would grab more wind.

Immediately he shouted forward to his navigator.

"Craig, backstay's busted! Find the best broad reach to the finish."

Craig swung off the rails and braced himself as he crouched down and climbed below deck to the navigation station, closing the watertight access way behind him.

A freight train roar started to grow as the wind grew stronger and pushed Onset dangerously off course. As she surfed over the crest of the next roller, a 40-knot gust pushed the bow down into the trough of the next wave, burying it in the sea. But the heavy bulb keel did its job, slowly bringing them upright and level. Bracing himself, Brett jammed his right boot into the drenched teak deck and pressed his weight down hard as he struggled to bring the wheel a full turn right to depower the sails. Onset's bow again pitched steeply down into the next trough as she slammed into an even larger roller. The huge wave spilled part of its enormous weight over the fore and mid decks. The rest surged to the stern, flooding into him and the hiked-out crew. Some were thrown across the deck, saved only by their safety harness.

The enormous force of the water stripped the wheel from his gloved hands and shoved him back hard against the transom safety railing. His head dragged along the coiled metal, and a large gash opened below his left ear. Blood spilled down his neck and shoulders, discoloring his yellow life vest. In spite of the blow, he managed to hold on and climb back up to the wheel. That's when he saw Jim sliding across the slanted topside deck with his severed safety strap trailing behind.

He lunged forward to reach him, anchoring his feet in the spokes of the big wheel. He missed, and Jim passed under the port side railing into the open sea.

Frantically, he scrambled back and activated the autopilot before leaving the helm and moving forward to spot Jim's position for a rescue pass. At that moment, the upper mast stays peeled away as another stiff gust clawed at the weakened rigging. With the added wind load, the mainsheet yanked free and ran through the winch. Unleashed from confinement, the heavy boom accelerated across the deck, slamming into his shoulder and back as he tried to avoid its fury. He went down hard, slowly losing consciousness. His last thoughts were how he would make a pass to scoop up Jim, and whether he would be able to pack up the battered pieces and ship Onset home.

Chapter Sixteen
Target Practice

Stewart Greenberg leaned back and admired the neat stack of spreadsheets on his cluttered desk. Then he swiveled his chair around to gaze at the Brooklyn Bridge from the window of his small office. He was in the heart of Manhattan's business district, and he was feeling on top of the financial world.

Satisfaction stemmed from his belief that he had identified the perfect target company for a hostile takeover. All he needed now was a deep pocket corporate raider that believed as he did—that Taurus Corporation was ripe for the picking. Never mind its blue chip standing, universally admired reputation, or respected management team that delivered steady earnings year after year.

That consistent earnings crap trotted out to shareholders every year was so old school. Particularly since he and his team had now found the proverbial fly in the ointment that would resonate with any raider, Taurus was worth twice as much if it were broken in pieces and sold to the highest bidder. But he had the genius to demonstrate that fact with unerring financial metrics. It had all been condensed to fourteen spreadsheets. As far as he knew, no other leveraged buyout analysis had been presented with the clarity and precision that now lay before him.

He was also convinced that the new reality for business investment decisions lay solely in the exploitive harvesting of massive amounts of financial data. Not just reams of information, but petabytes of data driven by hyper fast parallel processing power and business intuition. He and his MBA friends from the most elite schools in the country had secretly kidnapped that power from their investment firm employers, tuning up the preexisting computer software capabilities and processors to meet their new standards.

All of that analysis now told the tale of the tape with penetrating clarity: Taurus valuation $30 billion; break-up valuation $64 billion; fees and expenses to do the deal $2.5 billion (including his $500 million fee); net pre-tax profit, post breakup $31 billion; profit after tax $15 billion. The deal delivered an outsized 50 percent return on the initial valuation of the company. But Stewart's genius had been able to see and quantify that profit potential, when traditional linear valuation models could not.

And a raider could finance the whole thing with nothing more than $2 billion up front. That sum would line up the banks and the other sharks to circle in the water around the company. This was so much better than stealing, because you didn't go to jail in America for radically increasing shareholder value. In fact, you were feted as a hero. He chuckled at his own sense of humor.

All he and his team needed to do now was identify, persuade, and recruit the raider. And they had the plan and the connections to do just that. He reached for his phone and began making a few calls to confirm with his team the previously scheduled nine o'clock meeting that evening at his Upper East Side apartment.

He left the firm early to make sure he was on time. Leaving the office at eight at night would garner a few raised eyebrows from his coworkers, who would grind on until eleven, as they always did. But he planned to be in the office the following morning at five to balance out his apparent display of professional weakness. He might even arrive before Earl Hargrove, who had the reputation of sometimes sleeping at his desk to claim the first in the office prize. Some prize, he sneered. He and his fellow grunts were stuck at the lowest pay grade in the firm, barely making $300,000 a year before bonus. Not a substantial sum at all, when everyone knew that partners were making millions apiece based on grunt brainpower. When he factored in his $8,000 per month apartment, his car lease, and his summer house mortgage, he couldn't see how he would reach the top tier of his profession and begin to live in the princely manner that he had been raised to believe was his due. And he certainly didn't want to hear that middle-class malarkey about paying dues and slowly moving up the ladder.

He was surprised at the limo pool to see no waiting car to whisk him away. Then he realized that they must only begin to pool around eleven every night, the New York City witching hour when legions of bankers, lawyers, and businessmen called it quits and left for home, or left for other late-night pleasures in the city.

He flagged a yellow taxi and barked his address to the driver. Then he tucked into the back seat and started working through several client-related analytics. They were all due on the partner's desk first thing in the morning.

"Good evening, Mr. Greenberg," his doorman said in a crisp, efficient voice as he swung the door open. Stewart realized that he hardly knew any of the staff on the early shift, but they were all required to know him by sight. Guess that comes with the $8,000 rental, he thought as he keyed the elevator and ascended to the private entry lobby of his 36th floor apartment.

Soon, almost everyone was gathered. Cy Trowig, Harvard, known for having the highest combined GRE and GPA score on record there, was first to arrive. But beyond that, Cy was a real bore whose passion, competitive chess, seemed to overwhelm every other aspect of his life—with the exception being the greed portion. Stewart was thankful for that. And Cy, bless his heart, also knew how to stay focused on the end game. In this case, the end game was his share of $500 million.

Melinda Smith was an altogether different sort. Top of her class at Stanford, she used her first love and her aptitude with statistics to successfully fleece $800,000 out of several East Coast casinos—until she was banned for life. Running low on money, she was his easiest recruit. Her mathematics skills helped him build the computational algorithms that revealed the hidden value in Taurus. She had no objections on moral or other grounds to ripping the company apart and plucking out a golden nest egg for herself. But she insisted on being given a higher share of the spoils verses the others, because of her contribution to the analytics. Stewart held out against that, but finally agreed to her demands after she displayed exceptional focus toward his own personal, physical needs behind closed doors.

Just arriving, and late as always, was Chauncey Smith. He was the connections guy, and his connections were far more valuable than the contacts the others had. His personal and family contacts alone would lead to the raider. His father, Carleton Smith, was still feared on Wall Street despite being in his mid-eighties. Reliable rumor had it that he was recently paid a greenmail fee of $1 billion by a Fortune company just to go away and leave them alone. Chauncey was motivated by the simple drive to outdo his old man, who had lorded over his life and would lord over his future. I guess they just aren't that close, Stewart surmised with humor.

After serving wine and light snacks, he opened the meeting and passed around a package containing copies of the spreadsheets and related documents.

"We've each made invaluable contributions to this analysis. The statistical algorithms supporting the conclusions have been triple checked by Melinda and me. Cy tried to break them for two days without success. He's confident, as am I, that the profit picture is sound."

"As you know, and as a final check, I ran the entire package through my firm's super computer, using our shadow programs, of course. Each spreadsheet was confirmed, and all numbers tied out."

"Finally, I asked Chauncey to scrub the selling proposition one last time, using the assumptions in the ROI spreadsheets. He believes that we have a very saleable proposition. Chauncey's summary is on the last page in your package."

Pausing for a few minutes as they went through the documents, he asked for any objections before he proceeded.

As he patiently assayed each of their faces, he vaguely remembered giving a similar but not nearly as lucrative a presentation in prep school. Back then, he had led a financially well-heeled faction of his classmates to secretly buy the building owned by their cross-quad rival. This was one rivalry taken to the extreme, which was not uncommon in the elite prep schools across the nation. The only trespass that the other fraternity committed was to receive the school's ancient order of the coif, naming them the premier residence house for the upcoming academic year. That distinction, however, gave them a huge leg up in the recruitment of wealthy young scions of industry, whose parents wanted the very best room and boarding accommodations for their nine- and ten-year-olds. Although Stewart's ruse was successfully executed, meaning that they actually purchased their rival's building, they were undone in the end. Poor Blakie, he remembered. That chap had gone downtown to record the deed for them. But he melted under questions from the county clerk, who had never seen a sixteen-year-old attempt to do that. The scheme was exposed and foiled, but Stewart's reputation as a person of ideas, cunning, and guts continued to grow.

Those were traits that served him well, both in college and later in business school, where he honed his aptitude for risk and further developed his ability to attract talented followers.

Hearing no objections from his team, he moved to the most important topic: the small list of raiders and the tailored approach to each target that he had carefully worked out with Chauncey.

"As you can see, we pared the target list down to three names. These folks are known to each of you, I assume, as together they have garnered more than their fair share of financial headlines."

"But," he continued, "the important common denominator beyond media hound is that each of them has been deleveraging and generating substantial free cash flow in the past eighteen months. They can afford the two billion dollar entry fee to the contest, even if they have to put it all up in their own money."

"Equally important, they've all known Chauncey since birth. Raymond Krondike, for example, is Chauncey's godfather. When the time comes, Chauncey's bona fides will help us close the deal with the right target. His credibility will separate our pitch from the steady line of money-making deals that they hear on a daily basis."

Cy chimed in with a concern, always pushing to see through the gambit and plan several moves ahead.

"What are the odds, Stewart, that Chauncey's pedigree might actually work against us? Would the targets undervalue him, due to either age or experience, or might they shy away due to some loyalty to his father?"

Stewart anticipated that line of questioning and suspected that at least one of the others besides Cy had thought about the same issues. So his response was well practiced and to the point.

"Cy, that's a very perceptive observation, and Chauncey and I have given it a great deal of consideration. Here is where we land. In each case, the target has at some point in the past been cut out of a deal or otherwise royally screwed by Carleton Smith. That should checkmate the loyalty prong of your question, given the egos we're dealing with."

Then he stood up and walked over to the large picture window that looked over Central Park before turning back to face them.

"Will they consider Chauncey too young to assist them in making $15 billion?" he asked. "That is a realistic possibility. One, maybe two of the targets might take a pass. But the odds of three of them walking on this deal are extremely low. This is where our analytics come in. We have to discern who among the targets will say yes to the deal, and who will pass *before* we put our key cards on the table."

"Take a look at the last page in your package," he said. "This is the order of the presentation we'll make, from the earliest non-confidential reveal to the final moment when we show the spreadsheets."

"Our challenge again," he calmly emphasized, "is to know who will say yes long before that time, and to only put the key spreadsheets in front of that target."

After the meeting, he escorted them to his lobby elevator and keyed them down. He secretly winked at Melinda, who would circle back later and join him for the remainder of the evening.

Chapter Seventeen
Beginnings

Sailing the oceans of the world was hardly a birthright for Brett. Many would say that his captaincy of a 54-foot racing yacht was the most improbable of occurrences, in light of his modest beginnings. He would tell you, on the other hand, that he was at the helm along with a long line of early explorers in his family, who pushed against the barriers and boundaries that had confined previous generations. He always said with a smile that his family story was a typical American story—it just happened to pick up steam a few hundred years after the forced immigration from West Africa. Or at other times, referencing his Native American roots, he would joke that his ancestors had to take care of all that paperwork involved in donating the country to the waves of foreign visitors before they focused on their own agenda.

Despite his gallows humor, he was convinced that even in the face of generations of hardships and setbacks, the qualities his family exhibited were in no way significantly different from those displayed by many other immigrants. The only quantitative difference in his mind was freedom and opportunity. But he also believed that the qualities of endurance and hope in the face of hardship added special seasoning and strength to most family recipes—except, of course, to that significant number who never had a stake in the game in the first place.

If you were a close friend, he would have regaled you with his track meet analogy at one time or another. You had worked out hard before the race, he would say with intensity, looking you in the eyes. So you were ready to compete in what was billed as *the competition*. Your warm-up and stretching routine went well, and when the starting gun went off, you were out at a good pace. A top finish or even a win was possible. You jockeyed with the competition around the track, taking some shots and giving back a few, but you held your own. Not a bad race.

But after crossing the finish line, you noticed a whole crowd of other folks on the sideline who had already finished well ahead of you. Some of them had even changed and were already dressed in street clothes. But you never saw them at your starting line, *because they weren't there*. That was the historical advantage that he'd long ago realized was hardwired into the economic system. But you still had to run your own race, he believed. Because the race was worth running, and it sure beat standing on the sidelines complaining.

His appreciation of history helped to shape his outlook early on. It derived from the influence of several public school teachers under whom he was fortunate to study. The first was Mr. Valoriano, in 7th grade ancient history class. There he heard lively lectures about the Egyptians and Nubians, the Assyrians and Persians, and the Greeks and Romans. Mr. Valoriano brought passion to each class, and he brought the past to life.

Down the hall in Latin class, he studied the ancient Roman authors, historians and politicians. There were countless hours mastering the painful grammar, but during the more fun times, lessons involved reciting the words of Caesar, Cicero, and many others.

Although he could no longer summon up the Latin words, he continued to this day to carry with him and believe in the English version of a quote from Cicero that he invested long hours in mastering.

To be ignorant of what occurred before you were born is to remain always a child. For what is the worth of human life, unless it is woven into the life of our ancestors by the records of history.

His very first awareness of self began with his earliest memories formed as a young child in Boston. Among the most vivid was that he was the victim of an assault and robbery. At the time, he was five years old. He couldn't recall why he was in that vulnerable space at the time. But he clearly remembered the events, despite the passage of years.

For some reason, he was walking alone down the street from his family's rented first floor walk-up apartment. There was no reason he could later remember why he wasn't stopped from leaving his house. Thinking back on it, he suspected that his father was away at work as usual, and that his mother Clara may have been resting in bed. Resting in bed was something that she had started to do much more frequently.

He remembered that he left his house on a mission to go down to the corner store that was not too far away. He believed he could walk to it, even with five-year-old legs. He was motivated by the coins that made noise in his pocket. He knew that if he reached the store and handed the coins to the man behind the counter, the man would give him potato chips in a bag. So he walked down the sidewalk to his goal.

On the way, a young teenager walked up beside him and kept pace. Then he looked down and asked if he had change for a dollar. That moment was the beginning of the end of his innocence. He distinctly remembered feeling then what he would later know to be apprehension. Even at five, he knew that the boy next to him was not interested in change, which had no real meaning in his mind. But he could sense that something bad was going to happen. He looked up at the teenager and shook his head. At that moment, the boy lunged at him and slapped him hard across his face. Then, lifting him up, he rifled through his small pockets, grabbing the coins, and threw him roughly to the ground before running away.

He went back to his house in tears. He was scratched up, hurting, and really sad that he would not have any chips. After reaching the front porch, he trudged up the stairs to the door. He was halfway up when his second-floor neighbor and friend, a city bus driver, returned home. Seeing his little buddy's tears, the driver bent down and asked him what was wrong. He blurted out in one breath through his crying that a boy had taken his coins, had knocked him over, and that he could not get his chips in the bag from the man at the store.

Then his neighbor—he couldn't recall his name after all these years—did a remarkable thing. He took him upstairs to his apartment and brushed off the dirt. He washed the scrapes with a clear liquid that stung a little bit. He looked down and said, "Don't worry, Brett. We're going to go out with Kermin. We'll find that kid and get your money back."

He began to feel better, and he stopped crying and sniffling.

Kermin was his neighbor's dog, a magnificent Doberman Pinscher, who was also his good buddy. They rounded up Kermin from the back yard. The dog was happy to see both his master and his little friend. After his leash was applied, Kermin waited patiently at the door. They all soon headed out in pursuit of the thief. Kermin went into hunt mode.

His neighbor took him on a remarkable journey that day that helped shape how he would view the world. After they walked down to the area where he was attacked, Kermin sniffed the ground and tugged on his stout leash. The dog moved around the area, looking intently, and then came back to Brett, who patted him and hugged his head and his smooth black sides. After that, his neighbor started to signal passing buses that would pull over. The drivers all knew each other. Then all three of them would board the bus and walk up the aisle to the rear, and then back to the front. His neighbor would ask him whether any of the boys on the bus was the one who had taken his coins. Kermin sniffed energetically at every seat they passed.

They boarded at least four busses and conducted the same search before heading back home. They never found the thief. Many years later, remembering the episode, Brett realized that finding the thief was not the point. After all, why would the thief take a bus in the first place and use the few coins he had just stolen? And if he had taken a bus, he would be long gone by the time their pursuit started. No, the hunt was solely designed to make him lose his fear, to make him become the hunter verses the hunted, and to prevent the young five-year-old from becoming another cowering victim of urban violence.

Otherwise, his home was an unremarkable place in those years. He remembered the love and kindness of his mother. Before the emergence of memory, he could feel her spirit, and he recalled her tender affection for him. From pictures taken of her when he was a child, he could see that she was a beautiful woman. She carried within her half of the blood of the Cherokee nation. While his memories of her beauty had long ago faded, he could still remember the feeling of hugging her legs, and her calm and caring nature. Most of all, his memories revolved around the family play times and dinner times. He retained vivid images of delicious meals and the aroma of Sunday breakfasts. They seemed to always include his favorite, pancakes. After that, there was playtime around the house with his sister and brother.

His dad was a steady influence in the home. His father always kept an electronics room in the house, where he had tubes and wires and lots of stuff that helped him repair TVs, radios, and just about anything that could be plugged in. This was his hustle, he used to tell them, part-time work for extra money. He always bought them small gifts with some kind of science principle behind it. Brett's favorite was his gyroscope. His sister, Dee, also got dolls, and later in life became a collector.

He remembered to this day that his father had set up some kind of electric defense in the windows of his hustle room, made with stripped wires and plugs and things. Daddy told them that anyone coming in the window would be in for a big shock. Those things made him feel safe.

Though he didn't recognize it for a while, his mother spent more and more time in bed. Later on she would not cook like she used to, and the kitchen was dark a lot. She didn't make his favorite foods much anymore.

But the change provided him an opportunity that he took full advantage of. He quietly crawled into the unlit kitchen on his belly one late afternoon, and took down the sugar bowl that was shaped like a big round apple. Unfortunately he dragged the big apple too far off the shelf, and it shattered on the floor. His mother did seem to have the energy to come into the kitchen and warm his jacket. But the spanking failed to shake loose all of the sugar granules that had accumulated around his mouth. His mother stopped spanking him and hugged him to her while she laughed.

Her confinement to the bedroom continued for many months. He was not able to hug her legs. Sometimes he would hear his dad and mom yelling at each other from the room, where they were behind the door. Then Daddy would leave the house and close the door with a big, loud sound. Those times made him feel sad.

Chapter Eighteen
Lailani

Lailani leaned out to look around the corner of her narrow front porch as dusk fell over Albany. She had lived in the neighborhood all of her life. She purchased her home two years ago, after getting fed up with sexual advances from landlords and the endless drama surrounding other tenants and their family members. Though a struggle, owning the house turned out to be well worth the financial strain. And she was now much closer to her father's nursing home, and that made things far easier.

She shouted into the late spring breeze.

"Keisha! Keisha! Time to come in!"

Her nine-year-old niece and ward was at the far end of the street, playing Ring-O-Levio. The problem with the game, as Lailani knew from experience, was that as you frantically ran to hide from the other team, you could find yourself blocks away, hoping to elude discovery. But it truly was the best game ever invented. Everyone knew that.

Generations had played it in Albany. Some folks said the game was invented in Brooklyn. While she stood there, she remembered the many games that she'd played in when she was young. And she recalled with a smile her special friend Brett, who always seemed to know the best hiding places and the best routes to navigate back to free teammates from jail. Then she quickly put those memories away and called out again.

"Girl, you better get your behind back to this house before I count to ten."

Keisha appeared, as always, by the time she reached fourteen.

"Make sure you wash those dirty hands," she said as she caught Keisha inching up to the stove for a pinch of food. "And scrub under those fingernails."

"Yes, ma'am," Keisha said with a big, infectious smile as she lightly skipped away to the hallway bathroom.

Her sunny attitude was a blessing. When Lailani's sister died of lupus two years ago, everyone in the small, close-knit community believed that Keisha's best option, given her trifling father, was adoption by her aunt. So Lailani petitioned the court. But Keisha's on-again, off-again father made things difficult. Despite a history of loose living, he persuaded the judge that he was capable of providing consistent care and nurturing, so he retained full custody.

That charade lasted about four weeks, until attentive neighbors began to notice and document his absence from the house late each evening, and his return the next morning, if at all. Keisha was left alone at home to fend for herself. Based on the neighbors' detailed accounts, Lailani's petition was reopened, and she was awarded full custody. Full adoption was granted later, after her brother-in-law admitted to the judge that he really didn't envision being a full-time daddy.

But she knew that behind the sunny smile, Keisha longed for her father, who rarely bothered to take time to see her. She felt her niece's pain, because her own story included the same pattern of abandonment. Maybe abandonment was too harsh a word, since her mother died from lung cancer after a long illness. But the pain of living without her then felt the same as abandonment.

Trying to provide some stability and safety for Keisha invariably meant that she had a very stunted date life. Maybe non-existent was a better word, she admitted. Not that Albany was loaded with eligible bachelors. Most in that category had long ago put Albany in the rear view mirror. But the last thing she needed to worry about was her niece's safety around a man that she was dating and just getting to know. Based on her painful past experience, the *no man in the house* rule was the best policy, and she never made an exception.

Adding to her concern was Keisha's early physical development. Just last week, she saw movement in the child's chest as she skipped around. A training bra was a definite necessity, and she bought three of them the next day. And earlier that month she had to take away Keisha's favorite short shorts. They had become far too tight and suggestive for a nine-year-old with a figure that was developing early. She made a mental note to visit the department after her shift tomorrow. Keisha did need a few more things.

Then she quickly remembered that tomorrow wouldn't work. She was slated to take her RN recertification classes at Union Methodist in New York City. She had an early flight to catch, and she wouldn't return until late in the evening.

She reached for the phone and called Remy, her best friend and occasional day care provider. She needed to reconfirm that Remy would be able to meet Keisha at home at the end of school tomorrow.

When Keisha returned from washing up, they sat down at the supper table. They shared the baked fish, sweet potatoes, and fresh salad with fruit. And Keisha had her favorite, a slice of cornbread with sweet butter on it. She eagerly placed it in a bowl, forked it into pieces, and poured maple syrup over the whole concoction. Lailani smiled and remembered when her own grandmother had first exposed her to the very same gourmet dish.

James also watched Ring-O-Levio that day, and every day before for as long as he could remember. But he always watched from his secret place behind the window shade, looking out through his granny's crumbling back porch. They could not see him there in the shadows. He knew that they didn't want him to play the game. As he rocked back and forth, back and forth, he fretted that he'd never been asked to play. James was thirty-six, but his mind had long ago stopped developing. He had heard the names *slow* and *retarded* when the man in the white coat looked at him and poked him with cold things and talked behind his back.

He knew he would be good at the game if he could play. Sometimes the children would hide in his yard, behind the old rusted Dodge Rambler. Sometimes they would squeeze through the busted slates under the porch and wait, and then run away laughing. But they never saw him looking. One time he went to the eaves door under the porch and heard the children talking soft on the other side of the metal barrier. Then they were gone, squeezing back through the slates and running away laughing.

Chapter Nineteen
Croatian Navy

Below deck, the navigator listened to the thumping and scraping noises from overhead. He could also hear other disquieting sounds from topside, including the increasing howl of the wind. In addition, metallic scraping sounds were being amplified within the mast that passed through the ship's decks. He suspected they were an indication of severed support stays and ripped steel spreaders. Without that support, the mast would have already started to lean.

He was also growing certain that Brett had lost control of the helm. The jerking and circular recovery motions he could feel after each gust indicated that autopilot, and not his skipper, was in control. He knew that Brett had a finer touch at the helm in heavy weather. Rather than fully rounding up after absorbing a gust and roller combination, he always anticipated the load and cut into the roller early, then released to port or starboard before tucking tight back into the wind again.

If autopilot was controlling the helm, then the navigator was certain that some great calamity had occurred.

Fifteen years of blue water sailing allowed him to calmly and rapidly evaluate each of the factors and make a life-saving decision.

Grabbing the cabin safety rails, he inched forward and reached the offshore radio mounted on the nav station's far shelf. Grasping it with both hands, he flipped the red emergency distress switch. After bracing himself against the cabin wall to counteract the bucking deck beneath his feet, he opened the channel and broadcast distress.

"Mayday! Mayday! This is Onset. Our position is 43 degrees 10 minutes north, 16 degrees 27 minutes east. Mayday! Mayday...."

JB Gatling

Gjurin Ivan Llvala banked his Mi 171 helicopter hard right over the listing mast of the partially submerged vessel. He counted five brightly colored life jackets in the water, 50 meters off the stern. Then he spotted the faint outline of an additional crewmember 150 meters behind that group. He radioed the positions to his base commander. As he calculated next steps, he knew that he had only two choices.

The first and best option was an aerial rescue using a lowered basket. But in these conditions, it would take extraordinary skill and coordination by his crew to pull that off. The basket could swing in an arc that was sixty meters wide in current wind conditions. Anything but the most precise timing could jeopardize his crew, as well as the sailors they were attempting to rescue. Entanglement with the mast and rigging was the biggest danger. That kind of trouble could pull his chopper into the sea. And finally, he wasn't confident that he and his three-man crew were up to the challenge. This was the moment when all of the training that had been cancelled due to austerity measures would have made an enormous difference. He could not risk it.

But he was determined to try the only other approach, and he radioed his commander that due to the gusting winds and waterborne aspect of the targets, he would deploy the large inflatable rescue craft, and his team would attempt to drag the targets on board. Once in the water, the craft would power inflate, and its 200-horsepower outboard might be able to provide adequate maneuverability in these seas. He received the go-ahead and began barking orders. What he really hoped for was some small reduction in the Sirocco winds to give them a fighting chance.

Jason John Paul was the skipper of Invictus. He was keen to overtake Onset's lead and claim his third win, and he was chasing hard. Because Onset was high on the wind after its last tact, he calculated that he just might have a chance to pass her on his own, faster angle during the next turn. But his navigator notified him as soon as the distress call was received, and everything changed. After charting the broadcast position, it placed Onset 20 degrees off their port bow. The distance was no more than one-half nautical mile.

He had raced against Brett in BVI two years ago, and in the Regattas held annually in Bequia and St Vincent waters. With neither of them finishing in the top five down there last year, they weren't too interested in attending the trophy ceremonies. Instead, they shared a few beers on the stern of Invictus as they swung on the hook far out in Admiralty Bay. Love of the sea and competition was the bond between them, and they developed a mutual respect.

Jason didn't hesitate to break off his dash for the finish line, even though Regatta rules and the available support infrastructure in Croatia didn't require him to do so. Other skippers might have taken advantage of the issue to increase their finishing position, or to win. But for him, there was no decision to be made between the finer points of rescue and winning. He hand signaled to his first mate to join him at the helm. After being fully briefed by Jason, he went forward to alert the rest. Jason engaged his engine and cranked the helm to port. The rescue was on.

He knew that in these heavy weather conditions, his seamanship would be severely tested. Rescue would be treacherous. But more important than anything, he hoped that Brett and his crew could hold it together until they arrived.

As he closed in, the wind and rolling swells seemed to abate somewhat. Nevertheless, his greatest fear was running his boat over someone in the sea. He shouted to his team to keep a sharp eye out.

"Give me enough warning to bear off," he demanded.

Soon he spotted the leaning mast of Onset in the distance as it emerged from the dense gray mist. The port and starboard stays were ripped off and tailing around the dangling spreaders. She was gradually bearing off before the wind, being slowly pushed back to leeward. As far as he could see, no one was at the helm. But the boat was afloat, at least for now.

Must be set on autopilot.

That fact would enable him to approach with more confidence. Then he saw the waves washing over the deck, and he hoped to God that the below-deck companionway was sealed and the bilge pumps were working overtime.

Overhead, he heard the rasping engine roar and metallic blades of an approaching rescue chopper. It came at Onset from the starboard side. He ordered two crewmembers to keep eyes on the boat and on the chopper. In these conditions, he knew that losing sight of the target and rescue craft was always a major risk. Then a crewmember signaled to him that one man was spotted in the water. Jason brought Invictus dead into the wind, and ordered the crew to pull the main sheet in tight and take in the headsail. He used a steady throttle and managed to keep the boat pointing straight on the target as they advanced slowly toward the big man bobbing in the high rolling waves.

Once near, they let loose lines and floating buoys with sea activated lights. The man was able to snare one. Jason throttled forward, using his bow thrusters for alignment. When he was within a few feet, he moved off slightly and gently nudged Invictus past the man. Then the crew tossed over a heavy safety line. The hard, dangerous work of reeling him in through the bucking transom opening began.

Gjurin could see that the other racing boat was having success bringing aboard the trailing crewmember. His movements in the water confirmed that he was alive. This was good, he said. His crew had already fished out two sailors and harnessed a third that they were starting to bring on board the inflatable. He could see that of the remaining two in the water, one was not moving, and was being supported by the other.

He was pleased when they finally cleared all of them from the sea. His crew had performed well. He radioed base that a severely injured racer would be arriving among the five they had rescued. He also reported Onset's most recent position. Base acknowledged and confirmed that a fast 42-meter coastal patrol ship was closing on the position, and would intercept the stricken vessel in 10 minutes.

Gjurin banked and climbed high, pointing his chopper back to base.

Chapter Twenty
Dreams

It was a giant car, and seven-year-old Brett and his sister and brother felt like they were drowning in the back seat, except there was no water and only blackness outside of the windows. Dee was on her knees, peering intently through the large rear glass. "I think that's Aunt Pat over there," she said excitedly. Brett popped up on his knees and looked hard, but couldn't be sure. There were lots of people standing around way off in the shadows that he could faintly see in the glow of light coming from a big white building. Everyone over there seemed to have on different clothes, or at least different from what he knew from before.

The mention of Aunt Pat's name made him long for her tasty desserts. They were spending a lot of time with her lately. He loved the big flat wooden spoons with heaps of leftover frosting from the two or three cakes she used to bake every week. The bowl where the frosting was mixed always seemed to find its way into his brother Jimmy's lap. And then there was the strawberry shortcake. She would make the biscuits from scratch, using a lot of white powder from bags, boxes, and cans. She would also mix in butter and cream and his favorite, sugar. The leftover spoons never stayed around very long. Dee always seemed to end up with two of them. But Aunt Pat hadn't made any desserts for a long time.

After a time, his brother fell asleep. Soon the front door of the car was unlocked, and Daddy stood looking down at them.

"Okay," he finally said in a voice that seemed different to him. "We are heading home." Daddy got into the car, but not on the regular side. Another man, bigger than him, got in, and he slowly drove them away.

Once home, Daddy carried Jimmy up the front stairs, and Brett and Dee followed close. Brett turned and watched the giant car moved away like a big beetle bug. Inside, the house was quiet and empty. He noticed there were no smells of food. They hadn't been home for many days. As he trudged down the long rail car hallway following Dee, he felt like it would always be empty like this. He knew it was so, because Daddy told them all last week that Mama had gone away to a place called heaven.

"Time for bed, you two," his father said in his deep voice after he had carried Jimmy into the room that he shared with Brett, gently depositing him into the bottom bunk bed. They instinctively rushed to their father and hugged him hard around his broad shoulders. Tears rolled down both of their cheeks. Brett saw tears on his father's face.

He didn't know what Daddy really meant. He kept saying, "You all will make a new start, and we'll do it together." But what was a new start? Even Dee didn't know the answer, even though she seemed to figure out most stuff.

It became clearer when their father helped them pack their jackets, jeans, and other clothes into big cases. Then he put those bags in the back of his old station wagon. They went to a road where all the cars were zipping along fast together. Brett fell asleep, and when he woke up the cars were still zipping along.

"Welcome to Albany, kids!" Daddy said that with a big grin. "This is your new home, our new beginning. Let's go in and say hi to Grandma."

None of them knew that this grandma, who they only vaguely remembered meeting before, was Daddy's ma until he said she was. She was old and didn't smile at all. They didn't think that Daddy looked much like her. Brett wondered if she could cook desserts like his Aunt Pat.

But one thing they knew for sure when they met her was that she was not pleased to be with them. Or maybe she was just overwhelmed by the three of them. As they trudged into the small house, passing through dark rooms, they saw old, thick plastic covers on the chairs and on the couch. Dee whispered that it must keep things new. But nothing looked new to him, and he smelled a sour odor in some of the rooms that he would later learn was dried-up urine.

Daddy promised to visit them every week, but that only happened once in a while. He said that work came first and that Grandma would take good care of them. Maybe he believed it. They stared at the station wagon as it went back up the dead-end street and turned out of sight. They felt very much alone.

Onset: An American's Voyage Beyond Borders

"Ring-O-Levio! Ring-O-Levio! " Brett screamed as he scrambled back to the circle, dragging Lailani close behind him. They had just freed their friends from the prison circle, and they scampered off to hide again before they could be captured.

Although he was almost twelve years old now, the game always brought happiness to him. Holding Lailani's hand during the chase was his other special treat. He began to have warm reactions in his body sometimes from touching her. They were different from when he was younger, years ago.

He would spot a possible safe route and grab her hand, and they would tear away on a dead run. Her smile and faith in him always made him try his hardest to help his team win. And she was pretty, too. Though they were too shy to say it to each other, everyone knew they were together. They talked all the time, and shared books and stories about every little thing. They were just comfortable with one another.

On one visit to Albany, Daddy brought a strange lady with him. She had nice clothes and a friendly face. Daddy told them she would be their new mother, and they would all move to New York City. Everyone would all be together, he said. Dee later said to them, out of Daddy's hearing, that it was strange that this new woman was there because Mama had only gone away five years ago. Maybe Dee believed that Mama would come back, but Brett didn't. He looked closely at the new woman and thought that she looked a little bit like their mama, at least as far as he could remember. She had pretty red nails and smelled real good. Jimmy liked her right away. Brett thought she had a good smile.

Things moved fast after that. Daddy came back the following week. They all piled their clothes into bags and boxes and packed them into the shiny new station wagon he was driving. Some of the things had to fit on top outside. Daddy kissed his ma goodbye, and they pulled out of the small driveway. He thought Daddy's ma looked happy. He was happy as well, to be leaving.

But as they pulled away from the house, he felt a numbing pain throughout his body. He'd forgotten to tell Lailani that he was going away. He slumped back in his seat, not knowing what to say or do. Soon they turned onto the zipping road.

Chapter Twenty-One
Gone

Lailani never completely recovered from the shock back then of learning that her very best friend had left Albany for good. She had gone over to his place on a Saturday afternoon, because they had planned to go to the church picnic together. As she approached the small house, she knew right away that something was wrong. For one thing, the front door to the enclosed porch was completely shut, when it was usually left open while the screen door remained locked. For another, the large mesh screens around the sitting porch were covered up with the outside shutters.

She found that strange, because Brett and Dee always liked to keep the screens open to let fresh air in the house. She always giggled when he said he was tired of smelling dried-up piss all the time, and that fresh air made a big difference.

Concerned that something was wrong, she circled around to the back of the house, only to find it closed up tight as well. Brett usually stored his Schwinn bike in the small shed in the back yard. She peeked inside, but it wasn't there. Then out of the corner of her eye, she saw a small movement of the curtain at the back window by the stairs. She knew that someone was following her movements.

With a feeling of panic in her chest, she stepped up to the back door and rapped on it hard. Nothing stirred inside. Once again she forcefully pounded on the door, but no one responded. She shouted his name for quite a while before finally realizing that the door would always remain closed.

She ran away from the house and raced over four blocks to the church. The picnic bus was partially loaded, but several children remained on the outside. Seeing no sign of him there, she waited and was last to board. She remembers that moment because she thought he was probably hiding on the bus and playing one of his silly tricks. But he wasn't there.

She went to his house again on Sunday afternoon, after church. This time she stayed back and out of sight, but she still had a pretty good view. There was no sign of anyone and no activity. She couldn't wait for school to start the next day. She knew that he would be there, because he always prided himself on perfect attendance. He kept all of those certificates on the wall near the head of his bunk.

Monday morning finally arrived, and she marched straight over to his classroom. But his chair was empty. That's when she asked his teacher what happened to him.

Mr. Smale was a thin, effeminate man with a sweet perfume odor. She remembered Brett telling her that he used to gather the black children together in the classroom and tell them they should not focus much on school studies, because they were simply not that good at book learning. He wanted the black kids to be janitors, carpenters, and laborers.

But her friend didn't like Smale for an entirely different reason. Brett thought he was dishonest. He used to say that he believed Smale gave him and the other black kids a slightly lower grade than the only white girl in the class, who always came out on top and took home the first place certificates. He wanted some of those for his wall at home.

Looking down at her and pulling on his long, curled moustache, Smale seemed happy to break the devastating news.

"Brett was withdrawn from school last week. He won't be back, and he has left Albany for good. That's all I can tell you," he sniffed.

A thousand questions flooded her mind. But mostly, she was in shock. Why had he not mentioned he was leaving? Was he tired of their friendship? Maybe he was tired of her. Or perhaps she wasn't that much of a friend to him after all. Then she became angry. Her anger lingered for a good amount of time. But it slowly receded with the passing years.

His disappearance caused her to withdraw and turn inward. She began to focus much more on her studies and became sort of a bookworm. Rarely did she run and romp with the old crowd, who continued to play Ring-O-Levio on a daily basis. The game had lost its fun.

Chapter Twenty-Two
Awakening

Brett felt a cooling breeze on his forehead. It was a trade wind, laced with a little salt spray. And it seemed to increase in feeling. He heard a faint voice calling his name from the mist and saw a soft glow just beyond it.

"Brett, Brett, come back to me, darling."

He heard the voice speaking to him, but it was still coming from far away. The pressure on his forehead increased and became warmer. He felt his face flush with heat. Then his eyes twitched, but they seemed to be glued shut.

"Brett, come back to me, sweetheart."

He struggled to open his eyes. Then there was a warm feeling on his arm and in his hands. He was being touched. He managed to open one eye just slightly. A painful stab of light made him shut it tight.

The warm touch rested on his forehead and covered his eyes. He smelled a familiar fragrance.

Her fragrance.

He forced his eyes open again, blinking repeatedly this time to wet the dryness. Then he saw her, his lovely girlfriend Zena. She smiled down at him.

"Welcome back, sweetheart." She rested her head softly on his chest.

"Where am I?" he mumbled in a voice he didn't recognize. Zena sat up and looked down at him as she wiped her tears. She smiled and held his hand in hers.

"You're in New York City, darling, at Brent Memorial Hospital. You've been here four days, since they flew you back from Dubrovnik. You and your crew were rescued off the coast. Everyone survived, and they're all okay. Even Onset was saved."

It was then he became aware that his entire left side down to his waist was completely immobile. He was encased in something stiff and hard. For a moment, waves of claustrophobia washed over him. He feebly shifted against the binding body cast and reared his head to pull up and escape. But the effort exhausted him, and he fell back on the bed.

Moments later, Dr. Emanuel Stern entered the room.

"Mr. Howard, welcome back."

Still having difficulty forming words, he nodded and relaxed further back into the pillows. He was quickly becoming exhausted from the deluge of visual and physical stimulation.

"As you are certainly aware," Dr. Stern continued, "you are zipped up in a traction body cast. You suffered a spinous process fracture. And that fracture was coupled with a vertical body fracture of the superior end plate. All in all, you have eight to twelve weeks of recovery ahead of you, followed by many weeks of physical therapy to restore what will be a very weakened musculature."

"My best advice, Mr. Howard, is to put off any tennis or golf outings that you have on your calendar for four months." Stern smiled thinly.

"And by the way, I'm afraid that you'll feel like a sack of potatoes, in a cast that is, for the next three weeks at least. But your prognosis is excellent. Your strength and conditioning allowed you to endure a blow to your neck, shoulders, and back that would have killed or paralyzed most people."

He began to experience a swirling dizziness, and his eyelids grew extremely heavy. He also felt an increasing low-level throb in his back beneath the cast.

Dr. Stern then moved to the left side of his hospital bed and rested his hand on a small intravenous device that was connected to his arm.

"That is why we have arranged a convenient morphine drip that will let you self-medicate when the pain exceeds your threshold. Use it generously. But don't worry, it's diluted, and we'll be cutting you off in three days as a precaution against addiction. Meanwhile, squeeze away. Any questions?"

He had many questions, but before he could form them into words, he was crossing back into dreamland.

Chapter Twenty-Three
Sweet Home

Chauncey lurched his lava black sports car to the far end of the circular driveway in front of his father's immense Westchester County estate. He liked the way the throaty growl of the turbo-charged engine heralded to all that he was home. But the drive from Manhattan to the country always irritated him, and the pretentiousness of the one hundred acre property was a constant embarrassment. He knew that Stewart and the others would look at him entirely differently if they had any real idea about the opulence he had been born into and would one day inherit.

And that was the biggest rub for him. It all came for free with his birth, compliments of his old man, the great investment banker. His own efforts had nothing to do with it and never would. He would forever be Carleton's boy. He was the kid with the platinum spoon in his mouth. He believed that his own merit and accomplishments had always been overlooked.

But that will soon change when the Taurus plan is executed.

Entering the main house under the soaring, vaulted architecture leading to the great hall, he was greeted by Alfred and Wilemina. They each had 43 years of service to the Smith household. They were there well before he was born. They were there when his mother shipped him off to boarding school at the age of nine. And he believed that they would be there forever, because they never seemed to age. It must be a black racial thing, he figured.

"Good afternoon, Master Smith," chirped Alfred with his usual impeccable tone of servitude. WIlemina bowed slightly in her own manner of well-practiced deference.

He nodded in their direction with a clipped smile and continued striding purposefully to the west wing, where he occupied his own suite of seven rooms whenever he visited.

His first telephone call was to Nathan JoHanson, a trusted and discreet private investigator that he'd initially utilized several years ago. Nathan was an unattached freelancer back then, and Chauncey was one of his first high-end clients. He used Nathan to extricate himself from a messy affair involving an East Side call girl. Despite a three thousand dollar per night charge for her splendid services, she believed that his pedigree entitled her to so much more. Nathan was most helpful in putting together a complete dossier on the young woman, and even more valuable in persuading her that pursuing an extortion scheme would result in complete shutoff from all of her high-end clients in New York and elsewhere.

In the Taurus matter, he planned that Nathan would be the key to establishing the initial confidential lines of communication with the targets. The first step was to penetrate the phalanx of security surrounding them without exposing himself. Nathan knew the security heads personally, because keeping the princes of business safe and sound was a small cottage industry in New York. Everybody knew everybody. Once those lines of communication were opened, the choreographed sequence of tease and reveal would commence.

Over the next hour, he provided Nathan with the target names and exacting instructions about what to say and when to say it. As a kicker, he promised him a ten thousand dollar bonus if initial rounds of discussion were opened on time and as planned with all three targets.

After the call, he rang the kitchen and told Alfred to send up a chilled bottle of early vintage Rose Champagne immediately.

Unfortunately, before it arrived the private line from his mother's suite rang, and she showered him with the latest drivel that passed for polite conversation among the super wealthy. She finished by sweetly inviting him to officiate at her club's tennis event for charity next Saturday afternoon. Agreeing with her was always the better and more efficient approach, and he did so.

He poured his third flute and continued to enjoy the crisp, clean taste. Leaning back on the divan in his living room, he took in the expansive grand estate views beyond the ten open French doors of his living room. But his mind quickly turned back to business. As he considered Nathan's ruthless efficiency, he was confident that the first target conversations could happen as early as Wednesday. Then he thought about who might be the first of the targets to take the bait after the opening rounds and move forward to more detailed discussions. But gradually, the room began to fill with the distant sound of grinding helicopter blades. Soon the roar became deafening, signaling only one thing: his father and several fawning minions were landing on the south lawn.

Not wanting to confront his father at this delicate moment of treachery, because the old man always seemed to possess the eerie ability read him like a book, he quickly downed the last savory drops, grabbed his keys, and bounded out of the entryway into the bright afternoon sunshine. After firing up his car and slipping on dark designer shades, he navigated down the mile-long exit road from the estate before turning onto Grandeur Road back to Manhattan.

On the way in, he called his longtime partner. They were scheduled to go out to Long Island together for the weekend. Looking forward to the break from the intensity and stress of planning for the Taurus raid, he was calling to make certain that Robert had done all of the shopping and other chores for the weekend.

His relationship with Robert had to remain hidden. He hated the phrase *in the closet*. But it was the precise term that defined how he had to live, and how he had to conceal his love for Robert from the outside world. He understood that his motivation to upstage his father was matched by an equally strong, almost desperate need to come clean before the world and step from the closet into the light.

Taurus would provide him with the financial means to accomplish that. The dependent financial strings by which his father played puppeteer over him would be forever severed. He wondered if his father would strike him from his will. Very likely to happen, he concluded, and so what.

At the Long Island estate, he and Robert would enjoy complete privacy. The vast breadth of his family's 10-acre oceanfront property and carefully placed landscaping ensured that all prying eyes remained on the outside, where they belonged.

Chapter Twenty-Four
Ring-O-Levio

Keisha finished her science homework and placed it neatly in the pile of work for Miss Remy to check. She was quick in her studies, and the homework rarely challenged her. She usually completed all of it within an hour or so. Aunty Lai always preached about how the road to fame was paved with well-done homework assignments. She wasn't at all sure what that meant.

But with her aunt or Miss Remy checking her work every night, she had long ago grown accustomed to making sure that everything was completed accurately and neatly.

If not, she would be late for the early evening game of Ring-O-Levio, and she was only late one time before, when she rushed through a math assignment and had to do it all over again. Then she was too late to join a team and ended up watching the game from Miss Shirley's front porch. She never missed another game after that.

With her Aunty Lai away in New York City at the nursing class, she went back upstairs to her room and pulled out her favorite short shorts that were hidden under her gym clothes in her bottom dresser drawer. They were a little tighter now, and she did remember her aunt telling her to take them off and throw them away. But she had taken them out of the trash later that night and hid them.

After all, she thought, she wasn't the only girl that had short shorts on her block. Tiauna had three pairs in different colors, and her grandmother who she stayed with never seemed to mind what Tiauna wore. Aunty Lai was just too picky sometimes.

She also decided to leave her training bra home, because she believed could run faster without it. She liked feeling her small chest bounce a little when she ran. And sometimes she saw the boys staring at her. But she was okay with it, as long as they kept their hands to themselves.

"Keisha, bring me that math workbook that you were using over the summer."

She quickly pulled on her sweat pants and slipped into a loose-fitting cotton jacket to cover her tight tee shirt. She grabbed the workbook and went into the living room, proudly presenting it to Miss Remy.

"Now, girl, before you go skipping out of here, did you take your time and get all these problems right?"

"Yes, ma'am. Can I go out now?"

Remy looked down at the stack of papers in her hand.

"You know I got them right," she begged. "If I made any mistakes, you can tell Aunty Lai, and you know what will happen. Please can I go? I'm going to miss the team picks!"

"Okay, that's enough with the begging. I'll take your word that you did a thorough job. But I'll be checking these papers, so it's going be on you if you did some messy work. Now go on, and make sure you hear my call for supper. Give me a hug."

Pushing Keisha back and holding her out in front of her, Remy was curious.

"Aren't you going to be hot in those long pants and jacket, girl?"

"No, ma'am. I want to keep from skinning my knees and getting dirty during the game."

Keisha flew out of the house and down the block, to where the two teams were being formed up.

James watched the game from the shadows as he rocked back and forth. He heard the laughter spilling down the alley as the first group of children ran by his back porch at full speed. One of them saw the broken slates under the porch, and she squeezed underneath. He knew where she would be.

Then another set of children ran down the alley. As he rocked back and forth, he could see them trying to find the others, looking here and looking there. One boy spotted the porch where the girl was and he leaned down, looking underneath into the darkness.

James smiled then, because he knew he could join the game and play if he went fast. He ran down to the basement and quietly unlocked the eaves door. He leaned in and put his ear near the seam. He could hear the girl breathing on the other side of the opening. But he didn't make any sound. The boy out front had entered through the slates, and he started yelling.

"I know somebody's in here and there ain't no way out. You gonna get captured today, so you might as well surrender now."

The girl moved a few feet back, staying low and leaning against the eaves door to stay out of sight. It gave way under her weight as James released it, and she tumbled inside. He quietly closed and locked the door.

The darkness had partially blinded her, but she scrambled to get to her feet. As she stood up she saw old James Harper, the crazy man, grinning at her and rocking back and forth. Keisha started to scream, but in fear he grabbed her mouth and clamped it shut. As she kicked and jerked in his arms, he squeezed her tightly. She managed to get one of his fingers in her mouth and bit down hard, drawing blood. The pain flooded through his hand and he twisted and spun violently, throwing her headfirst into the unfinished earthen wall. The blow made a loud, dull thud. Her legs collapsed as she tumbled sideways and unconscious to the floor.

His eyes were flared open wide, and his breath came in short, rapid gasps. He stood there confused and afraid, rocking back and forth. He moved in closer to the still body and stared down. He saw her chest moving up and down, and her bare stomach and smooth legs. He kneeled down and looked real hard and rubbed her legs. Then he lay down beside her still form and pulled her closer.

Chapter Twenty-Five
School Days

The Howard kids were excited about the move to the Big Apple. It turned out, though, the move was to a place called Astoria Queens. But it was part of New York City, Daddy told them, so they were still excited. Their modest three-bedroom Cape house had been bought with what their father told them was a GI Bill from the Air Force. The kids thought it was really neat. The house even had a separate basement with paneled walls that they loved. And it belonged to them.

Their new mother set up her sewing room in the back area of the basement, where she made extra money. And Daddy had a shop down there with tools and things to help him with his hustle. Most of all, from the kids' point of view, they had a brand new house only 15 years old. Dee had her own room, of course, and that seemed to be an unwritten rule for girls, Brett thought. Even though he continued to share a room with Jimmy, it was a bigger room and he had his own study desk in the corner, just like his sister's. Study desks and what Daddy called *chair time* had always been important in the Howard household. The last thing he ever wanted to do was face his father with a poor report card. He knew that wouldn't be good.

With school activities, sports, and constant after-school cramming to catch up in his new Honors and AP classes, he forgot all about Albany and rarely thought about Lailani. In time, she faded from his active memory.

His new mom was full of energy and assignments for chores around the house. Her rules included clean clothes, clean fingernails, and clean rooms, as well as rotating sets of chores for which they were each accountable during the week. Dishes for one week, oven cleaning once a week, yard work with Daddy for a week, and on it went. But at the beginning of every week they received a two-dollar allowance, and Brett thought that was great.

Dee never fully warmed up to their new mother, and she carefully avoided calling her by that name. He thought maybe it was because Dee was older and she remembered more about their first mother. She was cordial most of the time, but that was about it. But sometimes he would hear them yelling at each other. Later, when high school was over, Dee moved out of the house to pursue her studies down in the city. He missed her. Of course, to his disappointment, he and Jimmy had to pick up her share of the chores.

Enrollment into the new junior high school happened quickly, and he later learned that his dad had been in touch with the school a lot. And for the first time that he could remember, he had new back-to-school clothes. His mother insisted that he wear a collared shirt and tie every day, even though he found out later that he didn't have to, according to school rules. He thought it was a good idea, though, and he kind of liked the new clothes. His dad showed him how to make a Windsor knot with his new ties, so he threw away all his old clip-ons.

When he stepped off the shiny new school bus on his first day of classes, he was confronted with two new realities. The first was that ninety-nine percent of the students were white. The second was that only the nerdy kids with thick glasses seemed to be wearing a shirt and tie. But he kept his tie on anyway, maybe out of respect for his mom.

But big problems would result from the shirt and tie combo, as he soon learned. At that point in his life, he still didn't know what his daddy meant when he would refer to someone as a "knucklehead." It was one of his dad's usual expressions. He just figured there must be a lot of them around, because his father used the term quite a bit.

He met his first knucklehead in person that morning in his seven-fifteen homeroom class.

Daniel Slate was a big, ruddy-faced, Scott-Irish kid who was three or four years older than anyone else in the class. He was only in school because he would be truant and arrested if he was found outside. Slate specialized in bullying and dozing off in his vocational education classes. With his shirt and tie and brown skin, Brett was an invitation to mischief that Slate couldn't refuse.

What are you, some kind of a sissy ass? Slate asked from three rows in back of him. His voice was just low enough that the homeroom teacher didn't hear it.

But the two rows of kids in between them heard it. They knew immediately where things were heading. He looked to his right behind him and saw Slate leering back. Then he turned back around and looked straight ahead. Maybe he wasn't the intended target that he thought.

Once again, Slate intoned toward him in sotto voice: *What are you, some kind of candy-ass darkie?*

Being the only black kid in the room, he now had no doubt that he was the object of Slate's scorn. He also had no doubt that failure to reply would make him exactly what Slate had called him.

In his almost six years on the racially segregated streets of Albany, he had learned some hard lessons about standing up to intimidation. He'd had more than a few fistfights, like just about every other kid in his neighborhood. Without those he would have been constantly bullied. Having no older brothers or cousins also meant that he and his sister Dee had to battle on several occasions to protect their little brother from some of the kids with big families.

Sometimes he wished that he had an older brother who could have been there to protect him. It wasn't the case, so he had to learn early to protect himself.

But he did have his older sister. She had put a big pair of sewing scissors in her pocketbook one time as she planned to confront four rough-looking girls who had threatened Jimmy on his way home from his elementary school. He still remembered Dee looking at him back then and saying that she had to go up to Witcomb Avenue to settle the issue with them girls once and for all.

Somehow he found his courage and went up there with her. He remembered feeling a little weak in his knees as they walked the half-mile to where the girls were usually found. When Dee pulled out those sharp scissors from her bag and told them that she would cut their throats if they ever messed with Jimmy again, he was really scared about what might happen next. But the girls backed down and backed away. He always admired his big sis after that, because he knew she must have been scared like he was.

He turned slowly around to Slate and looked him in the eyes. Then quietly, without any facial expression, he told him to kiss his black ass. Slate was momentarily stunned. He hadn't expected any reply, never mind an aggressive one.

But it didn't take him long to recover his rage, and he lunged out of his seat with a snarl, his right fist sailing at Brett's head. Brett ducked down, and the punch missed. He grabbed Slate around the chest and they grappled. They soon tumbled together out of his seat into the aisle, and continued to punch and claw. In an instant, however, the homeroom teacher was in the aisle, forcefully separating them. He called the principal's office.

Slate looked mean at him before he was ushered out of the room by security. In a voice heard only by him as he walked past, he told Brett that he would see him after school on the *hill*.

He had no clue where this hill was, but he knew he would have to find it. He wished that Dee was with him, but she was at her new high school two miles away. So he went alone.

Finding the hill turned out not to be an issue. Once he rounded the corner of the school where the gymnasium was housed, he looked over to the far side of the athletic field and spotted it. The hill rose to a height of forty feet. A group of twenty-five or so students were milling around on top. All were white. He wondered if he would have to fight everyone. As he approached and trudged up the incline, they all looked down at him. As it turned out, this would be the same hill his football coach the following year would use for sprint punishment for any player that he thought was dogging it.

Slate was in the center of the crowd with his slicked-back hair and attitude, watching him approach. Brett took his school bag off his shoulder as he neared the top. At the crest, he loosened his tie and dropped his bag. Within seconds they were going after each other. He tried to use the hill to his advantage, but mostly he tried to throw as many punches as he could. Slate leveraged his height and weight, grabbing him around the neck and twisting him down with a back leg trip. Landing on top, Slate clamped his arms around his neck in a chokehold. He struggled to get free, but he couldn't separate Slate's strong forearms. He started to lose consciousness as the hold sealed off his air supply. Then he heard the muffled sound of Slate's voice shouting at him.

You give up? You give up?

Somehow managing to think rationally despite the dire circumstances, he saw the question as an amazing development. Of course he would never *give up*, especially to the likes of Slate, but what would happen, he wondered, if he said yes? Would Slate release the chokehold?

I give up! I give up!

Miraculously, from his point of view, Slate released the hold and stood back from him. In that instant he pulled back and smacked him hard with a closed right hand, opening up a bleeding gash above Slate's left eye. After that they continued to fight more or less to a draw, before both called it quits after another half hour. Each could claim some measure of victory in the struggle.

The next day in homeroom class, Slate showed up with numerous black and blue marks on his face, neck, arms, and hands. His left eye was swollen, and he had a wide bandage covering sutures in his eyebrow. One of his knuckles had apparently been fractured during a glancing blow to Brett's skull, so the knuckle and fingers were wrapped up, and his right arm was in a sling.

But most telling of all, his usual swagger seemed to have deserted him as he walked into homeroom. He didn't look in Brett's direction.

On the other hand, Brett appeared in class that day as usual, wearing a button-down blue shirt and another nice tie that his mother bought for him. Perhaps benefiting from his darker complexion, there were no black and blue marks or other visible evidence of the brawl. But he was very much in pain from the fight. Everything was sore or tender. Yet he tried to move and act as if everything was normal, knowing that he had to show he would meet on that hill again, if necessary.

That was the last fight he had in Queens.

Part Four
Fulfillments

Chapter Twenty-Six
Semper Fidelis

Nathan pulled away from his driveway with only one thought in mind—how he would execute the plan that the kid, as he mentally referred to Chauncey, needed to get done. It seemed simple enough. Call some of his folks who worked in the security business, give them the spiel that the kid had outlined today *without mentioning the kid's name*, get his counterparts to agree to translate the message to their principals, receive a yes or no to next steps, and reply to the kid with his list of takers. Earning the extra ten K for getting this done was a sure thing.

As he waited in his lane for several city buses to enter the traffic flow thirty yards ahead, he wondered why in hell they all seemed to cluster together like giant misshapen ducks on wheels.

But he knew the answer to his own question the minute he thought about it. If they were all together, they could shoot the shit when they took their frequent breaks. If they were all together, no one could be accused of dogging it. If they were all together, no one stood out as working too hard, which made the union happy and made them happy. Go along and get along, thought Nathan, the happy road to mediocrity. It was the major reason he avoided those types of outfits when he left the Marine Corps.

He had totally committed to the Marines as a 17-year-old, wet-behind-the-ears recruit from San Jose, California. Thinking about how green he was back then, he shook his head and spit his chewing tobacco five yards out the driver side window. But he figured he was damned lucky to draw the right Cali recruiter who overlooked his phony ID. Filling his numbers was all that stiff was about, so he always knew his good looks and charm had jack shit to do with him making it to boot camp at Parris Island.

But once there, all the anger and frustration that had been woven into his soul since his old man first broke a glass ginger ale bottle across his thirteen-year-old nose found a place to channel. The drill instructors were fierce, all right, but after the beatings that he had endured at the drunken hands of his old man, they weren't as bad as most people complained they were. At least you didn't wake up the next morning to the same pattern of abuse. Parris Island abuse was always different and varied.

He excelled in close combat and perimeter infiltration. Those were fancy Marine code words for *charge in, blow up the camp, and take no prisoners unless the chicken-shit bastards force you to.* That worked just fine as Nathan's preferred method of dealing with the world. And every time he went on a mission, all he had to do for motivation was imagine the ruddy face of his drunken old man on the other side.

He saw some live action with his unit in Grenada, and he enjoyed it. But they surrendered so quickly down there that he only got to clean his M16 three times before his unit was breaking camp and preparing to ship out for home. Mission accomplished.

When he left the Corps, he decided to strike out on his own, not following the traditional path of many ex-servicemen who signed up with one large organization or the other, be it the post office, shipping or freight companies, or the like. The Corps had been his entire life and his family. He knew he could never duplicate that in some other outfit, no matter how much they advertised themselves as a home for ex-military.

He wanted to use his skills in the service of a small, private employer. And bodyguard was not of much interest, because from what he had heard, the body you were guarding could turn out to be a minnow or a whale, depending on the amount of illegal substance that had been snorted or pin-pricked or smoked that particular day. He wasn't interested in giving CPR to some overdosed celebrity that had yanked too much snow up his nose.

His break came when a buddy of his called who had left the service two years before him. He'd heard through the grape vine that Nathan was looking for a good security spot. They met later that evening for a beer at a joint called Shorty's. His buddy was in what was called the *private assurance* business, and he made the pitch to Nathan. The opportunity was his if he wanted it. Good pay, high risk, follow orders, keep your mouth shut. Other than the good pay part, Nathan thought it sounded just like the Corps.

Turned out it was the break he sorely needed. There was a whole different class of customers in need of good security. They appreciated military grade professionalism, treated their folks well, and generally operated with the utmost discretion. These were not the folks who needed to be carted away from social events or from an ex-spouse's home. They were mostly the old money crowd. Blue bloods was the name bandied about back then that he remembered.

His very first private assurance job was as a tag-along triggerman supporting his buddy. They were quietly inserting the client into the airport of a small South American country, using the client's private jet. This was right after the successful takeover of a popular regional company based in the capital. The local threat stemmed from the fact that the client publically announced he was flying in to personally fire everyone at the underperforming company. That client was Carleton Smith.

Back then, Nathan believed that every client deserved his absolute loyalty. On one occasion years ago, which he always recounted when the word loyalty came up, he walked off a job because his present client in a tax evasion scheme was about to entrap one of his former clients in an IRS sting. Nathan walked out because the target of the sting had been a good customer of his, and the thing just wasn't kosher.

But over time, competition for high-end business increased due to the large number of ex-servicemen returning from America's foreign battlefields. They engaged in a dog-eat-dog war to land business. No one had time for loyalty, and the newer, hungrier firms were aggressively poaching customers from their rivals, even staging security breaches against them that they would later sell against. And worst of all, some of the larger security firms were retained by two competing rivals. Sometimes the conflict was disclosed, but more often than not it wasn't. It was all highly corrosive, and it ate away at Nathan too.

Chauncey's involvement with the transvestite call girl provided a needed boost to Nathan's business at the time. Nathan was quietly steered to recruit Chauncey as a client by the kid's father. Carleton Smith had only one condition—that he be kept fully informed about his son's activities. At the time it seemed like a reasonable deal, and the double pay was especially sweet.

Carleton had no qualms at all about spying on his only son. He believed that information had always been and would forever remain the coin of the realm. His earliest successes in business were based on it. Not just exhaustive information about a particular transaction, but detailed personal background information about the parties on the other side. He always knew what was below the surface, and what emotional factors motivated or demotivated his adversary, including his adversary's associates and family members.

Consequently, he accumulated a vast storehouse of sensitive information about many of the captains of American industry. Given his tendencies, developed decades before his son was born, his decision to enlist Nathan to regularly report to him about Chauncey's personal life, habits, and associates was merely a reflexive rather than a calculated move. In fact, he often lamented, if he had started earlier, his son might have better managed a whole host of issues flared up by his immaturity.

But by far his largest concern was the growing belief that his son might be incapable of carrying forward the Smith legacy. The more information he accumulated, the more he became convinced that Chauncey lacked the business acumen and social consciousness that was essential to hold and enhance the vast fortune he had built.

Business school had provided the bare essentials, and at least the boy managed to complete a course of study at a top school. But Carleton knew that beyond reading financial statements and allocating capital, the Smith legacy rested upon political influence and public philanthropy, both essential and interlocking components for securing freer rein in the economic sphere. It saddened him that he had yet to see any indication from his son displaying an appreciation for the vital importance of supporting progress in the charitable world of giving, or in the arts. Both, he believed, were noble pursuits in and of themselves, notwithstanding their strategic business importance. His many efforts to influence his son in those directions had been ignored. So far greed, acquisitiveness, and selfishness were the only Smith character traits on display.

Perhaps it was the softness that came with the territory of his son's privileged position. Or perhaps he was guilty of spoiling the boy, rather than allowing him to sink or swim, as had the sons of other wealthy colleagues who succumbed to drugs, sex, or crime.

I've always bailed him out of his problems. Was that a mistake?

The matter was one of growing urgency now that Carleton had passed his mid-eighties. While he kept himself in great physical condition and had fine-tuned his diet to eliminate most fat, toxins, and wasted calories, he realized that at best he had perhaps only a decade or two left. Planning for the end occupied more and more of his bandwidth. Alternate plans would have to be made, if his son proved to be an unworthy heir.

Chapter Twenty-Seven
Betrayal

Stewart opened his apartment door and scooped up the thick bundle of newspapers that he religiously plowed through each morning. All told, he estimated that the extensive collection cost him thirty dollars a day. But starting each morning with a complete inventory of international and domestic financial news was essential in his line of work.

On top of the pile, one WSJ headline screamed at him as he stared back in disbelief.

Taurus Corporation Under Attack By Corporate Raider

He virtually inhaled the article as he retreated back inside. At the end, one thing was crystal clear: his takeover scheme had been stolen and was now being executed without him. He slammed his fist into the kitchen table, spilling his coffee and shattering his china cup over the large marble floor.

Frantically he grabbed his pager and tapped out a text message to his team.

"Jink's place 8:00 A.M. for a bfast mting, bck crner tble, no excuses. See A.M. WSJ!"

He then methodically devoured all of the other print sources and went online for any updated coverage. He took no notes, committing everything to memory.

As he waited at a rear corner table, away from the cued snatch-and-grab crowd who ate their breakfasts walking to the office or standing up on a train, he tumbled over in his mind the possible scenarios that had caused their downfall. Maybe a member of the team had gotten greedy and decided to freelance, and screw the rest of them. Or some miraculous coincidence resulted in an unaffiliated corporate raider simultaneously exploiting the same opportunity he had unearthed. Then again, he thought, maybe their scheme had somehow been hacked, and then exploited by a ruthless opportunist.

He eliminated coincidence as statistically improbable and decided to target his inquisition of the team on the other two possibilities.

When everyone arrived at the table with coffee or juice, he quietly asked his first question.

"Is there any reason why we can't trust each other?"

They all said *no* in unison.

He then covered the three options and explained why only a couple of them made any sense. Focusing on betrayal, he said that he found it a hard option to swallow. Although it was consistent with human nature, he was not convinced as yet.

"We each have our own motivations, which are vastly different, and which we discussed early on when we committed to each other to do this thing as a team."

"Moreover, I think we all remain pretty much incapable of pulling it off alone. That's why we joined forces in the first place. Betrayal would mean we would have to trust others to assist us, and on pretty short notice versus the eighteen months that we've invested together. Except for a larger share of the pie, why would we trust others on such short notice?"

He took a sip of water and continued in his calm, analytical voice.

"And why would others give us a larger share of the pie, when they were bringing to bear most of the resources to do the deal? So there's no motive that I can see."

"Does anyone still think that option is viable?"

No one chimed in. They all waited for his logic train to keep chugging down the track.

"Okay then," he said. "One last possibility remains. One of us was hacked. Our plans were stolen. Let's think deeply about this for a moment."

He looked at each of them with a steady gaze.

"What possible security breach could any of us be guilty of, even unwittingly so? Documents left out in the open, phone calls bugged, a casual conversation with a friend or acquaintance where a slip was made, perhaps a lapse on a plane with someone peeking over our shoulder at a draft document?"

He paused and sipped his juice. Then the entire solution to the mystery came to him with brilliant clarity. He explained it to them slowly and methodically.

"Whoever breached our security did that very recently, given the sequence of events reported in the press. If anyone had breached our security earlier, they would have attacked earlier. There would be no logical reason to sit on the information, and every reason to make haste before our next move."

Then he revealed the conclusion that he had arrived at moments before.

"The thief had to already have the capacity and resources to capitalize on our information. The timing makes that conclusion inescapable."

Looking directly at Chauncey, he delivered the final chapter.

"The thief had to have been an accomplished corporate raider himself, already in the game and capable of quickly mobilizing the necessary resources to exploit this opportunity."

"Checkmate," Cy whispered softly.

The blood drained from Chauncey's face as he realized that his father had hacked his phone calls, and perhaps hacked his computer to extract details of the plan. Perhaps he had also hacked Nathan, his private investigator, though Chauncey didn't think that was possible, given Nathan's professional precautions and loyalty.

As Chauncey recovered his composure, he looked around to each of his friends and acknowledged what they all had heard.

"Stewart's right. The bastard must have ripped me off…ripped *us* off."

Then his anger flared, and his voice lowered in tone with a threatening edge.

"But I'll be god damned if I let him get away with it."

Chauncey clenched his jaw and stood up. He paced the small enclosure around the table for inspiration. The others had never seen him lose his cool exterior veneer before. Everyone stared, but no one stated the obvious—that they had no cards to play in this high-priced contest, not now that their information advantage had been stolen.

Chauncey's mind raced. The thought of losing out to his old man after all of their work wasn't an option for him. Then he paused and came back to the table to look directly at Melinda as he spoke.

"My old man does have one major weakness. He can't resist a pretty young face. And that weakness has to be our leverage to get back in the game."

For the first time since he'd read the headlines that morning, Stewart began to feel a glimmer of hope. He suggested that they meet at his apartment that evening to complete the planning. Before then, he had to devise a strategy that regained their lost advantage.

Chapter Twenty-Eight
Pain

Lailani walked out of her last class, relieved.

Thank God it's over.

She reached into her purse for her cell phone. Of course, all phones had to remain off during the recertification classes. Such a silly rule, she thought, when muting the phone was equally effective. Finally she was able to check whether a confirmation call had come in about her flight home to Albany. With any luck she would be home by ten-thirty. Unfortunately, that would be well after Keisha's bedtime.

A slowly rising sense of dread took hold of her when she saw on her screen the multiple times that Remy had called her phone—at least six times in the last hour. There were also several messages, most left by Remy. Holding her breath, she skipped the messages and stabbed her callback button.

As the number rang, Lailana's hands turned numb. She felt a rolling spasm in her back and a sudden stiffness between her neck and shoulders. Those feelings of foreboding were justified moments later when Remy's tired and grief-laden voice answered and began to mumble.

"Keisha's gone, Lai, she's gone. She didn't come home for dinner. I called for her, I screamed for her and searched the streets for that child. The police are here now, they've been looking everywhere, everyone's looking together for her. I'm sorry Lai, so sorry …it's all my fault, my fault…" Then she heard Remy explode with sorrow and wailing. The sounds were muted, as if the phone had been dropped. Lailani screamed, shouting Remy's name repeatedly and asking for more information.

Three polished Albany police cruisers with flashing roof rack arrays swerved at high speed onto the Albany airport runway and gunned their engines. They quickly surrounded the slowing regional jet liner and nudged in close as it taxied to a stop.

Over the speakers, the pilot calmly ordered all passengers to remain in their seats during the emergency. Two of Albany's finest stepped out of the lead cruiser. They were tall, fit men with close-cropped haircuts under Bancroft hats. They boarded the plane. From her rear seat, Lailani walked stiff-legged toward the exit door with a stewardess supporting her. The officers rushed down the aisle. The police captain took her hand tightly and put his arm over her shoulders as he ushered her forward. He bent down and whispered in her ear, "We found her, ma'am, your Keisha. She's alive, but she's been hurt."

She looked up at him and tried to speak, tried to thank him. As she opened her mouth, her knees buckled and she slumped.

Later that evening, she stood in the inner waiting room at Albany Presbyterian Hospital providing her name and health care information. The RN on duty was efficient but seemed completely uncaring about the reason for her late-night visit. She was only interested in dotting every "i" and crossing every "t" on the hospital patient intake form. Keisha had been admitted without any payment information and that seemed to be a huge *personal* affront to this nurse.

Lailani was familiar with the utter lack of compassion in the process, and she quietly lamented the loss of genuine caring in her profession. Compassion was once the hallmark for why women entered the field. Now, many women as well as men entered only for the pay and benefits. She could understand why so many surveys indicated that patients felt an absence of concern and caring in many hospitals across the nation.

When she finished the paperwork, she was finally admitted beyond the nurses' station. She walked down the drab green hallway to the dimly lit intensive care waiting room. Five neat rows of chairs, twenty or so across, were aligned before a small television monitor that was mounted too high up on the wall. The monitor glared without sound and used scrolling subtitles to deliver the daily news feed. On the wall in front of the monitor, framed signs with black blocked letters warned against cell phone use, against eating and drinking, and admonished all to speak quietly, if at all. A separate set of signs on the sidewalls used the same style lettering to warn against rearranging the chairs and against sleeping in the chairs. She shook her head in disgust as she recalled from her own experience the need for some family members to keep long vigils in the ICU, to be close to loved ones.

But no sleeping allowed here.

In the far corner of the room, slouched low in her chair with her head bowed and barely visible, sat the room's only occupant, Remy. Lailani rushed over to her and held her close. Remy's reaction to the embrace was slow, but she recognized her friend through tired, red eyes swollen with grief. As she comforted her friend, she lifted from her spirit the huge weight of bearing up alone through the long, painful day.

After what seemed like hours, Dr. Kaplan emerged from the treating area and looked at Lailani with a compassionate face. He came right up to her and helped her stand, along with Remy.

"She is going to recover fully," he said right away. "We're going to make sure she has the best physical help, and the best psychological help. My colleague, Dr. Covert, practices in New York City. He is the best in the field, specializing in post-traumatic psychological reconstruction. I just got off the phone with him, and he has agreed to take in Keisha free of charge. She will have all the help she needs."

Dr. Kaplan smiled. "Come with me, my dear. She's still sedated. I know you've been waiting a long time to see her."

Remy followed along behind, continuing her silent prayers.

The semi-private room was small and spartan. A long, blue dotted cloth divider hung from a ceiling runner, forming an incomplete separation from the other youthful patient, who seemed to be sleeping quietly. Each section of the room had a vinyl gray chair and a high table near the bed. Lailani sat down softly on the bed and bent forward to kiss her sleeping niece on her bandaged forehead.

Remy moved quietly to the small chair and lowered herself into it slowly as she kept her eyes on Keisha.

Together they started a vigil.

After two hours, Remy stood and stretched. Lailani was asleep at the foot of the bed, making just a small incursion into her niece's space. Remy walked quietly to the hallway and down the corridor to the small elevator. She wanted to find a gift at the first-floor lobby shop. It needed to be something bright and cheerful, she thought, a gift that would bring some joy to Keisha when she woke up.

Let her gaze on something bright and hopeful.

The small shop had a surprising assortment of items, including stuffed dolls, small jewelry pieces, and the usual assortment of flowers and boxed candy. It also had a full wall of electronic items. One brightly colored camera caught her eye. It had a silver-plated chain that allowed it to be hung around the neck, like a locket. Best of all, the camera captured digital images that could be uploaded to a computer. Remy knew that Keisha would love the camera. The product tag on the camera was cheerful.

"Photograph the World and Make it Your Party!"

This was perfect, she thought. That child always wanted to go and see things she learned about in school. Now she could take her own photos.

As she walked to the front counter to pay, a rolling wave of sadness washed over her. She covered her face with her hand as the tears spilled down between her fingers. The young woman at the counter took her money and made change efficiently, placing the camera in a small gift bag. She saw tears like Remy's every day.

Chapter Twenty-Nine
Hunt for Keisha

It hadn't taken the parents in Arbor Hill long to organize the search after Keisha's teammates alerted some of them that she had vanished. The effort was organized and underway well before the Albany police appeared on the scene.

Looking in from the outside, no one would have predicted such a response. Arbor Hill looked like a typical rundown neighborhood, devoid of resources and largely devoid of spirit. According to the most recent census, 5 percent of the city's population of 120,000 people lived in the area. While 29 percent of Albany's population was black, African Americans represented 77 percent of the Arbor Hill population. Median household income was half that of the city at large, and almost 45 percent of the residents were below the poverty level.

Driving down the surprisingly wide major thoroughfares, the most prominent features were the number of closed business or properties long in need of basic repair and upkeep. But there were also churches, neighborhood centers, and cultural institutions that while less visible than the blight, formed a partially hidden backbone in the community. And there were individuals of merit who lived there and who cared.

Bill Truit was one. He was born and raised in Arbor Hill. He enlisted in the Army at 17, slightly exaggerating his age. From Camp Lejeune to Vietnam, Bill had seen his share of conflict and had taken his dose of the rest of the world. But in the end, he came back home. He came back to scattered family, nieces, nephews, and most of all to his childhood sweetheart, Sadie. They had two children, grown now and doing pretty good on their own downstate in the big city. Turns out, he would always say to anyone listening, that coming back home was the second-best move of his life, after getting out for a good stretch of time in the first place.

He happened to be sitting around outdoors playing bid whist with his other retired buddies on a well-worn table on the side of the Turner engine block repair building. On this day, his leadership qualities would place him in the hero's circle, along with many others in the neighborhood.

He first noticed a large group of parents talking excitedly over on the south side of Sheridan Avenue, but he paid little attention. As he looked up once more from his bid whist hand, something didn't seem right to him. Then he saw it—the unusual aspect was the ring of children that surrounded the parents. Bill knew from observation that the children always congregated and played their games together, and the parents watched them from various houses and porches along the route. It had been the same even back when his young ones were ripping and racing around the streets and alleys.

Bill told his buddies that something important was happening over across the street. He put down his hand and said he was going to mosey over to the commotion and reconnoiter. Long after the episode was ended, folks would joke with Bill that if he'd had a good bid whist hand on that occasion, he would never have poked his head into what was going on. Usually Bill just smiled at the joke, but sometimes he would nod his head and admit they were probably right.

As he approached the crowd, Shirley Holmes and old Gert Williams were shouting at two children that were part of the circle of kids around the grownups. Another woman that Bill recognized from the neighborhood, but didn't know personally, was near the center of the crowd. She seemed to be really shaken up, and she was crying in the arms of another woman.

As he got closer, he saw Shirley grab a youngster tightly by the shoulders. Bill could now make out some of what she was saying, something about *where did you see her last?*

The traumatized youngster was half in tears and was trying to describe the alley her team had run down at the beginning of the game. Half of the other kids were shaking their heads in disagreement, and others were talking over each other as the child nervously tried to tell Shirley everything she could remember. It was pure confusion.

He could now see from his close vantage point that Shirley was also traumatized by what was happening. Putting the fragments of conversation together, he surmised that one of the children, a girl child, had gone missing during the game.

That's when Bill Truit spoke up. He used his loud basso voice that had served him well as an Army sergeant to get the complete attention of his platoon.

"Folks, gather round here, gather round. Now, I'm gonna get right to the point, because we don't have a second to waste. What we do in the next couple of minutes is gonna save this here young girl, or what we do is gonna end up allowing her to get hurt."

Everyone turned to him and the whole crowd, including the children, hushed up.

"I want half the adults on this side of me, and the other half over there by Shirley."

"Now, I want half of the kids that were on the same team over there with Shirley, and I want the other half that were on the chase team here with me."

They responded quickly to his directions. He wasn't surprised, because he recognized right off that there was what they used to call in the Army a *leadership vacuum*. He had filled that vacuum with his voice and directions.

He continued to fill it.

"Here's what we need to do, and do thoroughly and quickly. Let's return to the start area of the game. I want the first team with Shirley to cover their route, and each child to point out every hiding place they used or that they saw someone else use. There should be an adult with each group of children to search and look for clues."

Bill called over his old Army buddies and assigned them to each search team to add additional support.

"You kids here with me need to point out the areas that you searched, even if you didn't capture anyone. I'm counting on you adults to ask questions about everything you hear. If we do this right," Bill said, looking into as many eyes as he could single out, "we gonna find that little girl. Now, let's go!"

When the Albany police finally responded to the call, they approached Remy after her neighbors pointed to her. She was halfway up the alley with her team, following the trail that the chase group of children had taken during the game. The police caught up with her and began their questioning. Remy was still distraught, but she responded to as many questions as she could. Halfway through the interrogation, Bill came trudging back, half out of breath. He bent over at the waist, drawing in air. Then he looked at the lead police officer and recognized the man's rank from his insignias. He looked him in the eye and spoke with precision.

"Lieutenant, one of our two search teams has isolated the last known location of the victim. Two witnesses confirmed that location, and the victim was not seen after that. We have identified a possible access point into a building basement. Please follow me."

The officers responded immediately to the clipped cadence and exactness of Bill's description. They all moved out and followed Bill back up the alley. One of the officers was shouting into his hand-held radio as he ran behind the others.

Within minutes, the neighborhood was overrun with what appeared to be a military assault. Startled residents who were unaware of a missing child feared the worst and expected live ammunition to rip through their thin walls. Two assault helicopters swept low and loudly up the alley, following the officers' path. They banked up suddenly and assumed an ominous circular pattern over the house that was the target of the assault. Squad cars screeched up the streets and alleyways, leaving a thick, acrid odor of burned carbon. From the southeast, a heavy, ominous-looking dull black van entered the alleyway and quickly accelerated forward. The words SWAT were written on each side in large white block letters. Affixed to the oval-shaped nose of the van was a battering, ram six feet high and eight feet across. Concealed gun turrets were embedded in the sides of the van, sheltering sharpshooters.

Bill watched the final phases of the assault from the porch of a nearby abandoned house. He admired the tactics used so far and hoped they were not too late to save the little girl. He could see that the home where Granny lived with her special needs grandson James was completely surrounded and sealed off.

But many other residents of Arbor Hill felt great apprehension at the intrusive police presence. They recalled the stories told by uncles, and parents, and others who had been caught up in such assaults in the past. Damage was not always confined to the bad guys. So they hunkered down, not fully comfortable with the next moves by the police.

The SWAT team was using a bullhorn affixed to the van to warn occupants on the inside of the rundown house to exit and surrender with their hands above their heads. Other police units ringed the small house, aiming all weapons.

Bill made sure earlier to tell them how many occupants there were inside the home. But neither Granny nor James responded to the bullhorn. Then he realized that he had forgotten to mention Granny might be napping, and may have taken her hearing aid out. He started to run down the porch steps, but he was too late.

He heard the *pop-pop* sound of tear gas canisters being launched into the building, and then the thudding hollow noise of suppression devices fired from several perimeter locations. He knew they were designed to shock, confuse, and disorientate. As the wave of projectiles nested into the house, they shattered and collapsed the glass in every window. Within no time, a spark from a stun device ignited in the living room and a fire began to rage, rapidly consuming the thin drawn curtains on the front windows.

Waiting fire trucks were called in.

Chapter Thirty
All Hands On Deck

The shrill ringing of the house phone yanked Brett from his deep sleep, and he glanced at the clock as he reached over for it. It was 4:45 in the morning.

The crisp nasal voice of Walter Kleine, the chairman's right-hand man, sounded in the receiver.

"Brett, it's Walter. There's been a sharp run-up in Taurus stock this morning on the Asian and European markets. Volume is way over historical norms. Premarket activity in the U.S. is also off the charts. Sam is certain it means big trouble. He activated the Four Square defense plan at 4:30 this morning. He wants you and your top lieutenants at the 57th floor boardroom at 7:00 A.M. By the way, don't worry, you won't be the only ones at the meeting."

Walter clicked off without waiting for him to reply. Brett remembered the long series of high-level executive meetings years ago that led to the defensive plan, later named Four Square. The name symbolized the strategic and tactical approach the company would use with key stakeholders if ever subjected to attack—profits, price, positioning and people. He always wondered back then why the people component came last.

Being in the office for a 7:00 meeting was the easiest part of it. He arrived every morning at 6:00. That allowed him ample time before the pace picked up to take care of discrete business matters and correspondence. It also gave him time to scour the international news feeds that were very important to the large Taurus overseas businesses. No longer were public relations and investor relations U.S.-centric pursuits. That was one of the innovations he had brought with him to Taurus. The outside impression of the company before his arrival was of one that only paid attention to what happened and what was said in New York, Chicago, and Los Angeles.

Capitalizing on the wee hours of the day was a trick he learned in high school, when it became clear that extra time was needed to finish his homework. Arriving home from sports and activities at five in the afternoon left inadequate time to complete his usual three-hour load, particularly with his mother and father enforcing the house rule that eight-thirty meant time to prepare for bed. The solution was painful at first, up at 5:00 A.M. But it soon became routine. That was how he was first introduced to the farm reports and pork belly auctions that populated the early morning airwaves. Those reports were also a source of humor for him with his classmates when he joked around about the latest farm topic of the day, or the high price of manure fertilizer in South Dakota.

He walked to the shower, still thinking about the implications of Walter's call.

The Taurus conference room occupied the entire 57th floor. Views from its tinted twenty-foot windows looked over the Hudson River, and the widening sprawl of New Jersey to the west. The East River, Brooklyn and Queens were displayed to the horizon on the opposite side. To the south lay shimmering New York Harbor, the Statute of Liberty, and the high-arching Verrazano Narrows Bridge. Winding north was the widening Hudson River, flanked on opposite banks by the Henry Hudson and Palisades Parkways. Between them was the gleaming double-decker expanse of the George Washington Bridge, an engineering marvel. This was the ultimate New York City power view that only disciplined and hardened corporate soldiers could sit in front of without taking a moment to glance at the beauty beyond the glass. No one at this meeting looked out of the windows.

Seated at the head of the sixty-foot white marble table that spanned the center of the enormous room was Samuel Patrick Winston, Chairman of the Board and Chief Executive Officer. Sam was the longest-serving Fortune 500 CEO in the country. Sustained shareholder growth had been his mantra over his twenty-five year tenure at the helm of Taurus. And Sam had delivered, year in and year out. For that he was paid a princely sum.

He was cool, calm, and composed in the center of the storm. The crisp white shirt with red tie, dark blue suit, and black spit-shined shoes signaled control and stability to the assembled management team. His jacket with white pocket square was draped on his chair behind him. Every other executive sitting at the big table studiously copied that habit. Surrounding them in an oval circle were two elevated rings of white leather chairs. Each one of them would soon be filled. All attendees within the room had their own hardwired PC screen, translation services, and speakerphones for hearing and, on rare occasions, talking.

Brett had earned his seat at the big table a few years ago. He was now the up-and-coming wonder kid who headed up the global public and investor relation functions. His organization was 1,500 people strong. Though he was the youngest executive on the top team, even the old veterans agreed that Sam had made a wise choice five years ago.

Winning his seat at the big table was not an easy battle. It did not occur without hand-to-hand combat in classic big corporation style. Among other fights, he had to go up against a well-pedigreed EVP that rumor said was the heir apparent to Sam at the time. The famous internal story about him, and the one that laid the foundation for his later advancement, was his clash with that senior executive who outranked him by three rungs on the ladder. To this day, he easily remembered his opponent's name: Stephen McInerney III.

He found out on that day several years ago that McInerney had raked two of his directors over the coals at a meeting involving public releases for a new Taurus product offering. McInerney was from the school that believed a few smacks across the chops was a far better motivator than professional coaching. He also believed that he was a much better writer than Brett's well-chosen whiz kids. Rumor around the building had it that he was ex-CIA. His imposing six-foot-four height and solid rugby build came with a squinting, taciturn face and short-cropped reddish hair. It was also rumored that he kept a service revolver in his top right desk drawer. Some folks actually feared him.

At the end of his contentious meeting with Brett's staffers, he imperiously dismissed them and their work product, but not before setting up a subsequent meeting in his office. He commanded that they take their poor drafts and incorporate all of his red-lined comments. As the staffers later reviewed the tense forty-five minute meeting with him, it seemed to Brett that the only thing McInerney failed to do was boot his team in their butts on their way out of his office.

He became part of Taurus corporate folklore when he personally cancelled the follow-up meeting. He then called McInerney's executive assistant and scheduled a face-to-face with her boss. After sitting down in his office, he calmly explained why his staff would not be appearing at any future meetings. He went on to admonish that no one on his team should ever be subjected to that kind of personal abuse in the future.

Brett admitted later that his palms were clammy during the confrontation, and that he had a thin sheen of sweat below his white shirt, especially when McInerney reached into his top right desk drawer halfway through the confrontation. He always smiled when telling the story, expressing his sincere relief at the time that McInerney was digging for a tissue, and not for the revolver.

Sam's personal staff hovering around his shoulders took their places in the outer leather chairs directly behind him. Sam looked at his watch, cleared his throat, and kicked off the meeting. In his usual self-deprecatory style, he thanked everyone present for clearing their busy schedules to meet him at such an early hour. The Senior VP of Finance, Sam's most trusted advisor, joked out loud that if he'd been aware that attendance was optional, he might not have gotten out of bed so early. That humor, typical of Taurus senior leaders, relaxed everyone in the room and set the tone for a productive session.

Brett noticed that most of the meeting time was taken over by the investment bankers. In the background and hardly speaking were the valuable product line EVPs, who delivered profit for the company year in and year out.

That's extremely odd.

The bankers' message was clear and very disconcerting. They were certain that within a day or so, the identity of the raider would be revealed under SEC rules. The raider had the ability to drive the Taurus share price well above current multiples, and the inflated price would be a very difficult bogey for Taurus management to equal. Drastic measures would have to be executed by management to deliver a share price in the target range of what the raider would dangle before everyone.

The phrase *drastic measures* seemed to imprint itself in Brett's consciousness as the meeting continued.

He met later that evening for an off-site dinner with his own senior management team. His goal was to communicate the messages from the chairman's meeting that morning.

All senior executives in the company were doing the same thing, either at dinners, in conference rooms, or by teleconference. They all delivered the same key talking points. Brett knew them well, since his public relations team had captured them at the morning meeting, refined them, submitted them to the chairman, HR and legal for editing, and pushed out the final version within two hours after the close of the 7:00 A.M. meeting. The package contained Q&A's, strategic themes, do's and don'ts, and multiple disclaimers folded in by HR and legal. This so-called playbook was forty pages long, and all executives were required to commit the broad outlines to memory and deliver the messages without notes.

He chose a small Italian restaurant on the Upper East Side for the dinner with his eleven direct reports. Many of them had to miss family events to be there.

When he first looked around the table in the cozy space of the private dining room, he momentarily imagined seeing vivid red X's across the faces of half his team. The phrase *drastic measures* once again echoed in his mind. But he recovered his composure quickly and started.

After opening remarks that closely tracked messages in the playbook, he opened the meeting up for questions. They all paused for a moment while the waiters poured more water or wine and served plates. After the wait staff left and closed the dining room doors, they resumed.

Marge Schnidier, one of his VPs, was relatively new. She blurted out a question that must have been on everyone's mind, just below the surface.

"Brett, how long before each of us here will be informed when the axe is going to fall?"

She didn't expect a truthful answer, but she simply had to ask the question, because the stress was tearing her apart and eroding her interaction with her husband. He also worked for Taurus. They stood to potentially lose both incomes.

He looked at Marge, and then he looked around the table, remembering the many campaigns that he and this team had successfully accomplished together. He decided at that moment to ignore the wordy non-answer that was outlined in the playbook, and tell them the truth.

"My best advice to each and every one of you here, and the best advice I can give you as you make plans to protect your family, is to begin operating tomorrow as if the axe had already fallen."

No one asked a follow-up question about that advice. They were all pretty sharp, experienced folks, and the message was now very clear. Brett had always been a straight shooter with them, so they had no reason to question his motives now.

After what turned into a long moment of awkward and unusual silence for this group, Jim McShefferty, the VP in charge of shareholder communication, cleared his throat and spoke up.

"Thanks for sharing that. It was refreshing. We all know that everywhere around the office after the big meeting this morning, truth seems to have taken a permanent back seat to spin, or maybe it took a leave of absence."

Most of the group chuckled at Jim's remark, but some were lost in thought, already planning their next moves for tomorrow and the day after. Jim's comment, though, seemed to open the floodgates around the table. Together with the good Italian wine, a number of very frank assessments were offered up about the executive leadership team. Brett felt no need at this point to act as the defender of his colleagues. Most of the opinions at the table were spot-on. A few others were misguided or just wrong.

"Look, Brett," said Karen Lambert, who directed investor communications, "the thing that gets under my skin is not the fact that Taurus is involved in a nasty takeover fight, one that it will likely lose. That's just business. It's what we signed up for."

She took a long sip of wine before continuing.

"What irks me is the amount of sheer propaganda that's already being cranked out from the highest levels of the corporation. I'm going to be required to meet with my team and give them the same half-truth messages. And you know what, nobody really believes it! It's almost as if we were all naïve children, and if we get fed the right amount of milk and cookies, we'll keep on putting in the seventy-hour work weeks."

She wanted to continue, but she pulled back because she was unsure whether her remarks would be reported later to executive management by one of her ambitious colleagues around the dinner table. Trust was another victim of the takeover battle.

Brett knew that he had to respond, if only to pull the meeting out of the nosedive it was in. "Let me share a story with you," he said rather loudly, pausing to get everyone's full attention.

"Twelve years ago, I was a director working in the real estate investment group at Baum Development Systems in Palo Alto. This was my first job after business school, and I had a couple of good annual reviews under my belt. I was also fortunate very early on in my tenure to help the company land a significant development deal. So I was a bit of a golden boy, despite my dark hair and complexion."

That got a chuckle out of everyone.

"Along with the other MBA's that started with me at the company, I felt pretty good about the future. Truth is, I loved it there. I fit in well with the people and the culture, and the Palo Alto area was a gem." He paused and sipped his water.

"But in my second year, the founder of the company grew disenchanted with the increasing amount of oversight and restrictions that resulted from his earlier decision to go public. That decision had made him several hundred million dollars. But I suppose you get accustomed to that kind of money after a while, and you get restless, as he did."

"After deciding to go private, he put together the plan to get there. We found out later that the plan had actually been shaping up for more than three years before the announcement. So in fact, I was recruited into a company where the owner knew that what I would face down the road would be radically different from the company I agreed to join. Hmm... corporate full disclosure?" he asked. "Should we ever count on that? I'll bet he and others could give us a long list for why depending on that would be naïve."

He could see the sobering impact that his story was having on his team. But he believed that the learning would be valuable for them as they kept trying to climb the corporate ladder, most likely somewhere else.

He continued his tale.

"The road map back to private company nirvana for my boss required a 40 percent cut in the work force, including me and all of the MBA folks. Despite my reviews, promotions, and track record, I found myself dealing with HR mavens who seemed to suddenly want to hang a lot of poor performance-related issues around my neck. Old complaints and once minor forgotten facts were dredged up to become important, unresolved matters. In their view, and remember that HR types are only the representatives of management that lurks behind the curtain, I was only a marginal performer. I almost wanted to ask them why the hell was I recruited and hired in the first place."

"Did I mention that when they first hired me, the CEO waived the interview and application process? Anyway, for a while I bought the stuff they were selling. If they spin it right, sometimes they get you to question whether you actually got up on the correct side of the bed that morning."

This got quite a few laughs and nods of affirmation from around the table. A few of them had already been approached by the drones, who were busily establishing how these highly recruited members of his team had grown incompetent, almost overnight.

"I came away from that company with three concrete lessons and a whole lot of hurt. The hurt came from the disruption and separation from colleagues and friends, as well as the lifestyle that I liked. Gradually that hurt went away. But the lessons remained, and they are three that apply to most every business, large or small. One, never grow complacent, and never believe that the waters will remain calm. Keep in touch with your external network. Two, keep your skills sharp and continue to improve in your craft. That's what each of you has done, and what has made our department award-winning and great. And three, despite the dislocation that will occur, believe that you will land in a better place down the road."

He looked at his team around the table with an expression of gratitude for their hard work and sacrifice. Making sure that everyone had a glass, he raised his own.

"I would like to propose a toast to each of you for your award-winning contribution to the company, and to me. To those of *us* who will be moving on, by choice or by direction, I toast to that better place, where we will continue to flourish."

Chapter Thirty-One
Crossing the Line

Melinda stepped down from the long black Benz, showing off her legs as the door was held open. She winked at Cy, who had assumed the role of her servile driver, while she was the young and classy dame who would soon light up the staid private rooms of the Yale Club.

This was the fabled Upper East Side haunt of the rich and famous, including Carleton Smith, a graduate and multimillion-dollar benefactor to the university. The exclusive Club offered its alumnae a respite from the dusty streets of Manhattan, and the privileged company of similarly situated and successful fellow graduates. Though only a stone's throw from the masses that streamed past the fifteen-foot high soundproof windows, those tucked safely inside the elegant brownstone were cocooned together in a world of understated comfort.

Because she had been pre-cleared and pre-announced to arrive at this hour, the hulking doorman recognized her image immediately from his daily security photos and swiftly allowed her access to the inner sanctum. Melinda smiled slightly while she breathed in the crisp, clean smell of old money that suffused the hallway inside the massive mahogany doors. That she was not the graduate whose identity she had borrowed was never raised.

Before her in large, stuffed gothic chairs around the great hall sat a motley collection of near octogenarians—all white males, all eager to point out the smallest indiscretion or infraction to any new visitor. Each of them, of course, remembered when women were not even allowed to enter the front door of the Club. Yet ostensibly they seemed busy reading and rereading their collection of crumpled newspapers in the muted light of green-shaded bankers lamps adorning each side table.

Any conversation in the great hall occurred in muted tones, as if speaking in a normal voice might disturb the ancient bones or violate some hallowed rule from the past. Even the tuxedo-clad butlers floated silently around, bending deeply at the waist to take drink or food orders without causing patrons to speak above a whisper.

All of this superfluity was precisely as Chauncey had described in his notes and diagrams. Because of that, she was perfectly at ease and glided through the halls of power with studied indifference to her surroundings. In an instant she was greeted by the lean, silver-haired day shift host, who welcomed her to the Club—in hushed tones, of course. He asked solicitously how she had fared through the brutal Manhattan traffic.

Melinda's eyes sparkled as she resumed her role-play and cooed, "Thank you so much for asking, Gerald. It was absolutely dreadful." Then, through her most lovely smile, she added, "But all is well now that I am here."

"Of course, my dear, we forever remain your oasis from the storm. Allow me to show you to our facilities, so that you may freshen up from the journey."

Chauncey's meticulous briefings allowed her to display the insouciance needed to play the part of the carefree, wealthy success story. Due to her own inadequate pedigree, she'd completely missed the highbrow aspect of life during her undergraduate education and later business career, because she was never invited into the right sororities. But a select group of her classmates had experienced these upper echelon trappings throughout college and even before, some starting within the wall of their family mansions. She had learned a long time ago that being middle-class and smart was no ticket to the rarified ambiance that now surrounded her.

But on the inside, behind the mask, her heart palpitations were increasing as the clock moved closer to 8:00 P.M., when Carleton Smith would arrive at the Club for his martini with almost military precision.

Inside the large marble-walled powder room, Melinda turned to a full-length expanse of mirrors and inspected her goods, which were carefully staged to ensnare him. To take no chances with any details, Chauncey accompanied her on the shopping mission to Bergdoff's, signing off on the black A-line dress, white silk blouse, and four-inch pointed French heels. They showcased her slender thighs and rounded calf muscles when she pressed on her toes. According to Chauncey, accessories had to be expensive, yet simple. The diamond studs and elegantly small diamond-crusted watch loosely draping her wrist accomplished that. Her neck was deliberately unadorned above the plunging neckline, but her bosom rested prominently beneath a black silk bodice, providing the tasteful and magnetic attraction that would capture his father's attention.

Her auburn hair was piled high on her head, Hepburn style. She twirled around before the mirror like a princess in anticipation of ensnaring him. After all, he was standing between her and a multi-million-dollar payday.

Meanwhile, back among the working stiffs, Cy nudged the big black limo into the back half of the private Club parking lot. Six spaces, ahead an area was outlined with four red cones. This was the space always used by Carleton Smith's driver, whose limo with its heavy smoked windows on all sides was identical to the one driven by Cy.

Thirty minutes after Carleton stepped into the Club, he was sending the wait staff over to her table. As she nodded courteously in his direction, she ordered a martini made in the classic style, but without the olives. He knew it was time to close in on his prey, and he approached her with his well-practiced grace and verve. They were a couple in no time.

After learning that she occupied a gorgeous suite at The Pierre whenever she was in the city on business, he suggested that they retire there, if for no other reason than to learn more about each other. That's when she used her most alluring giggle, the one Chauncey pegged as his father's primary weakness, and purred into his ear that learning more about him would be a marvelous idea. Needing no further encouragement, he reached into his pocket for a small, flat control fob. Without removing it, he pressed the panel, sending three one-second signals to his driver—meaning that he was ready to be picked up at the front of the Club in 15 minutes.

But Chauncey had reprogrammed his father's pager, and with the small electronic rerouter Melinda had strapped to her inside thigh, the signals went directly to Cy and bypassed Smith's driver, who continued to snooze in the rear seat.

Cy slowly pulled the big car out of the parking lot and around to the front of the Club. The efficient staff recognized the limo and directed it to a position at curbside, immediately in front of the private exit doors and the waiting happy couple.

Chapter Thirty-Two
New York City

Keisha held her aunt's hand as they boarded the regional jet from Albany to Westchester Airport. From there it would be a short thirty-minute ride to the hospital. Dr. Covert's assistant told her when she confirmed the arrival time that a sedan service would be waiting for them when they exited the gate. They were to look for the driver holding a sign with their names written on it.

After they were seated, she looked over at her niece and lifted the armrest so that she could be closer. As a nurse, she knew the healing power that simple human touch possessed, and she had been giving her plenty of hugs and caresses. She smiled and asked her how she was feeling. Keisha looked back at her with that all-too-familiar blank stare.

"I'm okay, Aunty."

She knew that it was the evidence of the trauma left over from the assault. Her niece was once so bubbly and optimistic. But now that spirit was stolen away. In the four weeks since the attack, the blunt physical wounds were almost completely healed. Soreness, swelling, and back strain had been largely alleviated by the therapeutic sessions conducted every weekday by her colleague, who ran the Physical Healing Institute. That kind woman had reduced the cost of the therapy so that almost all of it was covered by her health insurance. That had been a huge savings.

But Keisha's spirit was broken, and despite her initial reluctance to follow up with Dr. Kaplan's offer, she knew that intense work on the mind and spirit was the only way to find her niece again. But she was worried about leaving her alone at the hospital in New York City and only seeing her on weekends. She decided that leaving her unprotected for five days of the week was not an option.

In the end, she took a two-month leave of absence, so that she would be right there with her for every day of the rehabilitation process. Dr. Covert had been very pleased to hear that, and he promised to fully incorporate her into his tailored recovery program. But the hard reality was that the leave of absence would completely exhaust her savings. When she went back to work, they would be living from paycheck to paycheck, with no financial cushion.

She leaned back against her seat and tried not to worry about it as the small plane taxied out to the runway. She saw Keisha tightly close her eyes, shutting out the entire world as she did so. She was seeking her safe place and walling herself away from all intruders.

As the plane picked up speed and climbed out, she quietly thanked the Lord once again that the assault was perpetrated by a man who had no idea how to carry it out. While his semen was found on Keisha's clothes and on her legs, he didn't penetrate her, either out of ignorance or some unknown restraint. When the police crashed into the basement, they found him next to Keisha's unconscious body in a spoon-like position behind her. As they dragged him to his feet and shackled him, he started smiling and shouting with joy that he was playing the game. Lailani tried to stifle the bitter thought with prayer, but she could not—she hoped he played whatever game he had in his sick, twisted mind behind bars for the rest of his life.

"You know, Keisha," she said energetically as she turned to her. "While we're in the big city, we should do some sightseeing." She touched her niece's shoulder and smoothed out a wrinkle in her sweater.

"I know that you'll want to take it slow," she continued, "but there are a few sights that are really worth seeing. When I was your age, I took a trip into New York with my dad. It was such fun."

Keisha looked up at her aunt. She was grateful for the love and support through all the years, and especially now. She squeezed her aunt's hand in both of hers.

"Aunty Lai, I read all about New York City in my social studies class. I wouldn't mind seeing some of the places that we learned about. Did you know there's a ferry that takes cars and big busses on it, and that takes people over to an island that's part of New York?"

"That's the Staten Island Ferry, darling, and guess what? It's only a quarter to ride it!"

Keisha's eyes lit up at the bargain that represented. She realized that even with her small savings account, she could still take a whole lot of rides on it.

Lailani pressed forward, hoping that sightseeing might hold a small key to rekindling some of the sparkle that had been stolen.

"You know. I just remembered that they have a boat cruise that goes around the entire island of Manhattan. We took it when I was small. I believe it's called the Circle Line. You could take pictures around the whole of Manhattan and put a photo album disc together."

Keisha's eyes lit up again at the thought of using her new camera that Aunt Remy gave her for the first time.

"Aunty, we could also go all the way to the top of the Empire State Building and take pictures from there!"

She promised that would be the first stop.

Chapter Thirty-Three
Four Square

This was the first one-on-one meeting with Sam that Brett had been able to arrange in the five weeks since the attack on Taurus. His goal was to brief him on the current public and investor relations pulse arising from of the recent sweetened offer by Carleton Smith. That offer had cast a pall over the company, as it far exceeded the Board's recently reworked valuation and strategic plan to deliver greater shareholder value.

It was apparent when he saw Sam up close that the mental and physical strain of successive 18-hour days had taken a huge toll. He seemed to have aged another ten years. And why not, given the intensity of recent weeks. There were the endless stream of board meetings, late-night conference calls, special board committee meetings, and duplicated investment banker meetings. One investment bank had been hired to shadow and check the honesty of the other investment bank. The bankers alone had racked up a $50 million tab so far. Then there were the usual staff meetings, operational meetings, financial reporting meetings, and the list went on. Sam had to prepare for them all, attend, and then follow up on the details.

But he tried to keep up a good front from behind dark-etched, tired eyes. As Sam gestured to him to have a seat, a little of the old twinkle returned, and he poked some fun. "We don't have to have this meeting sitting down, you know, Brett. It's all Kabuki theater anyway, and when I was last in Japan, they seemed to stand through most parts of the play."

They laughed at that, but he wondered whether Sam was signaling him that despite their friendship, he wouldn't be able to speak his mind and lay his cards on the table. The cards that everyone in the company wanted to see were the ones that specified the restructuring plan and the number of heads that would be cut. Rumors circulated every day. The current number was a 35 percent headcount reduction: 45,000 jobs.

"So," Sam asked, getting right to the point in his usual direct style, "how are we faring in the court of shareholder and public opinion, Brett? How can we be more effective in getting our message out?"

He responded candidly.

"As you well know, Sam, our tracking numbers have been trending down for three weeks. The equity of our great brands, the steady profits that you and the operational team delivered year after year, have given us no traction. Short-term gain carries a huge weight with all of our key investor constituents. We're also losing that PR battle with the rest of our stakeholders, because our messages are muddled. And with my hands tied by the lawyers and HR, there's nothing I can do to reverse the slide."

Sam leaned back in his old brown leather chair that creaked beneath his weight. Everybody knew that he shipped that chair to Taurus decades ago. It was his lucky chair, the one he owned when was first elevated to CEO at Regional CP, Inc., a company that was later bought out by Taurus in a friendly deal.

"What do you need me to do with legal and HR to give you some running room?"

The answer to that question was exactly why he had requested this meeting, and he had a succinct answer.

"Sam, I need to be able to build a story around the continued viability and presence of Taurus in the marketplace. This will assuage our trade customers and a good chunk of our shareholders, who care about consistent returns and continuity."

Then he added his most important need.

"I also need to strangle the internal rumors about massive layoffs and restructuring. They resonate well beyond our corporate walls and deflate confidence in the permanence of our management team."

Sam looked quietly at him, and then turned away to gaze out over the Midtown skyline. He knew exactly what Brett was looking for. It was the same thing that he had been looking for years ago when he interviewed him as one of three finalists for his first executive position at the company. He was looking for the truth, and a company with a mission he could believe in. It was a fundamental component that allowed him to work the long hours demanded by the business. What had impressed him about Brett back then during the interview was the manner in which he was the ultimate straight-shooter. When he asked him the standard question *why would Taurus be better off hiring you,* his response was telling, and it foreshadowed how he would conduct himself in the executive role. He still remembered almost to the word that short, seemingly unpracticed reply to his question.

Mr. Winston, I really don't know if Taurus would be better off hiring me versus one of the other two finalists. That is, respectfully, your decision. What I can tell you is that I am ready to assume the position, that I am ready to embrace the role, and that my career so far has prepared me to be successful.

Later, that interview had turned into more of a relaxed conversation between them. The seasoned CEO and the young, upcoming executive got to know each other personally. That sealed it for Sam, and he signaled his choice to the department head.

How time zips by. Where have the years gone?

When he turned back to Brett, he came as close to the truth as he possibly could under the circumstances. He spoke in a quiet tone.

"Brett, the running room that you need, those are exactly the stories that we *cannot* circulate now, because our credibility would be completely destroyed on the street. Legal and HR have it right. Please follow their lead."

Brett didn't need to wait for Sam to end the meeting. He now clearly knew what the future held for his team, and for much of Taurus. He stood, politely thanked Sam for lending an ear, and walked out of his office.

When he got back to his own space, Velma stopped him and mentioned that Zena had called again. He was certain that Velma's consummate professionalism allowed her to omit that Zena was highly agitated on the call. Why wouldn't she be? Two weeks ago, he'd rented a hotel room across the street from Taurus, as had most of the senior executive team, including Sam. He had moved away from her and moved in with the company.

And he hadn't had an intimate moment with her in the past three weeks. Other than a couple of lunch meetings and the occasional telephone call, they were growing apart. He could see his personal life and his business life spinning away down the drain as he watched helplessly.

He left Velma's station and walked into his spacious office. His adjoining conference room alone was bigger than four cubicles, the standard workstations used in the open seating plan on all floors. His office was twice that size. As he walked to his desk, he ruefully thought that when the downsizing started in earnest and the barbarians came over the walls, his first offer would be the conference room and his fallback would be to slice his office in half. But he knew that was fantasy. He would not be part of the future, at least not here.

Once seated, he saw that Velma as usual had neatly organized the calls he missed. Fifteen messages in all, segmented by the corporate rank of the caller. Each of them was marked urgent or important.

He folded Zena's message in half and placed it in his shirt pocket. When he called her back in three hours, her answering service received the call. He knew the snub was deliberate.

Zena saw his number come in on her caller ID and almost answered on the last ring. But she was just too steamed that she had been treated like everybody else since this takeover business started.

And Ms. Zena Melody Jensen believed that she was far removed from anybody else. Her father and his father were graduates of Meharry Medical School. Her family lineage on both sides had migrated to Canada in the late 1680s and had produced a long line of successful professional and business people. This was well before emancipation of the slaves in the U.S., and well before liberalization in the North spurred on by the abolitionist movement. In private circles, the family would use the term *freeborn blacks* as a badge of honor, and to reinforce their distinction from the African Americans who were the progeny of slavery. Zena was never fully convinced by the stories, but at every family gathering, after a drink or two, one aunt or the other would sit back and wax poetic about the unique Jensen family lineage.

One of those same aunts pulled her aside at last year's reunion and discretely asked her if she was really serious about *that* Brett who had accompanied her. The aunt seemed completely unimpressed that he was an executive of a Fortune company. She was more concerned that she'd never heard of his family and was unaware of his genealogy.

After looking over her own shoulder, that aunt also quietly voiced her concern that his darker color might cause potential offspring to dilute the Jensen color line. Or more accurately, thought Zena to herself back then, it might add color to the Jensen family line. She didn't see this color thing, or his family history thing, as an issue at all. Putting her arm around her frail aunt, she assured her that she was a long way from deciding who her husband would be, and that she would base that decision on how good a man he was. Her aunt smiled, but remained worried nonetheless as she wandered back to the front porch with Zena's help for more wine and storytelling.

This current extended separation from him was especially hard on her when they seemed to have grown so close after his sailing injuries. She had taken out all the stops back then, virtually redesigning his duplex apartment with the help of a friend of the family who was an interior designer. In his weakened condition, he was unable to put any breaks on her natural tendency to go over the top. A lifetime of privilege had conditioned her to spend money like it was water. She still remembered the disbelieving look on his face when she told him that her cotillion coming out party had cost her father one hundred thousand dollars. He was stunned that such a sum would be spent on a sixteen-year-old.

What, she'd asked him with her radiant smile, did you expect me to come out on the cheap?

After he regained his strength, she noticed that he was gradually pulling back, both from her and from his upscale life style that she loved. He kept talking about simplifying his life, and not filling it up with expensive things and shallow people. She was shocked when he told her that his boat broker was managing the sale of Onset, which had been shipped back to the States and repaired in Marblehead. Whatever the simple life meant to him, it was profoundly troubling to her.

They were in many respects a most unlikely pair, and she was aware enough to realize that. They were about as opposite a couple as you might come across. But they were also the classic case cited for the old saw, *opposites attract.* As African American royalty, her view of life and its possibilities was unbounded, because through the generations that was exactly what her family had accomplished. He was only beginning the process, she realized, and he came from a family history comprised of hard-working folks of relatively modest means.

But her outlook was strictly current time: today, next week, or next month. It was that same verve and energy that first attracted him. She was unrestrained by convention, and she was beautiful, and she wanted him to know that. Those qualities seemed to captivate him for a time, but now she wondered whether they had become weighted points of difference between them.

She still loved his smoldering, earthy passion. For one thing, she had no doubt about his sexual orientation—completely heterosexual, unlike several of her previous affiliations among her social *peers,* where sexual orientation could sometimes be a fluid and changing thing. He knew how to take his time with her and make her sing. Some woman somewhere had taught him well, for sure. She got a warm, tingling feeling in her body just thinking about it.

What he really needed was some cooling off time, she resolved. A little bit of time without Zena, she was certain, would cure him of all those distractions. She looked forward to him telling her again that she was the best thing that had ever happened to him. And he needed to do that damn soon.

Chapter Thirty-Four
Laughter

Dr. Covert was pleased with Keisha's progress, and the day finally arrived for her first trip beyond the grounds of the hospital. He declared that the day was dedicated to moving beyond borders. Lailani's direct involvement in her niece's treatment program had showed her firsthand how much time and effort was devoted to Keisha's recovery. She gained a new level of respect for the doctor, and for his team. They all gave their time and compassion selflessly.

She appreciated again something that had been hard to feel for several weeks—that there was genuine goodness in the world. She and her niece were surrounded by it at the hospital. Dr. Kaplan back home had given them an enormous blessing with his referral. When she returned to Albany, she vowed to herself that somehow she would scrape together the money to organize a proper reception for him.

They walked out of the front hospital door hand in hand. They were heading to Midtown: first stop, the Empire State Building. Not just to see it, Keisha said excitedly, but to go all the way to the top, 102 floors high. The child was tickled pink over the adventure.

Lailani was truly amazed at the progress she continued to make. It exceeded everything she hoped for, and she prayed in thanks every evening after she kissed her niece goodnight.

Their trip began with a walk to the subway. While a taxi to their destination would have been more efficient, she was really counting her pennies now. She was entering her fourth week without a paycheck. Her main goal was to keep on top of every withdrawal, and to meter out her funds as slowly as possible.

The subway entrance was only four blocks west of the hospital. In that brief span of time, they were exposed to the great melting pot of Manhattan. First, a shirtless man wanted them to pay for his travel back to Wisconsin so he could see his daughter. Then several furtive-looking traders with huge green trash bags offered to sell them jewelry and handbags, and silks. Moments later a bebopper on gold-colored roller blades glided by them and did a 180 back in their direction, bowing with exaggerated flair. Circling slowly around them, he proclaimed loudly as if on some imaginary stage.

"My, my, my, y'all are some fine black mamas."

Keisha laughed and blushed, burying her head in her aunt's shoulder. And then they kept walking and disappeared into the endless river of busy city pedestrians who never looked at anyone.

Their ears were treated to the grand cacophony of sound that is Manhattan during the day. Taxis swerved in and out; massive trucks ground through a maze of gears; staccato car horns gave warning to every manner of hazard or annoyance; skateboarders oozed over the concrete sidewalks, making space where none existed; and construction projects crammed between buildings fired up enormous machines to build toward the sky. All those sounds were mixed up together with a dozen others and magnified by the tight matrix of city streets.

But Keisha was glowing and taking every bit of it in. Even when Lailani was pulling her along, she was snapping photo after photo. This was the Big City, and she was fully alive, embracing it.

When they entered the subway, the noises underground rivaled that in the streets above. At times it won the contest. As the enormously long train approached them and continued to lurch forward and accelerate past their position on the platform, Lailani momentarily panicked, thinking that she had mistakenly cued up for the Express and not the local. But at last the endless train began to slow and eventually stop. Metal doors opened, and a crush of people streamed by her and Keisha before they could board. After they pushed in along with the waiting crowd, the doors clanked shut and the serpentine train sprinted forward, accelerating to breakneck speed. Looking around, they saw that the subway car was packed with riders as far as they were able to see. They were surrounded by a sea of people of all kinds and colors, many of which Keisha had never seen before. She hugged her niece gently, drawing her close.

"It's not polite to stare," she whispered.

Keisha continued to bloom in the city. The energy and rainbow of color, motion, and sound captivated her completely and purged whatever illness remained within her mind. For the first time in over a month, her niece was all smiles, and everything seemed to make her happy again.

When they finally arrived at the Empire State Building, there were scores of people and families intent on going exactly where they were going, to the top. The revolving entry door limited the number of people that could enter the lobby at any given time to a trickle. The line was enormous. Hoping that there was another way in, she grabbed Keisha's hand, and they left to explore the side of the building.

She spotted an entrance door with no crowds halfway down the block.

Maybe this might just be a short cut.

But she didn't see the small gold sign that displayed *Private Office Entrance*. She ushered Keisha along and told her to push on the revolving door, and step out after it opened inward to the lobby. Keisha entered the revolving door and pushed a little too hard. The door careened around and she was caught inside, circling around the turnstile. In a panic, Lailani entered the spinning door, trying to stop its advance. At that moment a tall black man in a navy blue suit rushed in and forcefully brought it to a gradual stop. He pulled Keisha out unharmed, and then slowly brought Lailani around to him.

When they were face-to-face, they froze and stared at each other for several seconds.

Then Keisha heard the tall man speak.

Lailani, it's you.

Keisha watched her aunt's face as she looked up at the man. She could tell that Aunty Lai liked him. But how did he know her name?

Lailani realized she'd been much too stern in responding to Keisha's insistent questions about Brett after they left the chance meeting in the lobby. On the way back to the hospital later that afternoon, she took Keisha's hands in hers and promised her that she would share everything about him and answer all of her questions when they got back. The last thing she wanted her behavior to instill in her niece, she realized, was that relationships with men should be hidden from view.

Keisha couldn't wait to hear all about the tall man. She couldn't remember her aunty ever being involved with a man, let alone a man like Mr. Howard. No man had ever come to the house. But mostly she was happy, because now she knew for sure that the mean things some of the kids said behind her back about her aunt weren't true.

As the subway train approached their stop, Lailani began to lose the panic she felt from her promise to share a very private part of herself. For so many years, she realized, she had been hiding it away inside of her. Even most of her close friends in adulthood didn't know that he existed. Why was that, she asked herself, already knowing the answer? It was because she had loved him then, fully and completely as a young, innocent girl, and he had disappeared, leaving her childhood love for him to wither.

She hoped that by talking about it with Keisha, it would help her erase that long-buried pain.

Keisha was propped up in bed, wearing the new pink flannel pajamas that Lailani gave her when she first awakened in the hospital ward. She had her knees hugged up against her chest while Lailani finished brushing and combing her hair.

Putting down the comb, she sat at the foot of the bed and took a deep breath. She didn't really know how or where to begin, so she just started talking.

"Keisha, Mr. Howard, I call him Brett, and I met when we were seven years old. He had just moved with his sister and brother to Albany. His mother had recently passed away, and they came to stay with his father's mother. He lived close to my house, and we were also in the same school together."

Keisha's eyes sparkled. "Did you like him when you first met him, Aunty Lai?"

"Yes I did. From the very first moment that I met him, I liked him more than anyone else I had ever met."

"In those days we used to have dance class during recess at our school. Now don't laugh out loud, but back then the dancing we did was called square dancing. It's kind of like the line dancing you kids do today, but different because you could actually dance together with each other for much of the dance. The boy and girl danced together as a team, sometimes holding hands with each other."

Keisha was surprised to hear this. Even at nine years old, she was not allowed to hold a boy's hand, not even in school.

"Aunty Lai, when you used to hold Mr. Howard's hand in the square dancing, how did you feel?"

She knew this type of question was sure to come from her niece, who was very perceptive for her age. She also knew that her niece's physical development and maturity was ahead of her peers. She had to arm her with facts to protect her from the predators who would readily steal her innocence. This was the first of many stress questions that she knew she would have to answer honestly. But she had already decided that the truth was good for both of them.

"Whenever I held his hand, I would feel a warm vibration in my stomach, and it would feel like someone had turned up the heat in the room."

Keisha smiled broadly and hugged her knees tightly.

"But you see, Keisha, the very thing that was fun about square dancing, being close to and touching boys, was also the thing that made it hard, and sometimes dangerous. There was one boy in the class who wanted to do more than hold hands during the dancing. When the teacher's back was turned, he would grab the girls and feel them or rub himself up against them. The girls hated being his partner. But the boys could choose their partners, and it was only a matter of time before this bully might pick you. And then one day, he picked me."

Keisha's eyes were now wide open, and her face showed fear.

"What happened, Aunty Lai? Did that boy feel all over you during the dancing?"

"I think he would have Keisha, except for one thing. My friend Brett stood up to him. After that boy chose me to be his partner, Brett came over and stepped in between us. He was about the same height as the boy, but Brett was skinny. I remember what he said back then, and he said it in a low, steady voice, just loud enough for me and the boy to hear and no one else."

Lailani's dancing with me today, and every day after this. I hope that's okay with you.

"The boy, and I wish I could remember his name, Keisha, didn't know much about Brett, so he probably wasn't afraid or anything. But I think there was something about the calm in Brett that made that boy back away and say that he had no problem with Brett dancing with me. "

"Aunty Lai, was Mr. Howard a good dancer?"

Lailani responded truthfully, as she remembered her sore feet from many years ago.

"Well, Keisha, Brett was new to the school, and also new to square dancing. He used to stomp on my poor feet like he was trying to make mashed potatoes."

Keisha burst out laughing. It was the first belly laugh that she could remember her having since before the attack. She joined in with her niece, and they cracked up together. They laughed until their stomachs ached.

After that, she shared some of her many times together with him. She talked about the summer reading they did at the Albany public library, where the goal between them was to read as many books as possible during the summer and receive a blue star for each book, placed on their forehead. She talked about sailing and about school field trips.

Then Keisha asked another penetrating question. "Aunty Lai, what was your favorite time together with Mr. Howard?"

"My favorite time was when we used to play Ring-O-Levio."

Keisha was stunned.

"I didn't know you ever played, Aunty. That's a kid's game."

"Well, I was a kid then, dear. Brett and I were always sought after when the teams were chosen."

Keisha's knees lowered down to the bed, and she leaned back on her pillow. She looked at her aunt with a new sense of appreciation.

"Aunty Lai, why did he leave you?"

Chapter Thirty-Five
Destruction

Melinda dropped two small pills into Carleton's remaining martini after he stood up to signal for the tab. Chauncey said that he always did that, and then sat back down to drain his drink. If the timing held, he would pass out moments after getting into the back seat of Cy's limo. The timing held.

Cy kept the car at the speed limit as he took 57th Street down to Riverside Drive. From there he headed uptown to 89th and then west for two blocks. They had yet to say a word to each other. They were both silently contemplating the full extent of their felonious activity. Carleton slept peacefully in the back, his head resting on Melinda's shoulder. Soon they arrived at the prearranged townhouse, entering through the garage door just off the back alley.

Stewart and Chauncey were in position downstairs when they pulled in. They helped Cy lift the limp body upstairs to the first-floor bedroom. They blindfolded him, removed his clothes, and bound his mouth, hands, and feet. He would start to awaken from his drug-induced slumber in about thirty minutes as the powerful narcotic began to break down.

After making sure the bindings were secure, Stewart knocked on the adjoining bedroom door, where he had warehoused two hookers. They opened the door together with their arms around each other's waists, wearing nothing but party masks. Each of them held a half-empty wine glass.

"Okay, ladies, let's start the photo shoot. Follow me, please."

They entered the room, and he directed the girls to pose in the most suggestive and seductive manner possible. He took hundreds of images.

"Make it seem like he's having the time of his life, girls!"

For several shots, he removed the blindfold and hood. He mashed Carleton's face between both of the hookers' silicone-inflated chests, and took a series of other equally candid exposures.

When the session was over, he gave each girl five hundred dollars and warned them again to forget that they were ever at the house. They giggled, got dressed and quickly made their way past him and out the rear door. The trailing one winked at him and whispered to him with a smile that he should call her anytime, for business or pleasure.

With only ten minutes remaining before Carleton regained consciousness, Stewart returned to the living room, where his team waited.

He asked one last time if there were any questions, and if they were clear about the back half of the plan. Everyone nodded yes.

"Let's get at it, then," he snapped as he put down his drink and headed for the bedroom. Carleton was beginning to stir when Stewart hoisted him up and strapped him naked into the desk chair with three double-wrapped bungee cords.

Cy grabbed the voice synthesizer and placed it in his mouth. Stewart motioned for Chauncey to leave the room. He checked Carleton's bindings one last time and stepped back. Then, moving forward, he delivered a hard punch to the covered right side of Carleton's face. The head snapped to the side and then straightened up. He was awake.

Cy moved in close to his right ear, the good ear, and began his threatening monologue. His voice was amplified and distorted by the synthesizer. Even though Melinda knew it was playacting, the rasping hard-edged tone caused her to shiver momentarily. The effect on Carleton was equally chilling. He eagerly nodded in agreement to each of the conditions that Cy ticked off. When it was over, Stewart slipped behind him, grabbed his neck and clamped his mouth shut. Cy quickly shoved two drug-treated inhalers into his nostrils. He soon slumped backwards in his chair, unconscious.

Cy and Stewart headed back to midtown with Carleton passed out in the back seat. With his clothes back on and the attentive cleanup, he appeared to be taking a brief nap. The trip back to the Club took half the time, and Cy slowly nudged the car into the back lot. Carleton's car remained faithfully in place, with the glow of the driver's cell phone visible through the darkened windows.

After covering his palm and fingers with a handkerchief, Stewart reached into Carleton's pocket and withdrew the reprogrammed digital control fob. He pressed it five times and waited. Like clockwork, the driver ended his call and left the car, leaving the trunk slightly open and the car unlocked. He walked around to the front of the Club, waiting for his boss to come out and expecting to carry back some type of large package to the car.

As soon as the driver turned the corner, they looked around the lot for any activity. Seeing none, they got out, opened the rear door and hoisted Carleton up between then. To anyone watching, they appeared to be two chums helping an inebriated buddy into the back seat of his car. That was not an uncommon scene in the city.

Before the confused driver returned to his car, Cy rolled out of the lot, heading uptown and then over to 11th Avenue. He lined up outside of a twenty-four hour car wash, along with fifteen other black limos.

Chauncey and Melinda had remained behind to sterilize the townhouse. They were well on the way to finishing the meticulous task and removing all traces of what had occurred.

"You know, under normal circumstances this might be a blissful domestic scene with a loving husband and wife tidying up the house together," Melinda joked.

"I was thinking the exact same thing. Then it dawned on me that only a very ghoulish couple indeed would be using surgical disinfectant and an industrial-strength vacuum cleaner to accomplish their domestic tasks."

"You 're right on the mark. Only a couple that had recently completed some macabre act of cannibalism would be so engaged."

They both had a laugh at that and released a good deal of tension before returning to the exacting work.

Twenty minutes later, a text message popped up on Melinda's pager. She went to the back room and told him that Stewart and Cy would pick them in thirty minutes. They double-checked all surfaces for wipe-down and began readying the bags of trash. Those would be left on the curb for tomorrow morning's pickup. Most of it, however, would be scavenged and removed by the army of anonymous late-night trash pickers combing the streets.

As he approached the pickup point, Stewart was hopeful, but his mind was racing. He was profoundly concerned. He had crossed, and indeed trampled upon, his traditional modus operandi—brains, not brawn. Yet here they were, having already kidnapped, drugged and assaulted a man. Big-time jail issues there, he knew. But what choice did they really have? That bastard had ripped off his plan from his naïve son, who left all of that hard work exposed for the picking.

Damn Chauncey, he fumed.

But he also knew well the absolute truth that the highest rungs of the super-wealthy ladder were only reached in collaboration with those same moneyed classes that carefully guarded the access gate. Thus the essential recruitment of Chauncey that allowed him to exploit a brief crack in the gate, before it slammed shut.

Stewart and his family were very well off, but weren't close to that rarified top one-half percentile circle. It was a closed circle he had seen filled with mostly inherited wealth, where access to power and position was a birthright. He had watched the sons and daughters all throughout school and his career. No real intelligence, guts, or cunning required for entry into that privileged club. Only the right blood was needed.

He had asked himself many times before why he should trudge through the trenches for twenty years, kissing endless ass and bowing deeply from the waist on his way to the top. There was never a convincing answer for him. Sure, the big payoff might be there over the long haul—or it might not be. Trouble was that the game had changed, and the old rules were in shambles. The top tier boys had jacked it up, grabbing it all for themselves with no regard for the continuity of the financial system that had fed them and their families well for generations.

No, he would take his now, thank you very much. He began to relax a bit again as he thought about the endgame.

Chapter Thirty-Six
Conception

She was more anxious now than when she was a little girl. Back then, the thought of actually holding his hand was a big deal. But once they actually touched each other, it seemed like the most natural thing. Holding hands and running to hide with him made Ring-O-Levio so fun. When they were on the other side of the game and had to chase the other kids to place them in jail, they didn't hold hands, because it looked strange. But they were still together.

When he asked her yesterday if they could meet for lunch, her first thought was a practical one—she didn't have the extra money to buy food in fancy Manhattan restaurants. Then again, maybe he would pick a place that was reasonable. But who was she really fooling, she asked herself. No matter where he picked, she would be there, even if she had to do the dishes after the meal.

She was relieved when Keisha told her that she would be perfectly fine without her for one day, and that she should meet Mr. Howard for lunch. But Keisha made her promise to tell her absolutely everything that happened at the lunch, including what Mr. Howard was wearing.

Brett picked a modest place in the Empire State Building. He told her that he needed to be close, because there was major activity at his job and his time was not his own. She wondered what kind of work he was doing. He probably went into business, she thought, because he always acted like a leader when they were kids. He certainly looked and dressed like a businessman. He even had a small bit of gray around his temples.

Taking the subway train back to Midtown was easy to do after her trial run yesterday. She believed that she was making good time as the train barreled toward her station. Then it skidded to a stop, and for no apparent reason stayed immobile for several minutes. As it began to move again, she took out her small compact mirror and inspected her face and hair. She saw in the mirror a fully mature woman. There was strength there, she thought. And while she had long neglected the social circuit, mostly by choice, she felt confident that she could still turn heads. But he had always seemed to like to look at her back then. She put her compact away.

When she finally arrived, she went to the private office entrance and waited inside the small alcove set back off the lobby. She was ten minutes late. Overhead, she admired the arching art deco design of the lobby ceiling. She watched the endless stream of business people, delivery people, and lost people circulate in and around the lobby. Tearing her eyes away from that big city parade, she looked down at her watch and saw that it was 1:20 P.M. In a momentary panic, she wondered if he had arrived on time and left when he didn't see her.

The she heard his voice from behind.

"I'm so sorry I'm late, Lai. Please forgive me."

She turned around and faced him. He opened his long arms, and she moved into them. They held each other tightly for a moment.

Stepping back from his embrace, she chided him.

"Well, Brett, you disappeared from my life without a trace and you've kept me waiting for twenty-four years. I suppose I can forgive this last twenty minutes, so long as you promise it will be the absolute last time."

Brett stepped toward her again and held her close, somber in response to her kidding.

"I won't keep you waiting for me ever again."

Emotions stirred within her that she hadn't felt for many years.

The modest lunch was the beginning of their renewed friendship. They both sensed a connection during that first meeting, a coming together; almost, she thought, like separate strands of Christmas tree lights responding in glowing unison after being reconnected to each other. She expected those feeling to lessen on their second and third meetings, but they didn't.

Yet one troubling thought kept coming back to her during their times together. He would quite often look at her, sometimes with a romantic gaze, but she wondered whether he was really seeing her as she was. She began to believe that he was envisioning some romantic version of her, a version of her that had not lived and endured life for two decades without him, mostly on her own.

She became convinced that he wasn't seeing the woman who had fought and scratched out a living by herself, and who was caring for an infirm father who barely recognized her. And how could he really know that she was the high school girl who stabbed a man when she was attacked in her own home? Of course he couldn't. He hadn't been there.

Should she tell him that she struggled and budgeted every month to pull together the money to pay her mortgage, utilities and living expenses? Would he really care to know that she was desperately trying to enroll Keisha in a private school across town, but they only offered half the scholarship money she needed to make it a reality?

That was why she'd practiced her speech for what was now the fourth meeting between them. She looked at him and spoke in a quiet, somber tone.

"I wanted to meet you this last time to say goodbye."

They were walking in Central Park after enjoying a boxed lunch that he ordered from the Taurus executive dining room. He turned and looked at her in disbelief.

"What do you mean last time, Lailani? I don't understand."

She remained calm despite the sadness that this truth brought to her spirit. She was determined to walk him through the logic that convinced her they didn't have a future together. She had to break it off now, because seeing him was so wonderful, and yet so very painful.

"Brett, please let me explain what I mean, and why I think it's the only decision that makes sense. I've thought long and hard about it, and I really believe it's the right one for us."

Then she plunged ahead into her well-practiced speech.

"Being with you these last few days has been a joy for me. Finally knowing that you are safe, and why we were separated, has laid to rest so much pain that I carried through so many years. Seeing you, walking with you, watching you eat and laugh and breathe, has meant the world to me. But I had to wake up from the fairy tale."

"You see, Brett I now know that we live in completely different worlds. Our priorities are miles apart. I'm no longer the friend that you shared so much time with when we were children. I'm a woman with her own hopes and fears and challenges."

She turned to him and took his hands in hers.

"I still live in Albany, near the same block where we used to play. My priorities are very basic—raise my niece to be a successful young lady. I also love my nursing career, and I'm committed to my ailing father and to my church. My life is not a big movie production like yours. I don't have fame and power, and I don't live and work in the clouds. Those things are wonderful for you, and you've been successful doing them. I'm really so proud of you. But we have become different people, with different goals and needs."

Then she lost the smooth cadence of her practiced speech, and she struggled to tell him the last part that hurt so deeply.

"The innocence and profound friendship, perhaps even the love, that we had as children has passed us by. It's too late for us now. It makes me so sad to say it, but I know it's true."

She turned away and looked out over the green expanse of the great lawn, and to the skyward-facing architecture that rimmed the eight hundred acre park. A tear fell, and then another.

He touched her shoulder, drawing her close to his side, and they walked slowly over to an empty bench on the perimeter of the wide brick walkway.

They sat down together, and he looked calmly into her eyes. He had always found them so beautiful, even now through the tears.

"Lailani, I've made a terrible mistake during our few times together. Hearing you talk about the chasm between us has driven this home to me. My mistake was spending so much of our time together regaling you with my own stories about business and travel here and there, and all the other diversions. Even sharing the facts about my job and what issues are consuming me right now contributed to my mistake. I didn't talk about the most important things, including the things that are most important to you."

As he said this, he put his arm around her, resting her head softly on his shoulder.

"You see, out of nervousness I think, I displayed to you all the trophies and trinkets acquired during my battles over the past twenty years. I never thought to think that you didn't need to see those things to know who I am. In the world where I have spent so much time, everyone wears those badges on their sleeves for all to see and admire."

"But what I didn't reveal was who I am now, who I have become after passing through those fires. How could you possibly know, with all my bluster, where I want to go in the future and why I want to go there with you?"

She looked up to his face, waiting.

"What I am, Lai, is basically a modern-day business soldier who is ready to leave the arena. I've had some success in there, for sure. Right now I'm fighting my last battle. I'll be a victim in this particular fight, no question about that. But in the things that matter, I'll end up winning."

As he looked into her eyes, he could tell that she didn't yet understand what he was talking about.

"This is how I see it. I liken my time in college, graduate school, and the business world to hard time served in a very confining space. It took a lot of discipline and it took a lot of sacrifice, particularly of those things that I hold dearest. It wasn't prison, don't get me wrong, and there were some rewards. But my own personal freedom, my own agenda had to be placed on the shelf. The focus was on the institution, the organization, or the business. Their goals and thoughts, not my own. It's the price you pay, that we all pay to get ahead."

"If things go as planned, I'll soon be liberated from all that conformity. Liberation as I see it is the ability to lead a simpler, less complicated life, where I can evaluate things on the merits as I see them, versus using the lenses provided to me by others."

"And believe me, my path forward is to a life apart from all the trophies I described to you. I'm sorry I went on about them. Truth is, I've been shedding those things for some time now."

Then he turned and embraced her, drawing her near.

"My love for you never left me in all the time we were apart. I think I spent all of these years finding a path back to you. I don't believe for a moment that our meeting again was chance. And I think you must also feel that, deep within."

"But Brett," said in a soft voice, but she couldn't find any words to continue.

"Lai, when I walk out of the arena in the next few weeks, I want to walk into your embrace. I want to spend my life there with you in marriage, where we raise our family together in Albany. The first member of our family is Keisha. I'll protect her, and try to help her become the kind of young lady that we're proud of. And if we are truly blessed, there may be another member of our family for us to nurture, one that resembles both of us. Well, that hopefully takes after you more than me."

"Will you marry me, Lai?"

She stared at him through moist eyes. His question sent her back to the distant past and seemed vaguely familiar. It took her to early childhood, and she remembered all of her fantasies in a flood. She and Brett would get married, of course, was the story in her dreams. How could she resist his marriage proposal? They would wait until after high school and have a big wedding with five hundred guests. Then they would start their family and have a boy and a girl. And they would live happily ever after.

But this was no dream. He'd just asked her to marry him in real life. She looked at him, realizing that dreams sometimes come true. Her mouth moved, but no words were spoken. He looked intently at her and put his hands softly on her shoulders.

"Lailani, was that a yes? Was that a yes?"

She gazed up at him and nodded her head.

"Yes."

Chapter Thirty-Seven
Chaos

Brett stared at the large package. It was a thick, reinforced manila envelope. HR had distributed similar bundles to all top management. On the outside in bold red script it warned, **For Mr. Howard's Eyes Only**. Not even super-efficient Velma dared to open the ominous delivery. Because he had not received the courtesy of a phone call from Sam before it arrived, he knew that the envelope contained the fate of his entire organization.

It would be an ugly fate. One he would have to deliver to his top team, and they would in turn deliver down through their respective management layers. *Cascading the message* was the corporate-speak phrase of the moment for what would soon occur.

Just like the military, he thought as he lifted the bulky envelope in both hands. But he knew there would be many more non-lethal casualties to his team and their families than those suffered in a military operation.

He stabbed his intercom button and told Velma to hold all calls until further notice. Velma hesitated, and then asked if that included Zena.

"Including Zena," he said in a harsher tone than he intended "Velma, I'm sorry I snapped at you. If a call comes in from Ms. Lailani Aikins, please patch her through. Thanks."

Velma smiled. She liked the poetry of that name far better than the name of the high and mighty Zena Melody Jensen.

After ripping his scissors through the top seam of the thick outer skin and pulling it open, he saw a sealed white business envelope on top of the large binder-clipped enclosure. The envelope was addressed to him. He immediately recognized Sam's scrawling handwriting as it splashed his full name across the front. Unleashing some of his mounting tension, he sliced his letter opener hard through the top flap. He knew this first communication would answer for him personally the question that so many at Taurus were asking.

What will happen to me?

That simple interrogatory, the fact that it had to be asked at all, was to him the most troubling aspect of this big company business. It was a humiliating question, really. And why was that? Because hadn't the top performers worked so many grinding hours and sacrificed so much precious personal and family time, all for the sake of achieving first-class business results? That should have meant some measure of control over their fate, and that of their family. At the very least, it should have meant they were, to some degree, masters of their own destiny.

Shouldn't it have meant at the very least, according to the credo of the corporate high achiever and all the best-selling business books, that they were more likely than not to advance up the corporate ladder by the strength of hard work and merit?

Not necessarily, he understood, not even most of the time.

Staring at the envelope he finally arrived at the full realization of what he had gradually begun to comprehend over the years of fighting his way up the rungs. Nothing is promised, no matter how sweetly whispered or well intended at the time. Any CEO or group of underlings can change your whole life in a heartbeat, just because it seems to makes sense to them at the moment.

He opened the neatly folded letter.

Dear Mr. Howard, Brett:

The management of Taurus Corporation has completed a full and fair review of your functions, which include Public Relations and Investor Relations. This review uncovered a number of inefficiencies and redundancies that have grown more severe over the years.

To maximize shareholder value, management has asked for and received an independent assessment to deliver enhanced efficiencies. After careful review and appropriate adjustment to the aforementioned analysis, the following changes are effective in three business days:

    1. The position of Executive Vice President, Public Relations and Investor Relations (your position) is eliminated.

2. Public Relations and Investor Relations functions will report to the Chief Financial Officer.

3. All outplacement resources will be available to you from today forward, terminating in 180 days.

4. In a separate package, you will receive details of the Tier 1 financial settlement available to you.

5. Your financial settlement is contingent upon your execution of the cascade communication plan in the accompanying package.

Management thanks you for your dedicated service.

Very truly yours,
Judith Wang
Executive Vice President, HR
cc: S. P. Winston

He stared at the impersonal letter and let out a long, slow breath. He was genuinely surprised they would can him so soon. On the other hand, he would be spared watching the slaughter as thousands were shown the door, under terms far less favorable than his own. He was also surprised that his ostensible good colleague Judy Wang didn't give him a heads-up before the package arrived. But he realized with a wry smile that her dissembling approach came with the territory, and that she would be out the door not long after his departure, even though she probably didn't appreciate that fact yet.

The soft buzz of the intercom snapped him back to the present. He punched the speakerphone button hard.

"Yes, Velma."

Her voice seemed strangely elevated.

"Brett, there is a Ms. Lailani Aikins on line 1."

"Lailani, hi, darling. What a pleasant surprise in what's turning out to be a crappy day on this end."

"I'm so sorry to hear that. Are you okay?"

I'm fine, no real surprise on this end."

"Well, I had to call to see if you came to your senses after that dramatic marriage proposal that you made to me yesterday. I just want you to know that cancelling the wedding will cost you a bundle."

"There'll be no cancellation, sweetheart. In fact, what has happened today will give us much more time together to plan the kind of wedding that we want to have. Can't give you more detail on this phone, but suffice it to say that I consider today's news to be a positive development."

"Well, darling, as long as you feel good about it, I'm happy. Will you have time to call later?"

"I'll make time. I should be out of here by ten tonight, and I'll ring you from the hotel."

"Love you."

"I love you, Lai."

He turned back to the thick manila envelope and removed the large stack of documents. He knew that they contained hundreds of corporate death notices.

Drastic measures.

Chapter Thirty-Eight
Downshift

Awakened from his sleep by the increasing dawn light, Brett sat up and turned to the narrow bedroom windows set two stories above the small, rectangular backyard. He gazed out at the old brown picnic table and chairs casually strewn across the sparse grass-covered yard. Then he looked up and east at the Albany sky over the back line of low trees and hedges. A red tinge framed the high cirrus clouds as they paraded beneath the brightening azure sky.

He remembered the many times he and his crewmates would read those color-coded mariner's tea leaves to predict the daily sailing winds. That valuable knowledge always added critical information to modern computer weather forecasts. Strangely, and despite the years of separation, he continued to feel a strong sense of loss for Onset and his old sailing mates. Then he remembered how he had first purchased the boat from that old salt in Marblehead many years ago. It all began when that gentleman, out of sheer kindness, loaned him his brand new SUV just because he happened to see him and his crew on foot, leaving their boat at the docks in search of provisions.

A few months later, that same old salt with hundreds of years of sailing lineage in his bloodline, and the kid from the inner city and the Albany Clear Lake sailing club, closed a purchase and sale agreement for Onset. It was an all-cash deal and Brett couldn't have been happier. He had fallen in love with Onset's proud heritage of racing, and the many detailed seafaring tales that the Marblehead skipper shared with him as they chatted over the phone in the weeks leading up to the sale. Though from vastly different cultures, their mutual love of the sea and its daunting challenges melded the older and younger skipper together. He had kept in touch with him for many years, until one day, after failing to connect with him on a call, the elder son called back to let him know his dad had passed away peacefully in his sleep.

Oddly, he thought as he reclined back against the headboard, his imagination now whetted by thoughts of the sea, his old crew had all settled along with new families near either the East or West Coast, as if awaiting word from him to assemble at the docks for one more challenge.

But he knew that wouldn't happen, at least not for some extended time.

As he breathed in the cool, early morning air, a soft muted cry and a muffled burp rolled down the hallway from the back room. Lailani stirred next to him and then sat straight up, oblivious to the reaction that her lithe nakedness stirred in him. She glanced down at the sensitive baby monitor next to her. It hadn't activated. But somehow she had instantly responded to the baby's sounds from her deep sleep with a new mother's unerring instincts. Her wedding band flashed in the soft light as she quickly pulled her hair up and off her face, tying it into a bun. He always loved seeing her do this when they were kids, and it still intrigued him.

Already she was rapidly moving back to little Joshua's room, but not before a sideways glance at him that asked how long had the baby been fretting. He looked back at her with a slightly guilty expression.

He followed her round hips to the baby's room. Somehow he had always followed her, he realized, seeking a path to a simpler, more meaningful existence. How and why it happened would remain a mystery. But he realized that his love for her, nurtured in childhood, had never weakened over the decades of their separation. He had only buried it safely away and surrounded it with high, strong walls during the years of separation. Hearing this description of his love for her recently, she teased him that she was much too independent to be anyone's prisoner behind a wall somewhere.

But she also shared her own story of endurance, in one of their intimate moments together after their small wedding ceremony. For the long span of years without contact after he vanished, she said she would at times unwrap her precious memories of him, and of both of them together. Then she would breathe them in for a time and place them carefully away again. But she admitted to him that for most of those moments, she could only think about him for the shortest time.

Epilogue

Joshua's frustration could be heard in his voice as he called back to his father for help.

"Daddy, I can't yank this one up! It's really tight!"

Brett looked over to the dock area at the new fleet of sixty neatly aligned sailboats, and spotted his son halfway down the pier.

He's as itchy as I used to be to shove off and get out on the water.

Only three days remained before he and his staff would receive the first influx of two hundred overnight campers from the inner cities of New York. By summer's end, that number would surpass one thousand. And the boy had kept to his word to help with chores and boating issues, to assist him with making that happen. For the most part, the boy worked smoothly with the various work crews who had been in and out of the camp during the past month. He did light manual labor, and other times just stayed out of the way when the work was dangerous. He knew that sometimes it had to be lonely for the boy during the long workday, because of his limited opportunity to look in on him.

That's why Joshua was really looking forward to spending some time with his cousin Desmond, who would arrive from Boston in a few days. His favorite cousin was a couple of years older, and was more like a big brother.

Joshua was at camp this time only because he'd begged his mother. His arguments for why he should be there were well constructed, and Brett had to admit that they sounded convincing at the time.

Daddy needs a quality assurance boy who can test the boats from the point of view of the kids. I can also help Daddy finish the chores that need to get done when all the painters and workers have gone home. And I have good experience left over from my first visit last year, too.

She had finally agreed to let him go back. But her reasons were much different than the ones put up by him. In a quiet moment between them one evening, when Joshua was in bed and the house was still, she rested her head on his shoulder and shared her greatest fears—that her love for the boy made her want to keep him with her all the time. She realized that it was the surest way to turn him into a mama's boy.

As she looked at Brett that evening, she sadly resolved that this first multi-week separation would mark the beginning. He shook his head, not understanding her. She patiently explained that it was the beginning of a lifetime of their son striking out and slowly starting the process of living a separate life. She already knew that someday, home for Joshua would be somewhere far away. She had looked up at him back then, sad.

Time seems to be moving by so fast, Brett. I just wish it would slow down.

He had placed his hand on her belly to comfort her, and he felt the new life stirring inside. He gently massaged her round stomach. He told her that she would be busy raising the new one for many years to come, even after the boy became a man. She had smiled.

Another pleasant surprise on his horizon was the arrival in ten days of his younger brother Jimmy, who would join the staff as a sailing instructor for three weeks. Jimmy had turned out to be a pretty good skipper in his own right, competing successfully in the San Francisco, San Diego, and Bermuda regattas for several years. He had his own trophy shelf. Jimmy's stay would also allow him to see his nephew, Charles, who was coming along with his dad. Finally, and after some uncertainty, Dee had committed to be in camp for two weeks in June, arriving a couple of days after her oldest, Desmond. She would serve as a guest lecturer on the cultural heritage behind African American and Native American dolls. As more shore time learning for the kids, the lectures were part of a series of others that were incorporated into the summer curriculum. All were designed to reinforce the lessons given on the water.

He had been extremely concerned at first with making sure that Dee's doll collection arrived safely, and that it was stored in camp at the appropriate temperature and humidity. But he had a plan now that the empty wine cellar in the basement of the main house had finally been refitted with shelving and updated temperature and humidity controls.

I guess it's going to be a little bit of a family affair this summer, he mused as he tried to remember the last time he'd collaborated with his sister and brother on a big project.

He yelled back down to the docks.

"Joshua, loosen the red reef line and snap it tight, then let it run. There's a knot high up on the mast."

After the boy tended to the snagged line, he yanked the mainsail to the top. He quickly cast off lines and eased the boat back from the dock, keeping clear of the others. He was under sail moments later.

As Brett watched him smartly bring the boat about and head offshore, he sat back and rested for a moment on the porch of the boathouse cabin, leaning against the door facing. He breathed a sigh of relief as he looked over again at the neatly aligned fleet and the expanse of floating docks. The fundraising campaign had been more successful than even he had imagined. It had raised the two million dollars needed to transform the ten-acre property into a first-rate camp. That amount had seemed insurmountable at one time, despite his outward optimism.

And recently, another generous financial contribution emerged out of nowhere. Zena, of all unlikely people, was leading a private fundraising effort at her sorority. So far two hundred thousand dollars in pledges were recorded, with over half of that amount already turned into cash.

But clearly the most significant early hurdle overcome was not the money needed for construction or operations. It was the free gift of the property from a board member who was present years ago at his original presentation in New York City. After that speech, the board member had buttonholed some of his fellow CEOs, who were also excited about the potential for change from the campaign Brett presented to them. But Carleton Smith had jumped the gun back then, upstaging everybody by making the donation of the Long Island property and garnering all of the early publicity for himself. The land alone was probably worth ten million dollars. Because of that generous gift, he was able to eliminate the planning time for site selection, financing, and land purchase. Permitting and construction were then put on a fast track. The camp was set to open a year ahead of schedule.

He'd been looking forward to thanking Carleton in person at the grand opening. But he was informed two months ago that Mr. Smith would be unavailable for the indefinite future.

He got up and walked over to the far side of the boathouse, and grabbed a short ladder and a power screwdriver from his toolbox. Then he went inside and brought out the small bronze plaque that had been shipped to him by Mr. Smith's foundation director. The instructions were to place it where all the children would constantly see it. It was the only string attached to the generous gift of the real estate.

He looked at the words on the plaque again before affixing it over the boathouse door.

In Honor of C S

He also learned to sail when young

He would tell you if he were here

To only point your helm

To an honest and true course

Whatever was the complete meaning, Brett thought it was a pretty good message for his future sailors to see on a daily basis.

Stewart Greenberg's daring plan was perfectly executed by his team. But he had no way of knowing about the well-concealed night vision cameras installed around the perimeter of the parking lot. The expensive micro cameras were the lavish counter-measure to repeated property damage and urban affronts that had irked Club management for years.

New York City detectives used the video footage from those cameras to identify the entire team involved in Carleton Smith's kidnapping. Only his son escaped the initial round of arrests. But Chauncey's participation in the felony wasn't difficult for them to discover. High quality videos images from the several cameras at Stewart's luxury apartment building led to his identification and arrest soon after the others. Three of the four co-conspirators were sentenced to twenty-five years at the Attica Correctional Facility, and Melinda would serve equal time at Bedford Hills.

Brett's dismissal from Taurus Corporation left him with a hefty seven-figure nest egg as the value of his stock and options in the company skyrocketed during the looming take-over. He cashed out, and the proceeds gave him the freedom to permanently retire from the corporate wars, and to chart his own course going forward. The sailing center, and the teaching methods that he established, became a model for similar efforts throughout the country.

Lailani continued to advance in the nursing profession. She ignored the fact that she really had no financial reason to work at all after the marriage. In time she became a manager of nurses and medical personnel. Later, she started her own staffing company that helped meet the urgent demand for trained and motivated medical staff.

Carleton Smith received a vastly generous payment from Taurus to abandon his takeover bid. But his ability to enjoy the spoils of his attack was prevented when he suffered a massive stroke that left him paralyzed.

After several years of takeover battles and more rounds of restructuring, a weakened Taurus was finally broken up and sold off to the highest bidders. Thousands more were fired then.

Nathan JoHanson, Chauncey Smith's trusted security guard, took his own life with a single shot to his brain after seeing the full consequences of his lack of loyalty to both of his former clients.

CPSIA information can be obtained at www.ICGtesting.com
Printed in the USA
LVOW10*0345140814

399042LV00004B/40/P